14

SAVING RYDER (SPECIAL FORCES: OPERATION ALPHA)

SAVING SEALS, BOOK 1

JANE BLYTHE

Cover designed by TRC Designs

Dear Readers,

Welcome to the Police and Fire: Operation Alpha Fan-Fiction world!

If you are new to this amazing world, in a nutshell the author wrote a story using one or more of my characters in it. Sometimes that character has a major role in the story, and other times they are only mentioned briefly. This is perfectly legal and allowable because they are going through Aces Press to publish the story.

This book is entirely the work of the author who wrote it. While I might have assisted with brainstorming and other ideas about which of my characters to use, I didn't have any part in the process or writing or editing the story.

I'm proud and excited that so many authors loved my characters enough that they wanted to write them into their own story. Thank you for supporting them, and me!

READ ON!
    Xoxo
    Susan Stoker

I'd like to thank everyone who played a part in bringing this story to life. Particularly my mom who is always there to share her thoughts and opinions with me. The wonderful Cat Imb of TRC Designs who made the stunning cover. And my lovely editor Lisa Edwards for all her encouragement and for all the hard work she puts into polishing my work.

CHAPTER 1

June 14th

9:23 P.M.

The air was hot.

Sticky.

Even though the sun had set and thick clouds covered any moonlight that might otherwise light the way, making the jungle virtually solid, inky black, the temperature had yet to drop.

Ryder "Spider" Flynn adjusted his rifle in his hands as he crept through the Mexican jungle. His SEAL team had been dropped off about a klick back, the plan was that they would split up to find the kidnapped girls. The three young daughters of a US Senator were only nine, twelve, and thirteen, and the compound where they believed the children were being held was vast. The quickest way to find the kids and get them out was to cover as much ground as quickly as possible, hence the fact that he and his team had split up.

It should be a simple rescue mission, but if his years as a SEAL had taught him anything it was that *nothing* was ever simple.

A slight shift in the atmosphere had him freezing. He'd long since learned to trust every one of his senses, including his sixth sense, and right now it was buzzing a warning. Someone else was nearby.

Scanning the surrounding area, his night-vision goggles picked up two heat signatures only twenty yards or so to his left. Because he had to make sure that one of them wasn't one of the abducted girls, Spider veered off his course and silently approached the unknown subjects. As he moved through the jungle, he exchanged his rifle for a knife. The rifle would get a quicker result, but using it would alert everyone in the area that they weren't alone, and that wasn't conducive to a smooth rescue mission.

Hushed voices muttered in Spanish, and he could make out the orange glow of cigarettes. The accompanying smell nearly made him gag, it didn't matter how many years had passed since he'd been in that house that smell had the power to transport him back through time.

Shrugging off the dark memories, he dismissed the two men, they weren't a threat to him and he had to find those girls. The longer he and his team took to find them, the higher the chances that something could go wrong.

The men here weren't just dangerous, they were the kind of men who had no conscience, no soul, they would do literally anything to make money. Trafficking guns, drugs, women, and children, these men didn't care who they hurt, the idea of their victims having rights never even entered their minds.

Spider had seen the aftermath of what men like this did

more times than he wanted to count. This wasn't the first rescue mission he'd been on, these little girls weren't the first ones he had snatched out of the clutches of the devil. He'd seen things, and heard things. Things he could never wipe out of his mind, things that haunted him, things that crept into his mind when it was vulnerable in sleep.

Silently, Spider made his way toward the center of the compound. According to the maps they had there were at least a dozen buildings here, and any one of them could be where the Burns children were being kept.

Ahead of him, he saw what looked like a small one-room building made from concrete blocks. As he got closer he saw an empty hole where the door should be, and when he looked through it he saw one heat signature.

Someone was in there.

Praying it was one of the Burns girls—and that so far no one had done anything more than terrify her—he carefully stepped through the opening, cleared the room, and then approached the prone body on the floor. The room was separated into two halves, one had a table and chairs, the other—where the body was—had nothing. Metal bars ran from the floor to the ceiling, trapping whoever it was on the other side of the room with no hope of getting out.

The body was too large to be one of the Burns girls, but it was clearly someone who was being held against their will, and there was no way he was walking away and leaving them here. Rasping, shallow breathing told him that whoever this person was they were ill.

Removing his NVG he pulled a small flashlight from his pack, the light would be noticeable if you were looking for it, but it wouldn't draw any attention his way. Scanning the walls he saw a key ring hanging on the far wall and snatched it up, unlocking the gate that separated him from the captive.

As soon as he had it open, he dropped down beside what

he could now see was a very slight woman. She had a long tangle of bronzed brown hair, was curled up in a ball facing away from him, and she was naked.

His stomach clenched.

He didn't have to use his imagination to figure out what the woman was doing here and what had happened to her.

She hadn't stirred at his presence which meant she wasn't in good shape. He'd check to see what medical treatment he needed to administer to get her mobile then he'd radio his team and tell them they'd be bringing an extra victim with them.

Knowing that if the woman woke up to see a huge man in fatigues leaning over her, she was liable to freak out, and not only was he not good with hysterical, traumatized victims he didn't want to alert anyone to his presence.

Gently he laid a hand on her shoulder. "Ma'am, can you hear me? My name is Spider, I'm a US Navy SEAL, I'm going to get you out of here."

Carefully, he eased the woman down onto her back, noting the heat in her skin implying a fever, and her breathing was even harsher up close. Her body was tiny, she was nothing more than skin and bones, and he wondered how long she had been here to get to this condition.

Quickly and efficiently, he ran his hands up and down her body checking for broken bones or open wounds, when he found none, he reached up to brush a matted lock of hair off the woman's face, and gasped.

No.

It couldn't be.

Shining the light directly in her face a rush of shock flooded through him, followed by relief, then elation, quickly followed by horror. The rapidly changing emotions left him shaky although that probably had more to do with the woman lying beside him.

It was Abigail McNamara.

Baby sister of his best friend and fellow SEAL Eric 'Night' McNamara who was here somewhere on the compound.

Abigail had disappeared fourteen months ago.

"I just found Abigail," he murmured into his comms.

A series of shocked gasps echoed in his ear. The entire team knew Abigail, as a daughter of a SEAL and Night's only living relative they'd met her several times, and all of them had helped look for her when she first went missing.

But slowly after months with no progress, they had started to lose hope.

Even him.

And his history with Abby was more intimate than the others.

They'd given up on her and she'd been here, trapped in this hellhole, no doubt praying every day that someone would come for her.

That *he* would come for her.

"You found *Abby*?" Night demanded. "Here? Is she … is she *okay*?" he asked in a broken voice. Spider knew that if they weren't in the middle of a risky extraction that Night would have completely lost it.

"She's sick," he said vaguely, not wanting to say anymore because they couldn't risk this mission getting derailed, and if Night could see the state his little sister was currently in then he would throw everything else to the wind to come to her aid. "But I got her, I'll get her out, you guys good to finish this without me?"

"We got it," Owen 'Fox' LeGrand, the team's leader, said. "Get Abby to the extraction point."

"Look after my sister," Night said harshly.

"I will protect her with my life," he promised, and meant every word. There wasn't anything he wouldn't do for the fragile woman lying beside him. He would blast his way out, he would shoot his way out, he would kill everyone on the compound, if he had to he would grow wings and fly her out because one thing was certain; Abigail was going to go home.

* * *

9:32 P.M.

She was hot.

Too hot.

It felt like a fire was raging inside her, and Abigail groaned as she rolled over, desperately seeking anything that could cool down her overheated skin.

Her fever was getting worse, she was alternating between chills that had her shaking so badly she hurt, and burning up with sweat pouring off her. Unfortunately, once the chills came the sweat on her naked body felt like it turned to ice, making her even colder.

She was dying.

A cold had turned into a chest infection, and she was sure she was now slowly succumbing to pneumonia.

Her lungs seized at the movement, and she broke into a coughing fit that made it feel like someone was stabbing a hundred nails into her chest.

It hurt so badly.

The pain only made her cough more, and the cycle continued for several minutes until she finally sunk back against the hard concrete floor, drained, sore, and struggling to breathe.

It was only after she'd collapsed against the ground that she realized someone was touching her.

Someone was here.

In her cell.

No one had come inside her cell since she was thrown in here over a year ago.

Panic flared inside her.

Was this it?

Were they tired of her and ready to kill her?

Even though she knew she was dying, Abigail couldn't fight the fear inside her. She didn't want to die, especially here in the middle of the jungle, all alone, with no one ever knowing what had happened to her.

A large hand covered her mouth, not hard enough to hurt but enough to muffle the sounds of her screams.

Was she screaming?

Abigail hadn't realized, but now that she thought about it she could hear muffled pleas.

Her pleas.

As she begged for her life.

She had promised herself she would never beg and yet here she was, when push came to shove, begging and pleading for mercy from men she knew would show her none.

She was weak.

Pathetic.

Then slowly she became aware of a hand stroking her hair, and there was warm breath on her ear, and a voice was whispering something to her.

Words.

In English.

Not the Spanish she was accustomed to hearing.

The voice wasn't harsh or angry, instead it was the opposite—soft, soothing, calming, and comforting.

"Shh, Abby, I know you're scared, honey, I know you're hurting, but I need you to stay quiet, I'm going to get you out of here but I don't want anyone to know I'm here."

He knew her name?

How?

Wait.

She recognized that voice. It belonged to the man she loved and the man she hated. But Ryder couldn't be here.

Could he?

Ryder and her brother Eric were both SEALs, but she'd been here for so long, and they hadn't come for her. She'd given up hope that they ever would, so why would he be here now?

Was she hallucinating?

Forcing herself to relax, Abigail stopped screaming and sensing the change in her the man removed his hand from her mouth. She squinted through the near darkness and saw a large figure looming over her. He blended into the night, dressed all in black, even his face had been covered in something so it too blended into the night, and she wondered if she was looking at some sort of ghost.

She might have believed it if it weren't for the blue eyes.

They were the bluest shade of blue there was, and she could stare into them forever.

Ryder had blue eyes like that, but why would he be here?

She didn't even know where here was except that she assumed she had been brought into Mexico.

"Abby," the ghost man said on an exhale. There was pain behind that single word, guilt too, and she wanted to believe this was really Ryder, but she thought it much more likely he was nothing more than a figment of her imagination.

It sounded like Ryder, and those eyes were his eyes. Could he really and truly be here?

Abigail tried to lift her hand to touch his face, she needed to feel if he was solid and real and not going to disappear into a wisp of smoke the second she reached for him. She was weak and didn't have the strength to lift it more than an inch off the ground, her whole body was shaking and she hurt so badly, if she was going to die she'd rather it just happened than be hallucinating like this.

"Hold on, honey, I'm going to get you out of here. As soon as I do I'll get some medicine in you. Here drink some water."

Her shoulders were lifted off the floor and she was propped against a strong chest. A bottle was held to her lips, and when cool water began to flow into her mouth she eagerly swallowed. There was a tap built into one of the walls, but she'd been too sick to get herself to it.

A hand touched her forehead. "You're burning up," Ryder muttered.

It was Ryder.

It had to be.

If it wasn't it was the most realistic hallucination anyone had ever had.

Locking her gaze onto those blue eyes she licked her lips and croaked, "Ryder?"

"Yeah, honey, it's me. How long have you been sick?"

"Not sure. Days." She was tired and wanted to curl back up and go to sleep, but Ryder was here and she wanted to go back home so much more than she wanted to rest.

Ryder picked up her wrist, frowned as he took her pulse, then put his ear above her chest. "I don't like the sound of that," he muttered.

"I think I have pneum—" Abigail broke off as another coughing fit seized her. Ryder quickly pulled her into his arms, supporting her as her lungs spasmed, trying to suck in enough oxygen.

"Yeah, you have pneumonia," Ryder agreed when she could finally catch her breath. "Let's get you out of here and to a hospital."

"Can't." She jiggled her left wrist which had a metal cuff locked around it, unless he was going to cut off her hand—

which at the moment she would be willing to sacrifice if it meant going home—she was stuck in here.

"I have the keys." Ryder shot her one of his winning smiles, the one she knew made his dimples show, and held up the keyring that had been taunting her, hanging on the wall, out of her reach, all these long months. Once he had her unlocked he eased her back to the floor so he could rifle in his pack. "I'm going to put my spare clothes on you. If I take you outside like that we'll be a beacon to anyone else out there."

Right.

Because she was naked.

When she'd first woken up in this cell her clothes had been gone and they'd never been returned to her. It was warm enough in here that she hadn't frozen to death during the winter. She would have been embarrassed to be naked in front of Ryder, but he'd seen her naked before, and besides, right now, all she cared about was getting out of this room.

Ryder didn't bother asking her if she could dress herself, just propped her against his knee and pulled the black long sleeve t-shirt over her head, then he pulled on a pair of black pants and a thick pair of socks. The clothes felt weird against her overheated skin, and she squirmed uncomfortably.

"I won't roll these up," he said to her, "that way it will cover your hands. Even if I had a pair of boots they wouldn't fit you, and besides, I don't think you're going to be walking out of here."

He was right.

There was no way she had the strength to walk out of here which meant that Ryder was going to have to carry her. Carrying her meant that he would be leaving himself vulnerable, there was no way he could handle her and his weapon and protect himself if any of the men here saw them.

"Ryder, maybe you should leave me," she said softly. As

much as she wanted to escape—had dreamed about it every single day she had been trapped in here—she didn't want anyone to die making it happen. She was sick, and even if she got to a hospital she might not survive. Ryder should just save himself and forget he had ever seen her.

Ryder just scowled. "If you think I'm leaving you here you're crazy."

"But—" her protest was cut off when she began to cough again. The pain was awful, her chest was being ripped to shreds with each harsh cough, and the heat that had woken her earlier had turned into a chill and she was shaking badly, making her chest hurt more.

"Let's go," Ryder said briskly, putting his pack on his back then scooping her up into his arms.

All Abigail could do was hang limply in his hold. She hated it, wished she could do something to help, she didn't like to let other people do things for her. But as much as she wanted to do her part, she couldn't. Right now, she had to concede that Ryder was her only hope of getting out of here alive.

* * *

9:44 P.M.

Abigail felt as fragile as a baby bird in his arms.

She was a ballerina, had hoped to end up working professionally until she hadn't made the cut—that was what she said anyway although Spider sensed there was more to it than she had let on—so she had always been small, but now she was tiny.

The urge to track down every single person involved in

Abigail's abduction and imprisonment was strong. He was a protector by nature, but when it came to Abby …

Some things were better left untouched.

Like his complicated relationship with his best friend's baby sister.

Wanting to get out of here as quickly as he could, Spider carried the shaking woman in his arms out of her prison and toward the door. Abigail wasn't heavy and her weight wouldn't slow him down much, but if someone saw them it would be awkward juggling her and his weapon, doable, but he'd feel a whole lot better when he got Abby out of here and onto a helicopter.

At the door he had to pause when Abigail dissolved into another coughing fit, her entire body spasming, her face contorted in pain. Since she'd obviously been sick for a while, he didn't think her coughs would attract any attention but he couldn't be sure.

Cradling the back of her head in his palm, he pressed her face into his shoulder to muffle the sound as best as he could. Each harsh rasp only spurred his fear, she was coughing up mucus, her pulse was racing, her breathing shallow, and she was definitely running a high fever, she needed antibiotics, but he didn't have any in his individual first aid kit. The IFAK was filled with bandages and other things he might need to treat a bleeding wound in the field, not what was needed to treat a lung infection. That would have to wait until they were on the helo.

When she sunk against him she tilted her face to look up at him. "Ryder, if I'm going to slow you down just leave me here," she said softly.

What was it with this woman and her leave her behind attitude?

Had Abigail forgotten who he was?

"Hush," he admonished. "None of my team would leave

you behind and you know it, and Night or I would do anything to get you out."

"I don't want anyone getting hurt because of me," she murmured, her head drooping against his shoulder.

At least that made sense, and it was sweet she was worried, but his team had done plenty of rescue missions just like this one. "No one is getting hurt," he assured her.

"We got the assets," a voice spoke in his ear.

"Abby?" Night asked.

"She's going to need IV antibiotics," he replied. He wasn't a doctor, but he had enough medical training to know that if he hadn't found her here she would have lasted a couple more days at the most. With medical treatment she should make a full recovery, but he had to get her there first.

Night muttered a curse. "Tell her we'll have her home by sunrise."

"Will do." Looking down at the bundle in his arms, he saw her staring up at him. "Night ... uh, I mean Eric, says hi."

"I remember his nickname," Abigail said. "Yours too, it's Spider."

"Yeah, it is."

Before he could say more she was hit by another coughing fit, this one worse than the others, and by the time she could finally catch her breath she was shaking badly. Each gasped breath she took made his stomach churn, he hated seeing her like this, fighting so hard just to breathe, and seeing what had happened to sweet, sassy, spunky Abby gutted him.

She deserved better, and he couldn't deny that he and Night had failed her.

They should have found her long before this, and he dreaded hearing what else she had endured over the last fourteen months.

It was time to get her out of here, bring her home.

"I'm sorry, honey, I'm going to have to move you so you're over my shoulder so I can keep better control of my weapon, I know you're hurting and this won't be pleasant, but I promise to get you to the helicopter as fast as I can."

"It's okay," Abigail said tiredly. "I can take it, you don't have to worry about me."

Too late.

He'd been worrying about her for the last fourteen months and a long while before that. Abigail thought that no one saw her, that no one noticed that she was hurting, she tried to hide it, believed that she did, but he saw her, he'd just been too selfish and cowardly to do anything about it.

"Ryder," she said when he went to shift her into a fireman's carry, "don't call me honey."

Pain cut through him as cleanly and efficiently as any blade. He deserved that—and more—but it didn't make it any easier to hear.

As carefully as he could Spider maneuvered Abigail, doing his best to block out her quiet moans, and then he stepped out of the small building and into the jungle.

This time he didn't even notice the oppressive heat, his sole focus was getting Abigail to the extraction point. His team would get the Burns girls there, hopefully the children were uninjured, but either way their first stop would be a medical facility because at the least the girls would need psychological help.

Spider hadn't gone more than about four steps when he heard it.

Gunfire.

Looked like their cover was blown.

As much as he'd love to go tearing off through the jungle with no thought but getting Abigail to safety, Spider knew he couldn't do that. He had to go slowly, carefully, it was just him against an unknown number of subjects and he had Abby to think of. This cartel was known for being particularly brutal, they made an example of anyone who got in their way, and ruled this entire area with an iron fist making it one of the most dangerous in Mexico. This wasn't the first time that Spider and his team had performed a rescue mission on Luis Perez's compound, and he doubted it would be the last.

Slowly, he made his way through the jungle, it was a good five klicks to where the helicopter would pick them up and even though Abigail was small and not much extra weight, she *was* extra weight, and carrying her would slow him down.

He made it only a half klick or so from the building where he'd found Abby when he heard the sound that chilled his blood.

Footsteps.

Followed by voices.

Perez's men were nearby.

With Abigail on his shoulders he didn't want to engage them unless he was given no choice. Shooting them was out because he'd be broadcasting his location, but he couldn't hold onto Abigail and use his knife.

"Are they coming?" Abigail asked softly, and he could feel her entire body had gone tense.

"They won't find us," he said confidently.

"Ryder, put me down and leave," she implored. "I'm sick, I'm dying anyway, just leave me and go."

"I am not letting you die," he growled. Abigail was sick, and without treatment she would die, but if he left her here when one of Perez's men stumbled upon her she wouldn't be getting a quick death. They would torture her mercilessly until eventually her body succumb to her illness and the injuries they would inflict upon her. He was not letting that happen to Abigail, and besides he was a SEAL, he could keep her safe and eliminate any danger.

Hiding himself and Abby behind a large tree, Spider kept one hand on Abigail's hips to keep her steady while his other gripped his knife. Abby wasn't the only one who was tense, his entire body was coiled and ready to spring into action if they were found.

As the footsteps grew closer, Spider found himself holding his breath. He always knew there was a chance he wouldn't come back from a mission, he had accepted that fact, he did whatever he had to, to make sure he and his team made it home in one piece, but never had the stakes been so high.

Never had the woman he loved been here in his arms.

The sole responsibility for making sure she lived was on him.

The footsteps grew closer.

The voices got louder.

And then he saw them.

Four of them, armed, arguing with one another, annoyed that the security breach had interrupted their fun with one of the women.

Spider watched and waited and prayed the men passed without incident.

Just as he started to relax and believe that they had just bypassed trouble, Abigail began to cough.

He dropped to the ground, pulled Abby into his lap, supporting her weight as he clamped a hand over her mouth and prayed that the men had been far enough past them that they wouldn't hear the muffled coughing, but he knew that they would. The jungle was quiet and the sound traveled, the men would have heard it and be circling back this very second.

He had just failed Abigail.

* * *

10:06 P.M.

"I'm sorry," she wheezed between coughs. Abigail knew that the men who had just walked past them would still be close enough that her coughing fit would have alerted them to their presence here.

She had just signed hers and Ryder's death warrant.

He should have left her.

She didn't want anyone to die because of her.

"I'm leaving you my pack," Ryder whispered, already setting her on the ground and covering her with leaves and sticks. "If I don't come back, you take this and you get yourself out of here. My team knows you're here and someone will come for you. You just get to someplace safe."

There was no way she was walking away from here on her own and they both knew it. She was too weak, and besides, sooner or later one of the men here would stumble upon her.

Besides that she didn't want to be alone.

For month after month she had been trapped in that prison. No one talked to her, and whoever brought her food simply threw it in through the bars and left. Then Ryder had appeared out of nowhere and now he wanted to leave again.

Although she knew she was wasting whatever time he had to try to enact some sort of plan, Abigail curled her fingers into his clothes and clung to him. "Don't leave me," she begged, and she really hated to beg. She was a strong, independent woman who had been looking after herself most of her life, but right now she wasn't herself. She was a vulnerable, needy shell of a person who was terrified out of their mind.

"I have to," Ryder said briskly, but she saw the indecision in his blue eyes. "I'll be back as quick as I can," he promised.

She just stared at him.

They both knew he might not come back.

Abigail might not know how many men had just walked past them, but she knew there had to be hundreds of them out here, she didn't think she had seen the same man twice in all the months she had been here. Ryder was outnumbered and wouldn't want to shoot his weapon and draw every man in the area's attention.

Because he was trying to protect her.

"Trust me, Abby," he said, but as soon as the words were out of his mouth he flinched.

They both knew she didn't trust him.

At least not with anything other than her life.

He'd decimated her trust both times she'd offered it to him and she didn't think her heart could risk a third time.

Still, since she did trust Ryder to get her out of here alive she gave a small nod.

Ryder gently uncurled her fingers, straightened, then paused and stooped to kiss her forehead, then he was off, running noisily through the jungle.

He was trying to get their attention, lead them away from her, she knew better than most that Ryder possessed the ability to move silently, he was deliberately making a racket so that he could lead the men away.

He was risking his life for her.

His actions melted a little of the ice she had coated her heart in to protect it from being broken again.

Her chest burned, her head ached, her mind longed to check out and fade into nothingness but …

Ryder was here, and Eric too, no doubt the rest of his team as well, she didn't want anything to happen to any of them. They'd come here to rescue her. How could she live the rest of her life knowing that one or all of them had died in her place?

She was a McNamara. How many times had she had it drilled into her when she was growing up that McNamara's didn't quit? Her grandfather had been a SEAL, her father had been a SEAL, her brother was a SEAL, she hadn't had a hope of living up to any one of them or their expectations.

Look at her.

She'd been abducted and kept in a cage, she didn't even remember how it had happened. The last thing she remembered was leaving the dance studio late at night, she'd been working with a girl who was preparing for an audition, the child had been picked up by her mother, she'd closed up, set the alarm, crossed the parking lot, and then ... nothing.

The next thing she knew she was waking up in that prison.

She'd screamed and threatened and insulted until she was blue in the face, but no one had cared. No one had done so much as even acknowledge her and bit by bit she had given up.

But not any longer.

Abigail knew she was stronger than most people gave her credit for. She was short, and a ballerina, and most people interpreted that as not being as strong as other people. While Abigail knew she could never beat Ryder—or any of the men here—in a physical fight, she had learned how to use her smaller size to her advantage.

Right now the biggest advantage she had was the gun Ryder had shoved into her hands before he left. She hadn't even noticed it at the time, but now she felt its weight and saw the shiny black against the paleness of her hand.

Careful to be as quiet as she could, Abigail pushed the leaves and branches off herself and tried to focus enough to come up with a plan. She couldn't carry Ryder's pack, even if she was at one hundred percent she doubted she could carry it very far, but like this she wouldn't even be able to get it off the ground.

Which meant she traveled light, just herself and the gun.

Hiding here wasn't a survivable plan, it was only a matter of time before she started to cough again and one of the men would find her. She wasn't going back to that prison, she would rather die trying to escape than just give up.

Steeling herself, Abigail planted her hands on the trunk of the nearest tree and used that as leverage to get herself standing.

Her legs wobbled precariously and she very nearly landed heavily on her bottom, but somehow she remained upright.

Fighting against the dizziness, she pressed one hand to her temple while the other she kept on the tree. She prayed that her head cleared enough that she could see where she was going, it would be hard enough in the dark without it feeling like her brain was busy riding a rollercoaster.

Heading off in the direction Ryder had gone, Abigail clutched the gun like it was her lifeline, she knew the risks of using it, but she also knew it could be the only thing standing between her and Ryder, and certain death.

Her chest heaved, sweat poured down her body, even though it was warm out and muggy she knew that how hot she felt was not in proportion to the temperature.

Determination flowed through her veins.

She'd find Ryder.

She'd make sure he took care of those men.

And then she'd do her best not to be a burden and do her part to help them get out of here and back home safely.

Abigail stumbled over something, staggering and landing hard on her hands and knees, the gun flying from her hand.

A body.

She'd tripped over a body.

Ryder.

He must have taken out one of the men hunting them.

The thought of those men getting the upper hand never even occurred to her.

Her chest seized, and she tried to fight it, but there wasn't anything she could do to stop the next coughing fit. Abigail doubled over, sick to her stomach in addition to the sharp pains in her chest, darkness started to close in around her and she wanted so badly to give into it.

But then she thought of Ryder.

She had to find him.

Had to help him.

Somehow she managed to crawl around until she found the gun then got back on her feet and this time she started running. Well, as close to a run as she could get in her present condition.

Up ahead she heard sounds of a scuffle.

Picking up the pace, a moment later she stumbled into a small clearing, two more men lay motionless on the ground but there was another and he was fighting with Ryder.

Abigail didn't think she just acted.

She crossed the remaining distance between them and swung the gun at the man attacking Ryder. He had a knife in his hand, the blade pressed against Ryder's neck, but at her blow he spun around. She wasn't strong enough to have caused him any real damage but the distraction was all Ryder needed.

He grabbed the man's arm and in one smooth motion used his own knife to slit his throat.

The man gurgled then dropped to the ground clutching at his neck.

He was dying.

She'd never watched anyone die before.

It wasn't that she felt like he didn't deserve it, she knew

what these men did, she'd heard enough in her time here to know that they were traffickers of humans, drugs, and weapons, but seeing his life drain away made her realize how close Ryder had come to dying.

Her feelings for him might be complicated but she didn't want him to die.

Overwhelmed, her body shaking badly, her breath increasingly harder to catch, this time when unconsciousness came calling she answered.

* * *

10:20 P.M.

Abigail swayed, and then her eyes rolled back, and she dropped.

Spider sprung forward, catching her before she hit the ground, then lowering her carefully the rest of the way down.

Her breathing was shallow and rapid, and when he put his hand on her chest he could feel her heart thumping wildly as it struggled to keep her weak body alive. Moving his hand to her neck, he checked her pulse and found it racing, she'd overdone it getting up and following after him.

He'd had things under control, led the four men away from Abigail, circled back around so he was behind them, taken out two of them before they even knew he was there, then eliminated the third before the fourth was on him. Despite the fact that the fourth man had held a knife to his throat, he'd been about to overpower him when Abigail had suddenly appeared.

Although he could have killed the fourth man without her help, the fact that she had managed to get on her feet—not an easy task given her current condition—and tracked him down, then put her own life at risk to try to help him warmed him in a place he hadn't allowed himself to think about in a long time.

Still, she'd scared the life out of him appearing like that, and he wanted to throttle her for it.

It would be easier to be angry with her for risking her life when he was the trained professional if she wasn't lying there struggling to breathe. He needed to get her to that helo.

Scooping her up into his arms, he backtracked to where he'd left her to retrieve his pack. Quickly he strapped it on, lifted Abigail's wrist to check her pulse, then settled her on his shoulders and started walking toward the meeting point.

They hadn't gone far before he heard more voices.

Lights danced in the distance, right between him and Abigail, and the spot where the helicopter would be picking them up.

There was no way he could risk continuing in that direction, he spotted at least two dozen lights meaning there were at least two dozen men. If he was on his own he might risk it, he could probably get through them or go around them, but he wasn't on his own and Abigail hadn't stirred yet. Attempting to get past the men was too big a risk.

Which meant he needed a plan B.

Since they hadn't known that Abigail was being held here they hadn't been prepared for an extra victim, and even if they had known she was here they couldn't have known that she was in such bad shape.

He would have to find them somewhere to hide out until his team could come back for them. There was no way he would make it to the extraction point in time, so there really wasn't any other option. He'd find them a safe place, do what he could for Abigail, and pray that his team made it to them before she got any worse.

Heading off in the opposite direction to the lights, away from what might end up being lifesaving help, Spider prayed that he wasn't about to let Abby down again.

It was their pattern.

He'd met her brother when he was ten, Abigail had been five, and he remembered the little girl with the unusual eyes who would follow him and Night around everywhere they went. Back then he loved to tease her, driving her crazy, and she'd quickly become like his little sister. He and Night would look out for her, make sure nobody bullied her, and any boy who showed an interest knew that if he hurt her they would hurt him.

That all changed the night of her high school graduation.

Ever since then, all he'd done was bring her pain, no wonder she didn't trust him. If he was her, he wouldn't trust him either.

If he got her out of here alive, he would find a way to fix things between them.

The thought caught him by surprise because he'd thought he had already made his peace with the fact that he could never be with Abigail. You didn't have sex with your best friend's baby sister, and you certainly didn't fall in love with them.

Too bad he'd already done both.

Although he'd been surprised by his own decision to make things right with Abigail, he realized that he wanted to. Believing that he had made peace with giving her up had been nothing more than self-delusion. She deserved to be happy, and after a lot of therapy he had come to accept the fact that he deserved to be happy too, no matter what he had done in the past.

No more self-destructing.

Now he just had to remind Abby that once upon a time he had made her happy.

How he would do that he didn't have a clue, but he was a SEAL and solving problems was his job. He saved lives, but the pressure of having to save Abigail's life was nothing like he had ever experienced before. This was all on him, yes he had medical training, but no, he wasn't a doctor, and Abby was slipping away. He could feel it in how still she was, in the soft wheeze every time she breathed, and in the way her whole body shivered.

"Hang on, Abby," he whispered. "You can't die until we get a chance to sort things out between us."

He walked for at least an hour through the thick jungle, if he was alone he would have found somewhere to hide himself, but Abigail needed to be somewhere safe, and he needed her somewhere where he could treat her as best as he could with what he had in his IFAK.

A faint light up ahead caught his attention. It was different than the torches Perez's men had been carrying, it was larger, stronger, and not moving. It had to be coming from a building.

Crouching, he slid Abigail off his shoulders, covered her much the same way he had last time, and prayed that she wouldn't wake in another coughing fit and draw the attention of whoever was in that building.

With Abby tucked away he crept closer to the cabin, making sure to check for cameras or sensors as he went, anything that might be set up to alert the occupant of someone approaching.

Nothing stood out, and he advanced on the small wooden shack silently. He paused at the window, staring through the grime to see a single occupant in the one-room building. The man was sitting in a recliner, his pants were undone and he was touching himself, his gaze on the TV screen in front of him where several men were having rough sex with a woman.

For a second, bile burned hot in his stomach.

Was the woman in the video Abigail?

There had to be a reason why they'd kept her here for so long. Perez was a human trafficker, it would have made more sense that he would have sold her quickly. Abigail was stunning. Besides her bronze hair she had the most amazing eyes, she had heterochromia which would have been pretty enough in and of itself, but one of her eyes was a golden brown—inherited from her mother—the other was a silvery gray—inherited from her father. Those eyes alone would have been enough to get Perez a tidy sum of money when he sold her.

Unless he'd wanted her for himself.

He hadn't had a chance to speak with Abigail yet about what had happened to her, but he knew once he got her out of here besides treatment for her pneumonia she would also need a sexual assault kit performed, and treatment for any STDs these men had given her, and ...

His heart dropped into his stomach.

They would have to check to see if she was pregnant. Was that why Perez had kept her? Hoping that she would make babies with those same amazing eyes?

Fury fueled him, and he turned the door handle and covered the distance between him and the man in seconds. Grunting his release onto the floor, the man didn't notice he was there until the blade of Spider's knife pressed tightly against his neck.

"You're dead either way," he growled softly in the man's ear, "you can either have a quick death or a slow and painful one. Understand your options?"

"Yes," came the gritted reply.

"You're one of Perez's men?"

"Yes."

"You're keeping watch on this area of the compound. Or supposed to be," he added with a nod at the TV.

"Yes."

"How often do you have to check in?"

"Four."

"Every four hours?"

"Yes."

"What's the codeword?"

The man didn't answer.

Because Spider didn't have long, he wanted to get to Abigail as quickly as possible, knowing she was alone out there had him closer to panicking than he should be in the middle of a mission, he didn't bother to repeat his warning he simply whipped the knife up, slicing through half of the man's ear before returning it to his neck.

The man squealed in pain, his breathing quickening.

"Codeword?" Spider bit out.

"Whore."

"You earned yourself a quick death." While knowing this man was in part responsible for what had happened to Abigail, might even have taken an active part in torturing her, she was his priority. So true to his word he dragged the man outside and slit his neck.

Leaving him to bleed out, Spider turned and ran back to get Abigail. Half expecting her to be gone by the time he got there, instead he found her right where he'd left her.

Picking her up, he brought her back to the cabin where he set her down on the bed. Rifling through his pack he pulled out his IFAK and got the ibuprofen. He didn't have antibiotics in there so it was the best he could do to try to get a handle on her fever, and he had to do something because he wasn't happy with her racing pulse or the way she struggled to drag in enough air.

If this didn't work, how was he going to keep her alive?

If he failed her, how was he going to live with himself?

* * *

11:39 P.M.

"Abs, sweetheart, I need you to drink a little water for me and try to swallow this."

She was propped up against something, and something else nudged her dry, cracked lips then cool water was sliding down her throat.

It felt so good.

She was too hot.

Burning.

Like she had been thrown into a fire.

Only the fire was inside of her which meant there was no escape.

Abigail moaned in relief when something cool touched her. She had no idea what it was nor did she have the mental energy to figure it out, but she was so grateful for this minor reprieve.

Something brushed against her wrist and panic filled her.

Images flooded her mind.

Voices taunting her, arms holding her down, pain.

So much pain.

It started in her head, she wasn't sure what it was.

It wasn't until something came flying toward her face that she figured it out.

Fists.

Someone was hitting her.

Over and over again, not just in her face, her chest and her stomach too, until her whole body burned with pain.

A harsh cough seared her throat and tears streamed down

her cheeks as she coughed over and over again, each one felt like her lungs were trying to leave her body through her mouth. She didn't want to cough anymore, she didn't want to hurt anymore, she just wanted peace.

Peace and quiet.

You would think after so many months alone in that cell that the last thing she would want was peace and quiet, and yet it was what she had become accustomed to. The idea of being surrounded by too many people and too many sounds left her feeling panicked.

"Shh, sweetheart, it's okay," a soft voice murmured, and it felt like someone was stroking her hair.

The voice sounded like Ryder's.

He couldn't be here though because ...

No.

He had been there.

He'd appeared out of thin air and carried her out of that prison. He'd killed to protect her.

Ryder would make sure she got back home.

Unless ...

Unless she had imagined the entire thing. It wouldn't have been the first time she'd hallucinated since she'd been abducted.

"Honey, drink some more water, and I need you to swallow this pill for me." A finger touched her lips, urging them to part, and the pill was placed on her tongue before the bottle of water was at her lips again. She drank greedily and cool water flowed down her throat going a small way to ease some of the burning.

It *was* Ryder, he was here, she could feel his strong hands on her shoulders as he laid her back down. She remembered what those hands felt like touching her bare skin, teasing her, stroking her, buried deep inside her. She also remembered what it felt like when she had woken up alone in bed the morning after losing her virginity to him to find out that he had left without a goodbye.

The pain of that day had never really faded, and yet stupid woman that she was she had forgiven him and given him a second chance only for him to do the exact same thing to her again.

Two disappearing acts were enough, she would never trust him again.

"Go away," she mumbled weakly, pushing at the hands that lingered on her shoulders.

"Ah, baby, I'm sorry," he whispered, and she could have sworn that she felt his lips brush across her forehead. "You'll never know how much it killed me to walk away from you, how much I hated myself for hurting you."

Abigail might believe him, but he'd said those words to her before.

The night of her high school graduation was the night that her brother's irritating best friend, the man who teased her relentlessly and scared away any boy she liked suddenly morphed into something else. Despite his teasing, Abigail had loved Ryder since she was twelve years old, and when he finally kissed her and then made love to her, she'd thought that he had reciprocated her feelings.

That had been her first mistake.

She hadn't seen him again until she returned home after college, almost four years later. He had shown up out of the blue at her apartment with flowers and an apology. Of course she'd told him to get lost but he'd been persistent, sending her flowers every day, each bouquet accompanied by a note with an apology.

Eventually, she'd been worn down, let her guard down, and let him back in.

That had been her second mistake.

For a while everything had been perfect, she and Ryder

had gotten to know each other as two adults instead of the kids they had been. They'd had fun, gone on some dates, had the best sex of her life. She'd been falling in love with him.

Then one day about a year later he was just gone.

He didn't answer her calls, didn't respond to her texts, didn't come around again, and she hadn't seen him again until he appeared beside her in her prison.

There would be no mistake number three.

How could she ever trust him again?

No amount of flowers and sweet apology notes were going to convince her to let her guard down this time around. Once they were back home, she would be the one to walk away this time. Part of her wanted to give him a piece of her mind, he definitely deserved it, but she had shed enough tears over Ryder Flynn, she'd wasted enough anger on him, and she'd worked hard to get over him.

His hand was still touching her, and she suddenly couldn't bear it. It was worse than the awful burning up feeling. Jerking herself away from him, she felt something painful tug at her hand.

Looking up in fear she saw a large man standing above her.

It wasn't Ryder, this man was vaguely familiar but she couldn't remember where she had seen him, all she knew was that he felt evil.

He had a bald head, eyes as black as night, and lots of muscles, he radiated strength and she knew that he would use that strength against her.

"No," she pleaded, shying away from him. "Please don't hurt me again."

"I won't, Abby," Ryder said.

Ryder?

Where had he gone?

She scanned the room but couldn't see him, all she could

see was the bald man.

No wait.

That wasn't true.

There were more men standing behind the bald man, at least half a dozen of them.

They were going to kill her and Ryder.

No, before they killed them they were going to torture them.

Beatings.

Fists.

Pain.

"No," she sobbed, "I don't want to do that again."

Images of herself tied to a chair assaulted her.

Strong hands held her down, and she bucked and twisted against them, desperate to get away.

Abigail cursed her own weakness. How many times had she heard as a kid that she wasn't as strong and tough as her grandfather, as her father, as her mother, as her brother?

Each time she'd been told that another piece of her self-confidence slipped away.

She was strong.

Okay, so she didn't know how to shoot a gun, and she couldn't carry double her own bodyweight, she couldn't survive if someone dropped her on a deserted island, and she didn't know a hundred ways to kill someone, but she was strong in her own way.

Only now she didn't feel so strong.

She felt weak and helpless and pathetic, the exact same way her family had made her feel with their thoughtless words and unrealistic expectations.

As a child when she'd felt inadequate, she hadn't given up, she'd worked harder in school, she'd worked harder in ballet class, and she'd taken self-defense classes. She hadn't given up then and she wouldn't give up now.

"Let go of me," she screamed, fighting with everything she had.

"It's okay, baby."

"It's not okay." How could Ryder say that? Didn't he know that they would beat him too? Then maybe they'd lock both of them up and no one would ever see them again.

The fists came at her, hitting her in the chest over and over again until the pain became unbearable.

As the pain got worse it got harder and harder to breathe.

"Shh, sweetheart, you have to calm down or you're going to hurt yourself."

"Not worse than they'll hurt me," she countered. Nothing was worse than that, they'd broken her fingers and her arm, they'd cracked her ribs, they'd broken her cheekbone and given her a concussion.

They'd do it again.

And worse.

"No, baby, I won't let them hurt you, not ever again." Ryder said it so confidently that she actually believed him.

Arms wrapped around her and she was snuggled gently against a hard chest. The bald man and his army faded away into nothingness.

For the moment the horrible overheated feeling was gone, she wasn't hot and she wasn't cold, she just felt warm and comfortable. Her chest hurt and it was a little harder to breathe than it should be, but she felt … content … even safe.

She shouldn't.

Not here where they were still in danger.

And not with Ryder.

Definitely not with Ryder.

He wasn't safe, never had been and never would be.

Yet right now, she felt safer than she had in a very long time.

CHAPTER 2

June 15th

12:16 A.M.

Spider could feel her slipping away.

He didn't have what he needed to treat her, and from the looks of things the ibuprofen hadn't done a thing to help with her fever.

Her pulse still raced, each breath was clearly an effort for her, and while he might not have a thermometer to take her temperature he could tell by touching her skin she was burning up, and he feared it would climb higher. She was confused and hallucinating, and although he'd managed to calm her down he wasn't sure that next time he would be able to.

Abigail had been convinced there had been another

person here in the room with them, someone who terrified her.

Her tormentor?

A figment of her imagination?

He'd initially thought that she was talking to him, telling him to go away, and it had gutted him. He knew he'd ruined what they'd had not once but twice, and he knew that the chances of him being able to earn her trust back were slim to none, but he wasn't giving up on her. He would apologize every day for the rest of his life if he had to, he would send her flowers and find a million ways to say I'm sorry.

He loved her.

It was as simple as that.

When it boiled down to it, he could continue to believe he wasn't good enough and let other people dictate how he spent his life, or he could finally give himself permission to move on. While he thought he actually might have made it to that point in his life, he also had to accept it might have come too late.

He might have already lost Abby for good.

If he had then he had no one to blame but himself. He was the one who had walked away from her, he was the one who had betrayed her, he was the one who had thrown her and her love away.

Abigail whimpered in his arms, and the feeling of impotence that he couldn't fix this for her was overwhelming. He was a Navy SEAL, he saved people, protected people for a living, and yet the one person he loved the most he couldn't save.

"It's all right, Abby," he soothed, brushing her hair away from her sweat streaked forehead.

"No," she mumbled, "don't let him come back."

"He's not coming back, baby," he promised. He might not

be able to banish her hallucinations, but he could make sure that no flesh and blood man laid a hand on her again.

"If he does then kill me." Her eyes fluttered open and she met his gaze directly. "I don't want to go back, if he comes then kill me. Promise?"

His heart stuttered in his chest. The raw fear on her face ripped him apart. Whatever she had suffered here had led her to a point where she would rather be dead than go through it again.

"I promise you that I will make sure no one will ever hurt you again," he vowed. There was no way he was promising her that he'd kill her. They were safe enough here until a team came in to pick them up, he'd already made the first check in to Perez without incident, so as long as they believed that the man he'd killed was here and keeping watch over the compound then they weren't going to come out here.

Abigail's eyes fluttered and fell closed, carefully easing her down to rest against the mattress, he put his hand on her forehead. He could swear she felt hotter than she had last time he'd checked.

If her temperature climbed much higher, he wouldn't be able to bring it back down. It would be hours before the team could come to pick them up, probably not until tonight, and he didn't have medications on him to do much more for her than he already had.

He had to do something to break her fever.

His eyes roved the one-room shack searching for a solution. There was a small kitchenette, the bed where he had Abigail, there was a table and chairs in the corner, and the armchair facing the TV screen where he'd found Perez's man. There was also a small bathroom. It wasn't enclosed, just a tub and a toilet and a sink in one corner of the room with two screens offering some privacy.

The tub.

If he filled it with cold water and put Abigail in there it might help bring down her fever.

It was worth a try.

Standing, he walked over, put the plug in, and turned the faucet on. While he waited for the tub to fill he went back to the bed, and with as much professionalism as he could muster, he stripped the borrowed clothes off Abigail then scooped her up into his arms and carried her over to the bath. As attracted as he was to her now wasn't the time to be remembering the way they used to burn up the sheets, now he needed to keep a cool and calm head so he could do what he needed to do to save her life.

Abigail was unconscious. He couldn't put her in the bath on her own which meant he would have to get in with her. Setting her down beside the bath, he quickly removed his shoes and clothes, then picked Abby up again and stepped into the tub.

The water wasn't too cold, more a pleasant cool that wiped away the oppressive heat of the jungle that had been pressing down on him since he first arrived. Spider sat down, leaning against the back of the tub with Abigail between his bent knees.

She rested heavily against him, and he hated seeing her like this, so still and lifeless, that wasn't his Abigail.

His.

She'd always been his, he just hadn't realized it.

Walking away from her had been the biggest mistake of his life, and he wished it was possible to take it back. Walking away from her the second time, after he'd worked so hard to win her heart again had just been plain stupid.

Sitting with her like this in his arms, her hot skin against his bare skin, he couldn't deny that even with their lives in danger alone in enemy territory, and even with her body battling a high fever and an infection that could kill her, holding her again felt nice.

It felt right.

This was where she was supposed to be, and he was done with letting other people dictate who he spent his life with.

He wanted Abigail, he wanted to marry her and have a family with her, and whether it took him a day or the rest of his life, he would find a way to make it up to her for all the pain he'd caused.

Keeping one arm hooked around her waist to make sure she didn't slip down under the water, he used his other hand to scoop up handfuls of water and splash it over her head and chest.

"Come on, baby, come back to me," he murmured in her ear. "You're the strongest woman I know, Abby, you can't give up now. I've got you and I'm not letting go, you fought hard waiting for someone to come for you, now I'm here, and I'm going to take you home, but you have to hold on a little longer. You hold on for me, okay, sweetheart? You hold on tight and you don't let go."

Once he had her completely wet, Spider began to run his fingers through her hair, gently easing out the tangles. Abigail hated to have her hair messed up, in all the years he'd known her, even back when she was just a little thing, she'd always had her hair done perfectly. It must have killed her not to be able to brush it these last fourteen months.

One arm snug around her waist keeping her close against him, in an effort to make sure he didn't do anything Abigail might construe as taking advantage, he let his other hand settle on her shoulder. Her skin was soft and smooth despite months of being held in captivity, and he couldn't stop his fingertips from stroking along its silkiness, but then he froze.

Was it his imagination or was she feeling a little cooler?

Spider put his hand on her forehead and was convinced

that she did indeed feel cooler to the touch. Was her fever breaking?

He could only pray that it was.

Picking up a cake of soap that set on the edge of the bath, he grabbed one of her arms and began to wash away the grime that months of being held hostage had caused. He had to believe that being in the bath was helping and that sooner rather than later she would wake up, fix him in a hard stare those unusual eyes of her glittering with anger, and tell him off for walking out on her a second time.

After coming so close to losing her he would relish her anger.

* * *

2:54 A.M.

She wasn't burning up.

That was the first thought Abigail had as she slowly became aware of her surroundings again.

There was something cool lapping against her skin, she was resting against something warm, but it was a nice warm, a comfortable warm, it was vibrating and she could hear music in her ear.

It sounded like someone was humming.

None of the men who had brought her food every day had ever hummed so she knew it couldn't be them, but it took her brain a moment to figure out that it had to be Ryder.

She tried to lift her head, found it far harder than it should be, and moaned a little before prying open her eyes.

"Is that my girl finally waking up?" Ryder asked, taking

her chin between his thumb and forefinger and tilting her face up so she was looking at him.

Why did he have to be so sexy?

His hair was as black as coal, and he wore it just long enough that the natural waves curled around his ears. His cerulean blue eyes were impossible not to stare into until you got lost and forgot where you were, forgot who you were. He had just enough scruff to be sexy, and she wanted to brush her fingertips across it before pressing her mouth to his.

No.

Resist temptation.

She knew all too well what happened when you got sucked into the sex stratosphere of Ryder Flynn. Abigail had no intention of falling into that danger all over again. She wasn't *that* stupid.

"Abigail?"

"Hmm?" She flicked her gaze to his and found his blue eyes crinkled in concern as he studied her.

"How are you feeling?"

"Better," she answered honestly. Her chest still hurt to breathe and she was exhausted down to her very bones, but she felt better than she had. "But, Ryder, I'm not your girl."

His eyes narrowed and his lips pursed together into a straight line, she felt the ripple of denial move through his body, but he didn't address her words. "I think this bath did the trick, got your fever down. Do you think you could eat something?"

"Bath?" she echoed, glancing down to find that she was naked in a tub.

"I had to, Abby," Ryder said quickly. "You were burning up, your fever was spiking, I didn't know what else to do, I had to cool you down or I would lose you. I didn't touch you inappropriately, Abby."

She startled at his words.

Did he think so lowly of her that he honestly thought she believed he would take advantage of her when she was deathly ill?

Abigail swatted weakly at his impressively chiseled chest. "I know you would never take advantage of me, Ryder."

Ryder's eyes softened. "We haven't had a chance to talk yet, Abs, so I don't know what they did to you while you were here. I didn't want you to be triggered waking up to find yourself naked in a bath with a man."

"Oh," she said softly, touched that he was worried about her and wanted to make sure she was okay. She was no longer his responsibility in any way, shape or form, they weren't even friends, they were just two people who had known each other as kids and slept together. Given how easily he'd walked away from her, she didn't even think of what they'd had as a relationship. It was just sex. Sex that had obviously meant a whole lot more to her than it had to him.

Suddenly filled with an irrational need to make sure he didn't feel bad or worry about her anymore, she lifted her hand and placed it on his forearm. "It's okay, Ryder, they didn't do anything to me."

His forehead furrowed. "What?"

"They didn't do anything to me. They just put me in that cage and left me there."

Something in his gaze screamed disbelief but he quickly locked it away. "What's the last thing you remember before you were abducted?"

"I was leaving the studio late after working with a kid going for an audition. Her mom picked her up, I tidied up, turned all the lights off, locked up, and was walking to my car. The next thing I remember I was in that room where you found me."

Ryder said nothing for a long moment, but she could see the wheels spinning in his head. He lifted his hand and

41

pressed it to her forehead and then her cheeks. "You're still hot but your temperature is definitely going down. Let's get you out of here, dried off and dressed so you don't get chilled, and we'll see about getting you something to eat, you must be starving."

"Not really." Abigail shrugged, the idea of eating actually made her nauseous but she knew she had to keep up her strength. "But I will."

"That's my ... I mean, that's the spirit," he finished lamely, but they both knew what he'd been about to say. He'd been about to call her his girl again and she had no idea why he would want to, *he* was the one who left not her.

Twice.

She would have been his girl if he'd wanted her, she would have been his everything, his best friend, his partner, his lover, his biggest supporter. She would have loved him with everything she had, but he had thrown her away.

Ryder stood, keeping a steadying hand on her shoulder, then picked her up and wrapped her in a towel, carrying her to the bed. When he started to dry her off she put her hands on his.

"I can do it."

The look he shot her was doubtful, but he nodded and turned his back to give her privacy. "You tell me if you feel weak or dizzy."

"Okay." It was a fair compromise because she *was* weak and she *was* dizzy and she didn't want to pass out, fall over and hurt herself giving Ryder another thing to have to deal with.

It took her far longer than it should have but Abigail managed to dry herself and pull the shirt over her head before her strength gave out.

As though he could read her mind, Ryder asked, "You doing okay?"

"Actually, I could use some help," she admitted.

Immediately Ryder was at her side, he took hold of first her left wrist and then her right, and pulled her arms through the shirt's sleeves. Then he pulled the pants up her legs, lifting her hips to get them into place, before slipping socks back on her feet.

"There," he said and smiled as he perched on the edge of the bed beside her. "How do you feel?"

"Exhausted."

"No wonder, after what you've been through."

She nodded her agreement and watched as Ryder picked up her wrist. Was it her imagination or did his fingers caress her skin before settling on the inside of her wrist to take her pulse? They definitely lingered before he released her.

"Where's my brother?" she asked, looking around the small shack. There was no one here but the two of them and she wondered if Eric and the rest of the team were patrolling outside.

Ryder hesitated then met her gaze squarely. "We missed the helicopter. The others took the children and got out."

"The children?"

"We were here rescuing three little girls, a senator's daughters."

Realization dawned quickly.

They weren't here for her.

They hadn't even known she was here.

They had been looking for those children and stumbled upon her by accident.

Tears burned the backs of her eyes, and she sank deeper into the pillows she was propped up against. Maybe they had never been looking for her. She and Eric weren't exactly close, and Ryder had walked out of her life for the second time almost three years ago, she had friends and colleagues but no family, no one who loved her, who would move heaven and earth to find her.

"No." Ryder's harsh exclamation had her eyes snapping back up. "We looked for you, Abby. No one gave up on you. Not your brother, not your friends, and not me. We would have kept looking until we found you, okay?" When she nodded he reached out, hesitated, but then cupped her cheek in his hand. "I'm so glad we found you, these last fourteen months have been hell, knowing you were out there, not being able to find you, not knowing what was happening to you … I don't think I've taken a full breath until I found you in that cage."

Surprised to hear such heartfelt words coming out of his mouth, Abigail searched his eyes trying to figure out if he was telling her the truth or if he was just trying to console her, just trying to be nice because he pitied her. That wasn't what she wanted, she didn't want to be pitied, she wanted to find someone who loved her for who she was and didn't want to change her to conform with their own ideas on who she ought to be.

And that someone wasn't Ryder.

She would do well to remember that.

"How are we getting out of here if it's just you and me?" she asked.

"A team will be coming in to extract us in a few hours."

"What are we going to do until then?"

"You're going to try to eat something and then rest and conserve your strength. Your fever might be going down but you're still a very sick woman."

His hand was still on her face, and his thumb was brushing lightly across her skin making it tingle, and she could remember how his hands on her body had affected her when they had been together. He was staring at her like there was something he wanted to tell her, but he seemed to think better of it because he leaned in and touched his lips to her forehead, holding them there for a second before he released her and stood to rummage through his pack.

Ryder Flynn confused her.

He looked at her like he cared about her, like he wanted her like a starving man wanted food, but his behavior said the exact opposite.

Tired, her eyes fluttered closed and she was out before Ryder could give her anything to eat.

* * *

7:42 P.M.

The sun was setting, and Spider was starting to get antsy.

That didn't happen to him very often, his childhood had taught him how to remain calm even under the most horrible of circumstances because when you weren't calm you drew unwanted attention. Drawing unwanted attention could prove deadly—both in his childhood home and in his job.

But when something involved Abigail it threw him through a loop.

Since she was asleep again he reached out and touched her. Letting his fingers stroke her hair and then the soft skin of her cheek, he didn't want to wake her because she needed the rest, but at the same time he couldn't resist her.

He had it bad.

Always had.

He'd done his best to keep his distance, believing it was better for her not to be involved with someone like him, but now he knew he had been fooling himself. He could never stay away from her.

Abigail stirred beneath his touch and leaned into it making him groan. How he wished that they were anywhere but here, that Abby hadn't been abducted and held captive, that he hadn't broken her heart, that she wasn't lying there fighting for her life. He wished it was just the two of them, curled up in his bed, a fire crackling in the fireplace, classical music playing in the background, nothing in the whole world but the two of them.

"Ryder?" she mumbled.

"Here, babe," he assured her. Every time she woke up she asked for him and he couldn't deny that he liked it. He wanted her to need him, maybe it was a little caveman of him to want the woman he loved to need him, but he did, and it was nice to be needed.

"My head hurts," she whispered.

She'd been complaining about a worsening headache each time she regained consciousness and he was becoming concerned. Her temperature had fallen, but her breathing was still rapid and shallow, her pulse was weak, and although he'd managed to get her to eat a little it didn't seem to help her regain any strength. He'd held off as long as he could but it seemed like it was time.

Straightening, he grabbed a syringe from his first aid kit. "I'll give you a shot of morphine."

Abigail nodded, not even bothering to open her eyes.

At least she hadn't hallucinated again since her fever had broken. Seeing her fear so raw was enough to bring him to his knees. He'd do anything to make it so this never happened, but the best he could do was stand by her side as she dealt with the fallout.

And he was sure that would be a lot worse than Abigail thought.

She claimed the men here hadn't done anything to her but

throw her in that cage and leave her there, but that didn't make sense nor did it fit with what she'd been saying while she was burning up with fever. She'd been terrified of a man who had hurt her, she'd begged not to be hurt again and he had a feeling that something had been done to her between the time she was grabbed and the time she remembered waking up in that cage. If he had to guess, he'd say she'd been drugged and the drugs had wiped her memories, that or her brain was trying to protect her.

Luis Perez was a dangerous man, he wouldn't have just kept a gorgeous woman like Abigail in a cage for over a year. He could have gotten too much money from selling her to do that, and if he wanted to keep her for himself, he wouldn't have just stuck her there and left her.

Now wasn't the time to worry about that though, now he had to focus on getting her out of here.

The team should be here soon, not his team, there had been some complications when they'd gotten the Burns girls out of Mexico and they'd had to divert which meant that a different team would come to evac him and Abigail.

Giving Abby the morphine, he checked her vitals and checked her temperature, which still wasn't going down any further, but at least it wasn't climbing and he had to believe the worst was over now.

Weapon in hand, he moved to the doorway and looked out. So far everything had gone smoothly, he had made the four hourly check-ins, and no one had questioned him once he gave the codeword and said that he hadn't seen any activity. Just because everything had gone smoothly so far didn't mean that it would last. For all he knew they had picked up on the fact that he wasn't one of Perez's men and were simply planning an attack.

If that was the case then he would go down fighting.

And if the men closed in on them, would he do as Abigail

asked and kill her rather than letting Perez get his hands on her again?

No.

He couldn't do that.

Wasn't sure that he had it in him even knowing what might happen to her.

Did that make him weak?

A coward?

Taking a life changed you in ways you couldn't comprehend until you'd been put in that position. He loved Abigail, would do anything for her, would lay down his life for her, but killing her …

The slightest of movements deep in the trees snagged his attention.

Partially closing the door, he slipped his NVG on and aimed his rifle.

There.

He spotted three people approaching.

His or Perez's?

Only one way to find out. Wait and see.

His finger hovered on the trigger of his rifle, ready to fire if it wasn't his men who broke through the tree line and approached the shack.

The seconds ticked by in excruciating slowness.

One by one until his skin crawled with anxious anticipation. He was more than ready to get out of here, and he prayed that he was about to see friendly faces.

The green figures were coming closer, any second now he would have to decide whether to fire or not.

Spider realized he was holding his breath and forced himself to exhale slowly, clearing away everything until his whole focus was on the approaching men.

As they stepped out from behind the trees Spider relaxed.

Sliding off the goggles, he opened the door wider and

greeted the other team. "Hey, Wolf, Abe, Cookie." He nodded at each of the three men.

"Spider." Matthew "Wolf" Steel nodded then gave him a big grin. "You ready to get out of here?"

"Oh yeah," he said, finally allowing himself to believe that the worst was over. All they had to do was get Abigail ready for the trek through the jungle to the new evacuation point and then they were home free.

"Mozart, Dude, and Benny are keeping watch," Christopher "Abe" Powers informed him as the three men followed him into the shack.

"How's our girl?" Wolf asked, crossing the room to the bed where Abigail was sleeping. He and Night and their team weren't the only ones who had been hunting for Abigail when she disappeared, every SEAL team in the country had been in on the search. SEALs stuck together, they were family, and Abigail was Night's sister which made her family to all of them. They had checked out every lead, all lost sleep questioning anyone and everyone who was even vaguely related to Abigail from her colleagues and friends, to her neighbors, to her dentist, to the baker at her favorite bakery where she bought a loaf of fresh bread every day.

"She's hanging in there, she's tough," he said as he followed Wolf to the bed.

"Course she is," Wolf said. Perching on the edge of the bed beside Abigail, he touched the back of his hand to her cheek. "Hey, Abby Girl," he said softly.

Abigail's eyes opened with far more effort than anyone should have to use to do such a simple task. When she saw who was sitting beside her she shot Wolf a winning smile and Spider couldn't not be jealous that she never smiled at him like that.

At least not anymore.

Didn't matter that Wolf was happily married and only

looked at Abigail as a little sister, the green-eyed monster cared only that Abigail would probably never smile at him that way again.

"Hey, Matthew," Abigail whispered, "you our ride out of this awful place?"

"Sure am, ballerina girl."

"You got any injuries we need to be worried about, Abs?" Abe asked.

"No, just ..." she broke off as she began to cough, horrible harsh sounds that had the four SEALs in the room wincing in commiseration.

Spider moved to sit behind Abigail, holding her against his chest as she wheezed and struggled to regain control of her breathing. "Pneumonia," he said to the others, glancing at the red speckles on her pale palm when she lowered it from her mouth.

Three sets of concerned eyes met his and then moved to Abigail lying limply in his hold.

"Okay, Abs, I'm going to give you a dose of antibiotics before we move out," Hunter "Cookie" Knox said calmly.

Despite everyone's concerns no one wanted to say or do anything to make Abigail stressed, they didn't want to elevate her heart rate anymore than it already was. It was already battling to keep her alive.

While Cookie gave Abigail a shot of antibiotics, Spider held Abby like he could infuse his life into her. Will her to keep living just because he needed her and he wasn't ready to let her go for good. Maybe at the back of his mind he had always hoped that somehow, someway, they might reconcile, now that he'd made up his mind to make it happen he didn't want to lose her.

"You ready to head out?" Wolf asked, his dark brown eyes troubled.

"What's wrong?" Spider asked.

"We've got company coming," the other man replied.

Everyone moved quickly, preparing themselves for the trek through the jungle and removing any evidence that suggested anyone other than the man Spider had killed last night had been here.

Just as he was scooping up an unconscious Abigail into his arms, Spider heard the sound he had been dreading.

Gunshots.

* * *

8:01 P.M.

Gunshots.

Abigail tried to lift her head off Ryder's shoulder. "Was that gunshots?" she asked.

"Yes," Ryder said shortly, already moving with her in his arms.

"Put me down, carrying me will slow you down," she said, wriggling vainly in his hold.

"Hate to break it to you, sweetheart, but letting you walk will slow us down more," Ryder told her with an apologetic smile.

She hated that he was right.

She didn't want to be a burden, didn't want the fact that she was sick and weak to put the others in danger, but it was out of her control and that gave her that out of control feeling that she hated.

"Hey," Ryder said, waiting till she met his gaze before continuing, "we got this, this is what we do, we'll get you home safely."

It wasn't that she thought Ryder or the others were incompetent, she knew that they were all good at their jobs and highly trained, it was just that knowing she was a burden and couldn't pull her own weight made her feel like a liability. Being a burden was how her family had made her feel most of her childhood and it wasn't a feeling she liked revisiting.

"I know you will," she told him. The cabin suddenly went dark, and Abigail involuntarily curled her arms around Ryder's neck and held on to him tightly.

"They're approaching from the east," Matthew said to the others. "Spider and Cookie get Abigail out of here through the west window, Abe and I will hold them off."

"But," Abby started to protest, only to cut herself off when she realized that she was being ridiculous. She wasn't the expert here and telling the guys that she didn't want them to put themselves in danger because of her was pointless, they had already put themselves in danger by coming here and they would do anything—including give their own lives—to make sure she got home. It was noble and she respected them for the sacrifices they made and were prepared to make, but it still didn't seem like a good trade. She was the one who was sick if anyone was going to die out here it should be her.

Ryder carried her over to the window while Matthew and Christopher positioned themselves in front of the two front windows. Hunter quietly slid open the window then climbed through it, and Ryder passed her through it and into Hunter's waiting arms.

"Matthew and Christopher?" she asked.

"Will come once they know we're out," Hunter assured her.

He started moving with her and she wanted to ask for Ryder, but he was behind them, no doubt putting himself in danger by covering them as they ran the short distance to the concealment of the trees.

"Hunter?"

"Yeah, Abs?"

"I'm going to cough." She was trying to hold it back, she didn't want to do anything that would draw attention to them, but she wasn't sure she could stop it from coming. Before Hunter could reply she turned and buried her face in his shoulder, muffling the sound as best as she could.

The coughing made her dizzy, and the world spun horrifyingly fast revolutions around her.

Was it trying to throw her off?

It certainly felt like it.

She heard bullets continue to fly but they suddenly seemed very far away.

Voices murmured in rapid-fire above her but she couldn't seem to understand any of them.

Was it the Mexican men back? The ones who had held her captive? She spoke a little Spanish but not enough to have been able to comprehend much of what she'd heard them talking about.

She was moved, draped over something hard that dug into her stomach, and she very nearly lost what little food Ryder had been able to convince her to eat.

Then they were moving.

Fast.

Too fast.

Somehow she managed to get her hands curled into the hard sides of the pack belonging to whoever was carrying her. She hoped it was Ryder. When she was with Ryder she felt safe, well at least as safe as it was possible to feel in the middle of the Mexican jungle.

Ryder shouldn't make her feel safe.

Not after he'd ripped her heart out twice before.

Falling for him again meant letting him take a third crack at her heart and three strikes and she might be out forever.

Despite all that her body craved Ryder's touch. It was the

only thing that could soothe her right now. And it wasn't just her body that craved Ryder it was her soul. When they weren't together it was like a part of her was lost.

Why was she doing this to herself?

Why was she thinking of Ryder beyond the fact that he was here to save her life?

Letting herself fall for Ryder again was the equivalent of standing in an airplane, removing her parachute, and then opening the door and jumping out. It was emotional suicide and yet her logical brain seemed to have checked out and her traitorous heart was acting on its own.

This kind of thinking would get her hurt, only that was the problem, she wasn't thinking she was only feeling, and feeling was what led to heartbreak. If she'd had any sense at all she wouldn't have let her feelings for Ryder cloud her judgment when he'd come back to her, she should have known that if he could walk away from her once then he could do it again.

And again.

If she even entertained the idea of letting him back into her life she would spend the rest of her life just waiting for him to bail.

She'd always tried to live her life by the motto that people told you about themselves by their words and their actions, and you should always listen to them and believe them. Ryder had told her that he couldn't be trusted to stick around, she should believe that and accept it.

She had accepted it.

At least she thought she had.

Until he'd scooped her into his arms and carried her out of her prison.

"Abby? You with me? Abigail?" The harsh whisper slipped slowly into her brain, and she blinked and realized she had been set down on the prickly ground.

"Ryder?" It was dark, and while the sky must be clear because she could see the moonlight dappled through the leaves, the man in front of her was dressed in black with NVG on so it was near impossible to make out the features.

"Yes. Perez's men are moving in on us. There are at least fifty of them and only seven of us so we're going to hide out, let them go past us, then backtrack to the extraction point."

"Hide out?"

"Hide up," he said, tilting his head until he was looking up into the limbs of the large tree he'd propped her up against.

"Up the tree?"

"If we're lucky they'll never think of that and walk on by. Perez's men aren't smart or well trained, just bloodthirsty."

"Is everyone okay?" That was all she cared about at the moment. She would do anything Ryder asked her to do and if that was climbing a tree then so be it, she just needed to know that the others were all safe.

"Duke and Benny are holding the men back to give the rest of us time to get up into the trees."

"Will they ..."

"They know what they're doing, Abby, they'll make it up into the trees once we get up."

She tilted her head back so she could look up into the branches. How exactly did he think she was going to be able to get up there? "Ryder, maybe you should just leave me, I can't ..."

Lips crashed against hers cutting off her protest.

The kiss was hard and yet at the same time soft, but far too short.

"Up you go, Wolf is waiting for you. Between the two of us we'll get you up there." Ryder stood, bringing her up with him then hoisted her up toward the lowest branch where Matthew was waiting for her. He clamped his hands around her wrists and pulled her up beside him, keeping an arm around her waist while Ryder climbed up to meet them.

She was slowing them down.

Without her they would already be up safe in the treetops.

"I can climb on my own," she said, pushing away Matthew's arm as she reached out for the next branch. Her body trembled with the exertion but she managed to curl her hands around the branch and haul herself up.

When she reached for the next branch, trying to fight back a wave of dizziness, Ryder stopped her. "I know you don't want help," he whispered close to her ear so the sound didn't carry, "but it will be faster if Wolf and I help."

"Ryder," she said helplessly, she'd been alone for months now and it was weird having people around, besides, she'd been independent from the time she was a little girl, she didn't want to have to rely on anyone else.

"I know, sweetheart," he said sympathetically, before hoisting her up for Matthew to catch.

It didn't take them long to reach the top branches, and although she helped when and how she could, Abigail had to admit that without Ryder and Matthew she wouldn't have made it.

Exhausted, she was glad when Ryder wrapped his arms around her trembling body, she feared without him holding onto her she very likely would have toppled right back down to the ground.

Before she'd even managed to catch her breath, she saw lights approaching.

The men were coming.

* * *

8:29 P.M.

. . .

Spider had Abigail pressed between the trunk of the tree and his body, if they were spotted and shot at, then there was a chance that she would miss the bullets when they started to fly and survive.

Until he was hit and she fell.

He knew the only reason she was sitting upright was because the trunk was behind her and his body was in front, the combination of the two kept her propped up, but even so she was draped across him. Shivers wracked her body, and when he pressed his fingertips to her forehead he found her skin was still flushed, she was still running a fever, still in need of urgent medical treatment.

Voices wafted up to them as the men—at least fifty of them—began to trail past the trees where he and the others were perched.

Spider found himself barely daring to breathe.

One wrong move and this extraction would all go to Hell.

While he knew he and his team could sit up here for hours without drawing anyone's attention, it was Abigail that he was worried about. She was still running a fever so there was a chance that she could start hallucinating again, but what he was more worried about was that she would have another coughing fit.

Although she had tried to stifle the last one it had been loud enough to draw the attention of Perez's men, giving their position away, and they had only just managed to get away without anyone getting hurt. If she started to cough now every one of the men beneath them would know where they were, and every one of them would fire their weapons. He and the others would fire back, but they were basically sitting ducks up here, especially with a sick Abigail limiting their movements.

The men were passing by, fighting amongst themselves, they didn't bother to attempt to be stealthy, Perez's men were not known for their skills, but they were known for being bloodthirsty. He'd seen the evidence of what they had done to a rival drug lord when the man had attempted to takeover Perez's compound. It hadn't been pretty. Those men had been brutally tortured alongside some of Perez's own men who had been deemed to be traitors.

No way was he letting that happen to Abigail.

Just because they had kept her alive for fourteen months and, according to her, not laid a hand on her, it didn't mean that this time around she would be afforded those same protections.

The last of the men were passing by, and Spider was just letting himself start to relax when Abigail suddenly jerked upright, her panicked hands pressing to her mouth.

She was going to start coughing.

There was no way for her to stop it.

The best they could hope for was that the men's arguing amongst themselves and the fact that they had already mostly passed on by would be enough to save them.

Shoving her back firmly against the tree trunk, he put one hand behind her head to cushion the impact and pushed her hands out of the way to put his other tightly over her mouth. Spider winced because he knew he was hurting her but there was nothing he could do about that now. They had to muffle the sounds as best they could if they wanted to live.

Abigail pressed her hands over his as though they could further dampen the sound with three hands rather than one.

Then it came.

Tears leaked out the corners of her scrunched up eyes and Spider was sure they were from a mixture of pain and fear as her body began to spasm as coughs tore through her damaged lungs. Spider could feel Wolf watching them anxiously as the man moved slightly so he partially blocked them with his body.

No bullets came.

No shouts that they had found the intruders.

Nothing but the sounds of the men disappearing off into the jungle.

Abigail shuddered and slumped against his hold, and he cautiously removed his hand from over her mouth and pulled her closer, rubbing her back as he held her close. He knew how scared she was, how badly she was hurting, even if he bought that no one had laid a hand on her all these months—which given her hallucinations he wasn't sure he did—being locked in a cage, alone, for so long deprived of human connections, was a horrific form of torture. She had been isolated and broken down little bit by little bit, and when they got her back home he wasn't sure what kind of woman he would find.

That his Abby was gone was a given.

No one could go through what she had and come out of it the same person they had been before.

What he did know was the new Abigail would be every bit as strong as the old one had been.

He knew that without a shadow of a doubt because the Abigail he had seen over the last twenty-four hours still possessed the core of who she had always been. She was still fiercely independent, and she still cared more about others than she did herself. How many times had she begged him to leave her because she didn't want him to get hurt trying to save her? How many times had she worried over the safety of him and Wolf's team? Enough that he knew his Abigail was still in there, he just prayed that she wouldn't shut everyone out and instead let him and her brother and her friends be there to support her as she rebuilt her life.

They waited several minutes to make sure that the men had well and truly moved on before they started to move.

"Time to go, Abby," he whispered against her ear.

"So tired," she mumbled back.

"I know, honey, but not long to go now, the men are looking for us in one direction, and we're heading off in the opposite one. All you have to do now is hold on for a short walk then we'll have you on the helo and get you someplace safe where you can rest."

"A short walk?" She lifted her head and narrowed her eyes at him. "I know what you SEAL guys are like, a short walk for you is a grueling hike for most people."

Wolf chuckled beside him and Spider grinned, his girl was toughing this out like a boss. "Lucky for you, you won't be doing any walking then. All you have to do is hold on and enjoy the ride."

"I'm not going to enjoy going back down the tree," Abigail said and made a face.

"We got you up, we can get you down," he assured her.

She gave him a doubtful glance but didn't complain when Wolf dropped down onto the next branch and he lowered her down into the other SEAL's arms. Passing her backward and forward between them they got her safely to the ground where Spider sat her down and grabbed his canteen.

"Here, Abby, drink something." He took hold of her chin and tipped her head back as he held the bottle to her lips. She swallowed a couple of mouthfuls before pushing the bottle away. She was still dehydrated and would need IV fluids as soon as they got her on the helo.

While he was tending to Abby, he knew the other team was scouting around them, making sure they weren't about to walk into an ambush. He didn't think that Perez's men were smart enough to attempt to lull them into a false sense of security only to send them straight into a trap by dictating which direction they had to move in, but it was better to be safe than sorry.

Spider became aware that they weren't alone a moment before Abigail's eyes widened in fear as she stared at something over his shoulder.

He didn't hesitate.

He spun around, launching himself at the same time, and grabbed their would-be attacker, snapping his neck before the man had a chance to do anything.

Abigail must have scrambled up after him because as he let the body fall to the ground she clutched at his shoulder.

"He's just a kid," she whispered, her gaze fixed on the boy who couldn't be more than about twelve. The kid must have been told he couldn't go with the older men so he'd decided to sneak along behind them, wanting to be part of the hunt.

"No, sweetheart," he said, taking her and forcibly turning her around so she wasn't looking at the body anymore. "He's one of Perez's men, if given a chance he would have killed me and taken you back to that prison. It's my job to protect you, eliminate threats, and whether he looked like it or not that kid was a threat."

"He's so young."

"He is."

"It's not fair."

"Life often isn't."

"All good?" Wolf asked, returning to them.

"We had a little visitor, but yeah," he replied.

"Are we going home now?" Abigail asked in a small voice.

"Yep," Wolf assured her.

"Smooth sailing now, Abby, smooth sailing," he promised as he hoisted her onto his shoulder.

* * *

10:37 P.M.

They had been walking for a long time.

Well, she hadn't been walking, she was being carried, passed from one of the SEALs to another, draped over strong sets of shoulders. They stopped often and she knew it wasn't because any of the men were tired and needed a break. No, they stopped because of her, to try to get water into her, or to try to get her to eat something.

The more they walked the less they seemed to worry about her coughing. Now when a coughing fit attacked, whoever was carrying her simply eased her down to the ground and tried to help her as best they could by supporting her as she coughed and wheezed and struggled to breathe.

When they walked the other SEALs formed a circle around her, a little protective bubble, and she knew they were willing to die to protect her.

The thought made her misty-eyed.

She had grown up around her grandfather's former SEAL teammates, and her father's SEAL team, she was accustomed to big, tough, alpha men, but she had never experienced what they did like this. Before it had just been stories that her grandpa or Dad would tell her and her brother when they were kids, sanitized versions of some of their missions that were told in a manner making them suitable for children.

But this was so real.

Terrifyingly real.

Now she had seen firsthand just what the men in her family did for a living, and it gave her a new respect for them.

It even went so far as to wipe away a little of the lingering hurt that had built up inside her from years of living as an outsider in her own family. No one in her family had ever outright said it, but they had all known it was true. She was a girl so she could never have become a SEAL, but in their minds she should have become a warrior of some sort. There were plenty of military positions available for women and her family thought she should have pursued one of them.

Instead, she'd become a ballerina.

Her mother had accused her of choosing that particular interest and later profession just to stick it to her family, but it hadn't been like that. For her, there was strength in the beauty and control of dancing. It required discipline and power, it required you to spend hours to perfect every technique, to get it perfect, and she had worked hard at learning her craft. She'd given up time with friends, parties, and trips to the mall because she'd been busy in her dance studio. Abigail didn't regret her choices for a moment even if it had all come crashing down around her because of one momentary lapse in decision making.

That one moment had changed her whole life.

If she hadn't been forced to give up her dreams of being a professional ballerina and returned to California, then she never would have slept with Ryder, she never would have taken a job as a dance teacher, she never would have taken Ryder back and then lost him again, and maybe she never would have ended up in a prison out here in the Mexican jungle.

"Hey, Abby, how are you doing?"

She focused her weary eyes on Kason "Benny" Sawyer's face as he leaned over her. "Hanging in there," she assured him. She hated that the guys had to keep stopping for her, but she knew telling them it wasn't necessary wouldn't change anything. They would continue to stop to make sure she was remaining at least partially hydrated because they seemed to care just as much about her medical and emotional health as they did about her physical safety.

Yes, she knew these men personally, she often hung out with the SEAL families because it was basically the only family she had, but she had a feeling they were this sensitive with anyone they rescued not just with her because they knew her.

Sensitive wasn't a word she had ever associated with SEALs before now, but she liked seeing this side of them. They were big and strong and tougher than most people could comprehend, but underneath they had heart, and that was what made them really amazing in her mind.

Without her realizing it as she sipped the water Kason offered she scanned the group searching for Ryder. She knew how sensitive he could be because they'd been together for almost a year before he'd left her that second time. During those months he'd been sweet and funny, not afraid to open up to her and to let her open up to him about how her parents' disappointment in her had impacted her whole life. He had been thoughtful, paying attention to what she said and often surprising her with dates or gifts related to something she didn't even remember telling him.

Why had he left her?

Maybe if she could understand that, she could finally put him behind her and move on. Although it had been three years since they broke up, she hadn't been able to summon any interest in dating anyone else. Her heart was still firmly focused on a certain sexy SEAL with a mop of dark hair and clear blue eyes.

"Looking for your guy?" Kason asked.

She made a face at him. "If you mean Ryder, he's not my guy."

"Sure."

Abigail frowned. "You know he's not, you know we dated, and he dumped me without a goodbye or an explanation. Twice."

"I'll tell you what I know," Kason said seriously, "I know that Spider is crazy about you."

She huffed at that.

What else was there to say?

If Ryder was really crazy about her he wouldn't have left.

"Sometimes people have reasons for what they do, even if what they do is a mistake and anyone with eyes can see that. I won't ask you to cut Spider some slack because hurting you like he did wasn't okay, but I will ask you to keep an open mind. Spider has some stuff to work through, but maybe once he does, he'll be ready to be happy."

"Do you know something about him I don't?" she demanded.

"No. But I know a guy who's facing an internal battle when I see one. Abs, you're Night's little sister which basically makes you the little sister of every one of us. I don't want to see you get hurt, but Spider is my friend and I want him to be happy. So just hear him out if you can, okay?"

She would protest that she'd already given Ryder plenty of chances to tell her anything he needed to tell her, but her lungs seized again and she started to cough.

Abigail wasn't sure how much more of this she could take.

She was so tired of feeling sick and miserable, she just wanted to lie down on a soft, comfortable bed and go to sleep and then wake up feeling human again.

"Here, I'll take her," she heard Ryder say, and when strong hands lifted her she knew they were his. "Hold on, Abby, not much longer, okay? We're almost to the extraction point, and then we'll get some medicine into you and get you away from here."

This time when he carried her he didn't put her over his shoulder, instead he cradled her gently in his arms. "Ryder?" she asked.

"I want you to be comfortable and we're nearly there," he explained.

Tired, she rested her head on his shoulder, now that she wasn't being bounced around with a hard shoulder pressed into her stomach she was able to doze a little. The world faded around her and she let herself stop holding on so tightly. She was tired of being strong, tired of fighting to get through each day … she was just plain tired.

Something loud began to cut through the otherwise quiet night and her sluggish brain couldn't process what it was.

To be honest, she didn't really care what it was.

She was finding it increasingly difficult to care about anything.

The sound got louder.

She started to cough again, so hard it hurt her already aching chest.

Why did breathing have to be so hard?

It was supposed to be something your body did automatically, you weren't supposed to have to fight for each breath of air.

Then she was set down on something soft, something was put on her face and she could breathe a little easier. Someone was fussing about her, she felt a tug on the back of her hand, and something wrapped around her arm, fingers touched her wrist, and something cool brushed against her forehead.

"Let go, sweetheart," Ryder's soft voice urged. "I've got you, you're safe, you don't have to fight alone anymore, I'm right here beside you, so it's okay to let go."

For once she didn't argue, didn't attempt to protest that she could do it on her own, she just let his words ease her final finger hold on consciousness, and she drifted quietly away.

CHAPTER 3

June 16th

12:12 A.M.

Fourteen months, two weeks, and three days after Abigail had been abducted, the helicopter touched down on American soil.

She was home.

Spider felt a sense of relief, he and his team had been on a mission when Night had gotten a call that his sister had been abducted. Over a week had passed by then, and by the time they were able to get back to the States, she'd been missing for almost a month. The trail had already long since gone cold, and the local cops hadn't seemed to be overly concerned even though it was completely out of character for Abigail to just up and disappear, plus her car had still been in the parking lot with her purse sitting on the ground beside the driver's door.

He and Night and every single person on their team, and most of the other teams, had done everything they could to try to track her down but they had been met with dead end after dead end.

Now he could finally take a deep breath and relax.

Abigail was home.

Safe.

The rotors stopped spinning, and Spider finally lifted his gaze away from Abigail's face. The whole journey he'd sat beside her, holding her hand, allowing the others to tend to her medical condition while he kept himself just there for her support.

That was his role in her life now.

There was no more walking away, no more letting other people meddle in his life, no more feeling guilty for past transgressions. He and Abigail needed a clean slate, and they were going to get one.

"We're going to transport her to a house where we can stay for a few days while she recovers her strength, and maybe we can try to figure out why she was taken," Wolf said as they opened the helo doors.

"I have some things I need to tell you guys," he said as they lifted the gurney Abigail was lying on and carried her out of the helicopter and to the waiting transport van.

Abigail didn't stir as they moved her, she hadn't stirred since they had sedated her. They'd been pumping fluids and heavy-duty antibiotics into her system and hopefully they would clear up the chest infection without her needing to be admitted to a hospital.

Since he didn't know why she had been taken or why she had been held so long, Spider wasn't comfortable with anyone knowing that she was back until they knew a little more about the situation. He couldn't get her hallucinations out of his mind, he was sure there was something in there that would give them the answers they needed.

Once they had her settled they would need to do a more extensive examination, checking for old injuries that she might have sustained during her captivity and anything he might have missed. He had a feeling that if they x-rayed her they would find several healed broken bones because he was positive that someone had roughed her up—badly—before throwing her in that cage.

The drive to the safehouse where they would hang out for a few days was quiet, Spider's focus on Abigail, watching the rise and fall of her chest, his hand positioned holding hers so his fingertips rested on her pulse which was drumming weakly against his fingers.

She was alive.

It would take some getting used to. After fourteen months of believing the worst it was hard to accept that it was over and they'd gotten her back.

When they arrived at the safehouse, Spider gathered Abigail into his arms while Faulkner "Dude" Cooper grabbed the IV bags, and he took her upstairs to the master bedroom, where he set her on the bed. Before he could tell them what he knew they had to make sure there weren't any other medical issues to deal with.

With quick, efficient movements, he and Wolf stripped off her clothes, and Spider ran his hands up and down her body, checking for injuries. He didn't find any fresh ones, but two of her fingers were slightly bent out of shape. Breaking someone's fingers was a common method of torture and he wondered if that was what had been done to his sweet, precious Abby.

There was nothing else that concerned him, so he grabbed one of his spare t-shirts and slipped it over her head, then he tucked her in under the covers while Dude reconnected the IV.

She was still running a fever and Cookie put a cool, damp washcloth on her forehead, then while Spider settled into the only chair in the room, a chair he wouldn't be moving from until Abigail opened those stunning eyes of hers, the other men stood guard around her bed.

Although she was safe, out of Mexico and back home in the States, all of them seemed to feel the same sense of foreboding like this wasn't over, and they had barely scratched the surface of what was really going on, and all of them wanted to be prepared and make sure that Abigail wasn't hurt again.

"What do you know?" Wolf asked, getting right down to business.

"Abigail says that she doesn't remember how she was abducted. Said that the last thing she remembered was packing up after work and walking to her car."

"Someone grabbed her in the parking lot," Sam "Mozart" Reed said.

Spider nodded. "Her car and purse were found there. Whoever took her wanted to make sure that there was no way we could trace where she was taken so he left behind her car and her cell phone, both of which we might have been able to use to at least point us in a direction."

"What's the next thing she remembers?" Abe asked.

"Waking up in the same cell where I found her."

The other men exchanged confused glances. "What did they do to her while they kept her in there?" Wolf asked.

"Nothing."

"Nothing?" Cookie repeated.

"That's what she said. She said she was just left in there and someone came a couple of times a day to throw her some food, but no one would interact with her at all."

"That doesn't make sense," Wolf said.

"Agreed."

"So they just took her and put her in a cage for fourteen months?" Dude asked.

"That's what she said," Spider confirmed.

"But?" Abe asked.

"But her fever spiked when I had her in the shack, I had to put her in the tub to try to bring it down. While she was delirious with fever she was hallucinating. She thought someone else was in the room with us, and she begged him not to hurt her again, said she couldn't go through that again."

"You think they beat her before they put her in there?" Mozart asked.

He didn't even have to consider his answer, as much as it made his gut churn he nodded. "Yes."

"They drug her maybe? That could have wiped out her memory," Benny said.

"That would be my guess," Spider confirmed.

"Why?" Dude asked. "Why would they kidnap Abs? Perez deals in drugs and guns, dabbles in human trafficking, as far as we know Abigail isn't involved in anything like that."

"It feels like she was targeted specifically," Wolf said thoughtfully. "I mean, a typical abduction site isn't a dance studio parking lot. They beat her up instead of either selling her or Perez keeping her for himself. And fourteen months is a long time to hold her prisoner. What did he have to gain from keeping her?"

"I don't know," Spider said, and that feeling of impotence he'd had while Abigail was missing returned. If he couldn't figure out why she had been targeted then he couldn't keep her safe.

"Abigail is beautiful, if he was smart he would have sold her quickly, she would have brought in a bundle," Abe said.

"From what we know of him, Perez prefers blondes," Cookie added.

"Could the hallucinations have been just that, hallucinations? Not anything related to her abduction and imprisonment?" Benny asked.

"Anything is possible, but it was like she was seeing someone specific," Spider replied.

"Either way none of this makes sense," Wolf said, running frustrated hands through his dark hair.

Spider echoed those frustrations.

Nothing about Abigail's abduction made sense. The idea that she was targeted, the fact that she might have been beaten, that she had been kept so long and yet never touched even though she was on the compound of a known human trafficker, all of it tied together and yet he couldn't seem to find the start of that piece of string. How could he unravel this if he didn't know where to begin?

"We're not going to get any answers until she wakes up," Wolf said, gesturing to the unconscious Abigail. "When she's strong enough we'll debrief her, see if she remembers something now that she's safe and feeling better."

As much as he hated to admit it, Wolf was right.

There was nothing more they could do right now. Abigail needed time to rest, heal, and regain her strength, they weren't going to be able to get any answers until then. Even once she was better there were no guarantees that Abigail would remember anything, they didn't know what had been done to her or what drugs she'd been given, and the mind was a funny thing, it could block things out to protect itself.

The others filed out of the room leaving him along with Abigail, and he did the one thing he'd been longing to do since he walked out the door three years ago and never came back. Kicking off his shoes, he lifted the covers and slipped in beside Abigail. Careful not to disturb the IV lines, he pulled her into his arms and fell asleep holding the woman he loved.

* * *

3:44 P.M.

Abigail groaned and tried to roll over, but instead she just rolled into a big, warm, solid wall.

No.

Not a wall.

A man.

For a moment panic flooded through her veins. Where was she? Who was the man? Why was he in bed with her?

Then just as suddenly as it had come on her, the panic faded. She knew that smell, she knew that body, she knew those arms, it wasn't someone here to hurt her, it was Ryder.

"You're awake." His voice rumbled through his chest, and she hated how much comfort she got just from being held in his arms.

"Yes," she replied.

"How are you feeling?" He shifted as he asked the question, releasing his hold on her and propping himself up on an elbow so he could touch the back of his hand to her forehead.

"Better," she replied. She felt weak, drained like she didn't have an ounce of energy left inside her body, but she felt cooler, no longer plagued by a fever, and her breathing felt a little easier too.

"Your temperature is definitely down, and the antibiotics you're on seem to be working." Ryder sounded satisfied like he had hoped that the medications would make her better, but hadn't allowed himself to believe it until he saw it with his own eyes.

"We're home?" she asked hopefully. She knew that they had gotten onto the helicopter but she didn't know where they had landed. Were they back in the US or had they had to fly someplace else?

"We're home," Ryder said, smiling down at her.

She opened her mouth to ask a question but started coughing instead. It hurt, but it wasn't as bad as it had been which was a plus. "What time is it?" she asked when the coughing finally subsided.

He glanced behind her then said, "Nearly four in the afternoon, you've been out for about sixteen hours give or take."

"That long?"

"You needed the rest. Actually, you need a whole lot more rest. Why don't you close your eyes and go back to sleep?"

"Can't."

"Can't?"

"I need to go to the bathroom," she said simply. It would be so nice to go to a real bathroom, use a real toilet. After so many months of going in a hole in the ground, she had realized just how lucky they were to have running water and plumbing.

"I'll carry you," Ryder said, climbing out of bed and unhooking the IV bags from a pole beside the bed.

"I can walk," she said firmly.

"Sweetheart, I don't think you can stand on your own let alone walk."

"I can," she contradicted.

"You can't."

"I can," she overemphasized each word. She didn't want to argue with Ryder, but after so many months of being locked up alone she wanted to have her independence back, she wanted her life back.

"Abs," Ryder said overly patiently, "I know you, and I know how independent you are, how much you like to do things on your own, but you're going to have to face facts, for the next few days you're going to be weak and need help. Now I understand if given our history you don't want me helping you, but you need someone, so choose, me or one of the other guys?"

Her natural instinct was to keep arguing until he saw that she was right and let her go to the bathroom on her own, but her logical side had already accepted he was right. She'd only been awake for a matter of minutes and already she felt tired enough to curl up and sleep the rest of the day away.

"You, I guess." She sighed.

Ryder grinned and folded back the covers. "See, accepting help wasn't so bad now was it?"

"Don't gloat, Ryder, it doesn't suit you," she glowered as he curled an arm under her knees and one behind her back and lifted her up.

Ryder laughed as he carried her across the room and into the attached bathroom, lifted the toilet lid before setting her down, and put the IV bags on the vanity. "I'll close the door, and you call me when you're done. If you feel weak or dizzy you tell me okay, I don't want you being stubborn and keeling over. Hitting your head and knocking yourself out isn't something your body needs to be dealing with right now when it's already battling pneumonia."

Abigail rolled her eyes at Ryder's mothering side but nodded. "I'll call you if I need you," she promised.

Satisfied that she was telling the truth, he turned and left her in the bathroom, closing the door behind him. "I'm right outside," he called through to her.

"Okay, Mom," she muttered as she did her business. Ryder

turned into such a mother hen when someone was sick, she remembered when they had been together and she'd had appendicitis. Once she was released from the hospital after having her appendix removed, he had fussed around her every day for a week while she recovered. He'd fluffed pillows, cooked soup, baked bread, sat and watched Disney movies with her, cleaned the house, carried her to and from the bathroom when she was too weak to make it on her own, made sure she took her medications on time, and slept in a chair beside the bed so she had space to stretch out.

He had been perfect, so sweet and attentive, he'd cuddled with her, and taken such good care of her. If she was honest he'd been a better mother hen than her own mother had ever been. As a child, when she was sick her mother had subscribed to the sleep it off philosophy. She would tuck Abigail into bed and then tell her to stay there until she felt better, there was no fussing, no hanging around to keep her company.

Finishing up her business, Abigail debated whether she could make it the three or four steps across the room to the sink on her own or if she needed help. Deciding that it was a small enough distance she could do it on her own, she stood on trembling legs and flushed then took a deep breath and gathered her strength and walked to the sink.

There was a mirror above the sink but Abigail avoided it, not sure she was ready to take her first look at herself in months.

Would she look the same?

She'd no doubt lost weight, and her hair was probably a horrible knotted mess, but it was her eyes she was most worried about.

What would she see in them?

Fear?

Despair?

Hopelessness?

Would she see the strength and determination she would need to get herself through this?

Did she have what it took to pick up her life where it had left off?

Could she go back to teaching like nothing had happened, knowing that was where she had been kidnapped?

Did she have a home anymore or had it been sold because she had been presumed dead?

And all her stuff, had it just been thrown away?

She didn't know when Eric had been told of her abduction, but she knew when he was off on a mission it could be months before she heard from him again. She wasn't close with her big brother, but she was sure if he could have he would have boxed up her possessions and stored them someplace, but she could have been gone for months before he'd been told.

As the cool water ran over her hands she fortified herself and did it, like ripping off a Band-Aid, she looked up and saw herself looking back at her.

Or a version of herself she hadn't seen before.

Her skin was a horrible shade of white, the few freckles sprinkled across her nose and cheeks stood out in stark contrast to her deathly pallor. Her hair wasn't as bad of a mess as she'd thought it might be like someone had run a brush through it, and she wouldn't be surprised to learn that Ryder had brushed her hair for her while she'd been sleeping.

It was her eyes that gutted her.

They were empty.

There was no spark in them, no life, there was nothing.

They stared blankly at her reflection like she was dead inside.

Was she dead inside?

So far she'd been too sick to really process everything that had happened to her but that couldn't last.

What would happen when the dam finally broke?

Could she survive that flooding of emotions?

Tears built in her eyes but she held them back from practiced force of will.

"Abigail, you okay?"

The voice outside the door anchored her, kept the lid on her emotions locked. She couldn't cry here, not with Ryder and the other SEALs in the house. Later, when she was alone, when there would be no one there to hear her cries, then she could fall apart.

"I'm okay, I'm ready for you," she called back.

Ryder opened the door as she turned off the tap, he gathered her up into his strong arms and carried her back into the bedroom and over to the bed. She watched him as he tucked her in and put the IV bags back onto the pole, he was her own personal guard dog. He'd watched over her in the jungle, and in the shack, he'd kept her safe as they made their way to the helicopter. Could he protect her from herself? From the emotions she was afraid of?

Sleep tugged at the corners of her mind and Abigail gladly gave in to it, thankful for the temporary reprieve it would give her from having to feel anything else.

* * *

8:18 P.M.

"How's she doing?" Wolf asked as he walked into the bedroom, a plate of food in his hands.

"She hasn't woken up again, but her temperature is down, and she seems to be breathing a little easier. She'd going to have quite a road ahead of her to rebuild her strength and her life, but she'd tough enough to do it," Spider replied, his gaze fixed on the sleeping woman in the bed. He had faith in her, he just prayed that she had enough faith in herself to get through this.

"How are you doing?" Wolf asked, handing him his dinner then leaning against the wall by the window.

"Me? I'm fine. It's Night who's freaking out because he can't be here with his sister."

Wolf made a scoffing noise. "It's no secret that you and Abigail used to have a thing, also no secret that you've been pining over her ever since."

"She's my best friend's little sister," he said. And that was the only reason why he had stayed away for all this time. If it wasn't for Night and everything he and his parents had done for him then he would never have given Abigail up.

But what's done is done, he couldn't go back he could only go forward, which meant finding a way to make things right with Abby and a way to sort things out with his best friend so Night understood.

"Didn't stop you last time," Wolf said.

"Maybe it should have." Perhaps if he'd been smart about how he went about things, made it clear to both Abigail's brother and her father that he truly loved her rather than jumping into bed with her and taking her virginity then slinking away because he got caught, then everything would have turned out differently.

"Night is a good guy, he would want you to be happy even if that meant dating his baby sister."

Spider wished that was true, but Night's father's dying wish had been that Spider leaves his daughter alone. How could Night deny his father that? As far as his friend was concerned, whatever had been between him and Abigail was in the past.

"So you just giving up on her?" Wolf demanded, and Spider caught the protectiveness in his tone. Everyone loved Abigail and he knew that the guys thought of her as a little sister, one they would protect even if it meant protecting against one of their own.

"No. I made that mistake twice already; I won't make it a third time," he said firmly. He wasn't sure how, but he would have to find a way to convince Night that he and Abigail loved each other and deserved a chance to see if they could make it work without anyone else interfering. Spider was actually more concerned about that than he was about convincing Abby to give him a third chance.

"Good, because the way that girl looks at you like you're her hero is reason enough not to walk away."

"She doesn't look at me like that," he protested.

"When we were out there, every time we stopped for a break, Abs would look around for you, she needed to know where you were at all times because *you* were what made her feel safe. Didn't matter about the rest of us, we could have had every other SEAL there, all of us armed to the teeth, and she still would have looked for you."

"I messed up, broke her heart. Twice."

"When Caroline and I first got together I messed up, almost ruined the best thing that ever happened to me. But I pulled my head out of the sand, got myself together and got my girl. You'll do it too."

"It's not going to be easy." It was in fact probably going to be the hardest thing he'd ever done in his life and that was saying a lot.

"Neither was BUD/s or anything else we had to do to become SEALs. You'll find a way, besides the hardest hurdle is already accomplished."

"Yeah?" Spider asked, looking at his friend.

"She already loves you. Everything else will fall into place eventually because of that simple fact." Wolf patted his shoulder and then walked out of the room leaving him alone with Abigail.

Could it be that simple?

Could he believe that everything would work out because he and Abigail loved each other?

Did she still love him?

Spider wanted to believe that she did, but he'd hurt her so badly it was hard to believe she could want anything to do with him.

Picking up the hamburger, he ate even though he wasn't hungry. If there was one thing you learned as a SEAL, it was that you ate when you could and slept when you could because you never knew what was coming or when you would get another chance.

Abigail shifted in her sleep, her brow had creased and her fingers curled into the blankets.

She was dreaming.

Nightmares.

He'd certainly had enough of them to recognize the signs.

Setting the plate down, he slid into the bed beside her and pulled her into his arms just like he'd done last night. "Shh, baby, you're just dreaming," he soothed, pressing a kiss to her temple.

She began to thrash in her sleep, and a low moan escaped her lips.

"No," she begged, "please stop, I don't know, I don't know anything. Stop. Stop," she shrieked.

"It's okay, Abby, you're safe now," he promised, drawing her gently into his arms.

The bedroom door flung open, and Wolf and Abe stood there. "Everything okay?" Abe asked.

"She's dreaming. Did you hear what she said? She begged someone to stop, said she didn't know anything."

"You think she's dreaming about what happened to her?" Abe asked.

"Yes."

"What does that mean?" Wolf wondered aloud. "She doesn't know anything? Could she have been taken because they thought she saw something that she shouldn't have?"

About now that made as much sense as anything else.

"Call if you need anything," Abe said as he and Wolf left, closing the door behind them.

"No," Abigail moaned, "no, no, no."

He couldn't take any more of this. Sitting up, he grabbed her shoulders and gave her a firm shake. "Wake up, Abigail, now," he said firmly.

"No, no," she murmured, trying to shake him off.

"You're dreaming, Abs, wake up," he begged. He couldn't handle seeing her like this. "Abigail, wake up."

Her eyelids snapped open, her eyes wide with fear as she looked through him, still trapped in whatever hell she had been reliving in her dreams. Her skin was cold, and she was trembling, her hands clutched at him, clinging to him as though he were her anchor even when she didn't know where the waves were tossing her.

"Abigail, you're okay, sweetheart, safe now," he assured her. Cradling her cheeks in his hands, he stroked her cheekbones, attempting to soothe her in any way he could.

Her eyes refocused, seeing him, and relief washed over her. "Ryder."

"Here, babe, always gonna be right here. You were just dreaming."

"I was?"

"Yeah, you remember what about."

She shook her head. "I just remember being afraid."

"You don't have to be afraid anymore, Abby. I know it's going to take time for you to adjust to being home, to being safe, but you are, okay? You have seven Navy SEALs in this house. You think anyone could get through us to get to you?"

"No."

"So you see, you're safe."

"For now," she agreed, "but what happens when we leave here? Where will I go? I don't know if I still have my apartment, or my stuff, or my job."

"I can't say about the job, but you still have your apartment and your stuff, Night and I made sure of that."

That seemed to pacify her a bit and she nodded, then yawned. "I'm tired but I don't want to go back to sleep, I don't want to dream again," she said on a shudder.

"I can stay in bed with you if you want, hold you while you sleep, your body really does need the rest."

"Ryder," she said like she didn't think that was a great idea.

"Or if you want I'll sit in the chair and watch over you." He was prepared to give Abigail as much time as she needed to get used to the idea that he was back in her life, this time for good.

"Ryder," she said again, "I'm not sure that's a good idea. I have to rebuild my whole life and I don't know how I'm going to do that, but what I do know is I can't let myself get used to you being around because sooner or later you'll leave again."

"No, sweetheart, I won't ever leave you again."

"You said that last time I took you back," she reminded him, but she said the words matter-of-factly without any heat.

"I know it will take time for you to believe it, but I'm never walking away from you again."

"I'm sorry, Ryder, I don't believe you."

"I'll prove it to you, I'll earn your trust back."

"We've been there and done that, I ended up with a broken heart last time, this time won't be any different."

"It will, Abby."

"Why?"

"Because I'm different, I'm ready to let go of the past."

Her brow furrowed in confusion. "I don't know what that means."

"I know, but you will, when the time is right, when you're stronger I'll tell you everything." He tucked a lock of hair behind her ear and let his fingers trail down her neck to settle back on her shoulder. "You need sleep now, my beautiful ballerina. Lay down, close your eyes, relax. I'm here and I'll keep your nightmares away."

When he moved to get out of bed, she reached out and grabbed his hand. "Stay," she said before lying back down and rolling onto her side.

The pressure in his heart eased just a little as he lay down beside her, spooned her against him, and began to hum her favorite song.

CHAPTER 4

June 17th

6:23 A.M.

The warm arm around her stomach and the hard body pressed against her back made her feel like she was waking up wrapped in a blanket of security.

When she'd been a very little girl, Abigail had had a special blanket that she'd carried with her everywhere she went. It had been pink and yellow striped with a picture of the moon in the middle. She'd loved that thing, she'd slept with it, and she'd taken it in the bath with her. It had gone with her on her first day of kindergarten, and when she'd moved to New York City to pursue her dreams of dancing professionally she had packed it up amongst her belongings, feeling safer knowing that she had it with her.

The blanket was torn and tattered now, but it was folded

up neatly and tucked away on the top shelf of her bedroom closet.

As special as it had been, as safe as it had made her feel, it couldn't even come close to providing her with the same feeling of security that Ryder's arms gave her.

Ryder was breathing deeply, and he appeared to be asleep so she wriggled in his hold until she was lying facing him. Was it wrong that when she looked at him all she could think about was kissing him?

It was probably just everything that had happened the last few days messing with her emotions. Being rescued, being alone with Ryder, being so sick, it made sense that since he was the one who had saved her life that she'd be thinking about kissing him.

Old memories.

That was all it was.

Gratitude and old memories.

"I miss seeing you like this, all sleep rumpled and sweet," Ryder said, watching her with those expressive blue eyes of his. She'd never known anyone with such expressive eyes as Ryder had, he could have a whole conversation with them without having to utter a single word.

"You miss seeing me with my hair a mess and bad breath?" she asked, deliberately ruining the mood because she couldn't handle the way Ryder made her feel on top of everything else.

"Sure do." He leaned in and kissed her forehead.

"You're crazy."

"Crazy in love," he said with a smile.

He'd told her last night that he would never leave her again, that he would earn her trust back, but she didn't think that was possible. She didn't want to give him false hope and let him think that there was a chance they could get back together, and yet she couldn't bear to tell him to leave because she needed him.

It was selfish of her.

She knew that she just couldn't make herself send him away.

"It's okay, I wouldn't leave anyway."

"Did I say something out loud?" she asked.

"Nope, I just know what you're thinking, and it's okay. You don't believe me yet but you will, and even if you never take me back I'm still happy to be here for you. I love you, Abby, I always did, I didn't leave you because I didn't love you, I left because I do love you and because I let myself believe that you were better off without me."

"Better off without you?" She didn't understand what Ryder was talking about.

"A story for another day, but just know that I loved every second I spent with your control freak, independent, sexy little butt," he said, reaching around her to give it a swat.

"I'm not a control freak," she grumbled.

"If you say so." Ryder laughed and then got out of bed, pulling the covers away with him. "Your temperature is down to just about normal and the antibiotics seem to be working. You still have to get your strength back, but you're doing much better. Do you want to try a shower?"

"A shower?" she squealed, scrambling up onto her knees, realizing as she did so that the IV had been removed. In her cell back in Mexico all she'd had was a tap in the wall and cold water, she'd washed as best as she could every single day right up until she'd been too sick to move, but a hot shower with soap and shampoo was something she had been dreaming about since she'd been abducted.

"I thought you'd be excited, but there's a catch."

"A catch?" she asked warily.

"I don't want to leave you alone in there so I'm staying. If you want I'll keep my back to you, but I don't want you passing out on me, and you're still weak, one slip in the shower and it could set you right back."

"Fine, whatever," she said, already swinging her legs over the side of the bed and cautiously standing up. Right now she would go along with pretty much anything if it meant getting properly clean.

"Alrighty then, let's get you clean and then some food into you."

Ryder stayed beside her ready to catch her if she fell as she teetered on her feet toward the bathroom. She appreciated that while he stayed close he kept his hands to himself, knowing how important it was for her to do this herself. He'd always understood her independent streak, he knew her parents, knew how they'd always been disappointed that she wasn't more like them and Eric, and how hard she had worked to prove she might not be SEAL material, but she was still a strong and independent woman who could take care of herself.

"Shampoo, conditioner, body wash are all in the shower. Wolf asked Caroline to go by your place and grab some of your clothes, so once you're clean you can get dressed into your own things."

"Matthew and Caroline are such sweethearts," she gushed.

"Don't let Wolf hear you call him a sweetheart," Ryder said with a grin.

She laughed and then immediately sobered when she realized that was the first time she had laughed since she was kidnapped. "Ryder?"

"Yeah?"

"How long was I gone? I counted the days at first but then it got too depressing."

"Fourteen and a half months," Ryder replied.

Abigail gasped. Fourteen months? That was so long.

"You're home now, Abby, try to focus on that."

She nodded. She'd try but it wasn't like her memories of being alone in that cage day after day were ever going to go away. They were part of her now, and the best she could do was to find a way to live with it.

Ryder turned on the shower and when the room began to fill with steam, thoughts of her imprisonment faded, and all she could think about was how wonderful it would feel to have the water drumming down against her skin.

"Arms up," Ryder said, standing before her.

She complied, and he took hold of the hem of the t-shirt that was more like a dress on her and pulled it up and over her head, leaving her standing naked before him. She wasn't embarrassed; he'd seen her naked too many times to count, including just a couple of days ago in the shack in the jungle.

Heat flushed through her that had nothing to do with the steam from the hot shower. Three years might have passed since she'd last been with Ryder, but to her body it was like a day. She still craved his touch, still remembered what it felt like to have his mouth on hers, his fingers on her skin, him buried deep inside her.

He was watching her closely, fire and desire flamed in his eyes but he stood rock still, his hands hanging loosely by his side. He wanted her, but he wouldn't do anything about it unless she initiated it. She already knew that part of his game plan from last time around.

It wasn't a conscious decision on her part, her hands just lifted to rest against his pecs, and she stood on her tiptoes and brushed her lips across his.

Ryder hesitated for a moment, and then his hand was on the small of her back, pulling her in close so she was flush against him, and then his mouth was devouring hers with the same pent up emotion that three years apart had left them both with.

When his hand trailed down to cup her bottom she started and jerked away.

What was she doing?

Why was she kissing Ryder?

Was she so stupid that she would really risk her heart a third time?

Was she so stupid that she had to be beaten over the head again and again until she learned her lesson?

She was supposed to be angry with Ryder for what he'd done to her, not be kissing him like a starving woman just because he'd saved her life. Which had been an accident. He hadn't known she was there, hadn't been there for her, she could be grateful for what he'd done for her without throwing herself at him like she was that desperate for a man.

"I should get in the shower before the hot water runs out," she mumbled, embarrassed about how she had behaved.

As she went to turn away from him Ryder gently grasped her shoulders. "It's okay, Abby, you need time. I didn't mean to pressure you, it's just when I kiss you I lose all common sense. Have your shower, sweetheart, enjoy it, we have the rest of our lives to fix this mess I made."

With a kiss on her forehead he released her, and feeling confused and all mixed up inside, she stepped into the shower, and the second the water hit her skin the rest of the world and all its problems faded away.

This was heaven.

The hot water soothed muscles that were still tense from over a year of lying or sitting on nothing but hard concrete. Abigail filled her hand with shampoo and washed every inch of her hair and then repeated that twice more. Conditioner was next, and it took three goes before she could get the comb through her hair without it getting snagged on a tangle. Then she washed every inch of skin, scrubbing it over and over again until she finally felt like she was clean.

Tired, she sunk to the floor of the shower, resting back against the warm tiles and just let the water cascade over her. As good as this felt she couldn't stop tears from brimming in her eyes again. She fought them back with everything she had. She couldn't cry now, not with Ryder on the other side of the room.

"You can let it out, Abby, you need to, you need to purge those emotions so you can start to process them," he said like he was hardwired to feel her emotions.

"I can't," she said simply. She wasn't going to cry, it wouldn't change anything. She was just going to pick up the pieces of her life like she'd done before and put them back together. They might not make the same life that she'd had before, but at least she was alive and free again.

"Abby ..."

"Can you pass me a towel?" she asked, cutting him off as she stood and turned the water off.

"Sure thing."

"I'm going to dry off, get dressed, and I'll meet you in the kitchen. For the first time since you found me I'm actually hungry," she said, dismissing Ryder because if she didn't she was likely to break down and sob until she was empty inside.

He studied her for a moment then nodded. "Kitchen is downstairs through the hall and to the right." He paused at the door. "Abby, when you're ready to let go I'll be there to help you put yourself back together again."

His sweet declaration just about shredded her resolve.

* * *

7:36 A.M.

. . .

"Wow, you look great," Spider said as Abigail stepped into the kitchen.

He'd been waiting for her, his gaze fixed firmly on the doorway while he half-listened to what the guys were saying as they sat around the large kitchen table eating breakfast. He was worried about Abby and her desire to reign in her emotions, not let herself feel anything, not allow herself the release of tears. She needed to cry, needed to let go, needed to purge fourteen months of fear and anxiety and sorrow and take that first step toward healing.

Bantering with her, kissing her, sleeping with her in his arms, he knew he was getting his hopes up that he still had a shot with her and he would have to be careful to make sure he kept her as the priority. She needed time to process, time to heal, he wouldn't burden her with the story of why he'd left her until he was sure she was ready to deal with more baggage.

Looking at her right now, he realized that she was a lot stronger than he gave her credit for.

Her skin was still pale but there was pink on her cheeks now, she had braided her hair and it hung in a long rope down between her shoulders. She was dressed in a pair of yellow yoga pants and an oversized pink sweatshirt, she looked sweet and sexy, and if he hadn't just commanded himself to wait until she was stronger before focusing on their relationship, he would have dragged her into his arms and kissed her senseless.

"Thanks," she said, touching her hair self-consciously. "After using a piece of stone to file my nails and not shaving or washing for fourteen months it feels really good to be clean. Matthew, thank Caroline for me for going and getting my clothes and toiletries."

Wolf opened his mouth but Spider shut him down with a single glance, he wasn't looking for Abigail's gratitude so there was no need for her to know that he was the one who arranged to get her stuff brought here.

"I'll tell her," Wolf said.

"Come and sit," Spider said, standing and resting his hand on the small of her back to guide her to the table. He could feel her trembling beneath his touch, and he knew she was using all the strength she had to remain on her feet, but he hoped a little of the trembling might be her body reacting to his touch. His body certainly reacted to touching her. "What do you want to eat?" he asked as he pulled out a chair for her.

"What have you got?"

"You don't want to ask that question," Benny replied with a grin.

"Since it's your first breakfast back home we may have gone a little overboard," Dude added.

"What he means is we have every breakfast food known to man," Cookie told her, moving to the counter where there were plates full of food. "So, what do you want?"

"Fruit," Abigail replied.

"Fruit?" Mozart made a face.

"Hey, I'm a dancer, fruit is what I've eaten for breakfast since I was a kid, but I might have my fruit on a pancake please."

"Fruit on pancake it is." Cookie made a face like he couldn't believe anyone would want to put fruit on their pancakes, but he served her up a plate.

"Mmm." Abigail's eyes closed as she popped a fresh strawberry into her mouth. "I dreamed about strawberries while I was eating that awful stale bread they gave me, but this is even better than I dreamed."

Spider and the rest of the men in the room tensed at her words, they were all protectors and none of them could stand the idea of a woman being hurt in the way that Abigail had been. None of them wanted to upset her or ruin this moment for her, so they all pasted on smiles and ate in silence for a few minutes.

Abigail hadn't been fed properly in fourteen months and she made it through only about a third of the pancake and halfway through the fruit before she pushed the plate away.

"Drink some more water," Spider said, pushing a glass closer.

She rolled her eyes at him, but picked up the glass and downed nearly half of it. Then she set it in front of her and began to spin it between her fingers. "Let's get it over with."

"Get what over with?" Wolf asked.

"The questions. I know you guys are dying to ask me stuff and I'd rather just get it over and done with, I just want to put all of this behind me." Abigail finished on a defeated sigh as though she knew this was far from behind her but wished it could be.

"We can wait till you're stronger, Abby," Spider said because as much as he wanted answers for him, her emotional wellbeing came first.

"I don't want to wait, Ryder, I just want to do this." Determination shone in her eyes and she straightened her spine, leaving the glass alone and clasping her hands together on the tabletop. "So, go, what do you want to ask?"

"Some of this you'll already have gone through with Spider so try not to get frustrated if we ask you something you've already told him," Wolf told her as they all set their utensils down and gave Abigail their full attention.

"Okay," she agreed. She covered her mouth as she coughed then looked at them expectantly, waiting for their questions.

"I want you to start with the last thing you remember and go through everything in detail. I might stop you to ask about something specific, okay?" Wolf asked. They had agreed that he would lead the questioning because Spider wasn't sure he could push Abigail if they needed to.

"Okay. I was working with a little girl, she was nine, and her name was Susan April, she was very talented and reminded me of me when I'd been her age so I kind of took her under my wing a little. Her mom picked her up at around eight-thirty, and I tidied up, turned the lights off, set the alarm, locked the doors, and left."

"What had to be tidied up?"

"She was using a few props and I returned them to the prop room along with her costume, then I cleaned up my desk. I'd been working on choreographing some dances and I always write it out on paper, I didn't like to leave with my desk a mess."

"What's the last time you remember seeing?"

"Eight forty-four because I remember thinking four plus four equals eight, it's silly but those times stick in my mind." She shrugged like she was embarrassed, but everyone had little quirks like that and Spider remembered her mentioning similar times often when they'd been together.

"When you set the alarm, locked up, and stepped outside were the lights in the parking lot on or off?"

"They were on," Abigail replied confidently.

They'd asked her that question because often times in an abduction the perpetrator would set it up so that their intended victim didn't see what was coming until it was too late to do anything about it. That Abigail's abductor hadn't done that meant that he might have either used a ruse in order to put her in a vulnerable position or she knew him.

The second possibility chilled him.

Were they looking for one of Abigail's friends or colleagues?

"Are you positive?" Wolf asked.

CHAPTER 5

June 18th

10:39 A.M.

"So?" Abigail asked, watching Ryder as he set the blood pressure cuff down. He had checked her vitals, taken her temperature, and received the results from the blood tests they'd had done, now she was waiting for him to tell her how she was doing. She knew how she felt, she was doing better, but she still wanted to make sure that she hadn't picked up some awful disease while she was imprisoned in Mexico.

"You're doing much better." Ryder was crouched before her as she sat on the edge of the bed, his hands rested lightly on her knees, and although she should tell him not to touch her, she didn't. She didn't want to lose the comfort his touch brought.

"Temperature is down to normal, vitals are all normal, blood tests all came back ..."

"Normal," she finished for him.

"Right." Ryder grinned at her. "It's going to take time to build your strength up so you're going to need to take things slowly. Once you go back home, you should visit your doctor and get a proper medical professional to check you out. And, Abby," Ryder's face and voice had sobered, "I think you should go have a, uh, gynecological exam done."

Abigail jerked backward.

Why would he say that?

No one had touched her while she'd been held captive.

No one had done ... *that* .... to her.

"Why would you say that?" she demanded. Was he trying to freak her out? Trying to lash out at her? Push her away?

"Honey, I'm not trying to hurt you, and I'm not saying anyone touched you there, but you don't remember some of the time you were missing, and we don't know what happened to you during that time."

Right.

Her fingers.

Absently, she lifted her left hand and looked at her slightly crooked fingers. Had she broken them trying to fight off her attackers or had someone done it to her on purpose?

A flicker of a memory drifted through her mind but when she tried to reach for it, it floated from her grasp.

For the first time since she had been found, she realized that she didn't have any answers about her abduction. How many times had she wondered why her when she was curled up in that cell? Why had that happened to her? Why hadn't it been someone else? Not that she would have wished what she went through on anyone else. Now she realized there might have been more to her abduction than she had thought.

"Ryder?"

"Yeah?"

"Do you think someone chose me specifically? Was I targeted?"

"Abby ..."

"Don't lie to me, Ryder. After everything you put me through the least you owe me is an honest answer to my question." She knew she probably wasn't being fair, from what Kason had told her while they were in the jungle, Ryder had a reason for leaving her, but she knew that if she played the guilt card he would fold like a deck of cards.

"Yes. I think you were targeted."

She gasped even though it was the answer she had been expecting. "Why?" Why would anyone target her? She wasn't special, there was nothing about her that should make anyone want to target her. She went to work, hung out with her friends, went shopping, and loved to go to the movie theatre just up the block from her apartment building. She ate out more than she should, and she had a favorite café where her friend Lavender worked. She had a slight obsession with Halloween and went a little overboard decorating her apartment and her small courtyard.

She was normal.

Boring.

"I don't know why, Abby." Ryder reached out to touch her, his hand hovering between them for a moment before he touched the side of her head, letting his hand smooth her hair before settling on her neck. "But I promise you I'll figure it out. For now your job is to rest, heal, and get better. And I'd like you to consider finding a professional to speak with. I have the name and a number of someone I trust to help you. What you went through was horrific and I know you, you'll try to brush it under the carpet, plow on like nothing happened. This is serious, Abby, it won't just go away because you want it to, you need to deal with it and that starts with talking to someone."

Because she knew Ryder and she knew how stubborn he was she huffed. "I'll take the card." It wasn't a lie, she'd take the card she just wouldn't commit to calling the number on it.

"Good," he said, seemingly satisfied.

His long fingers curled around the back of her neck, and he applied just enough pressure to move her slightly forward. He leaned in and of their own accord her lips parted. He kissed her on the forehead then released her leaving her feeling oddly disappointed. She didn't want him to kiss her and yet she did. It was silly. Crazy. Definitely self-destructive, after he had left her the second time she had promised herself she would never get dragged into Ryder Flynn's orbit ever again.

"I have good news for you," Ryder told her, standing and setting the medical kit on the chair by the bed.

"Yeah?" If there was one thing she could use right now it was good news.

"You can go home tomorrow. You're feeling better, getting your strength back, there's no reason why you shouldn't be able to go back to your place."

The grin he gave her told her that he thought he was giving her great news, and he was. Right?

It should be good news.

She should be happy to be going home and moving on with her life.

She should be thrilled that Eric had made sure to keep her apartment and all her things, that he had no doubt made sure all her bills got paid and her bank accounts and everything remained open.

She should be excited that she had her life back. She could call her friends, call the studio and see if they still had a place for her, or maybe start her own dance studio like she had always wanted to do.

She should be a whole lot of things, but she wasn't.

What she was, was scared.

The idea of going home alone terrified her.

It shouldn't, she had been alone in that prison every day for fourteen months with no one to talk to, no one to hold her when she got scared, to snuggle up with when she got cold, to get angry with and scream about how unfair it was.

She should be used to being alone.

"Abby?" Ryder's hand touched her shoulder.

"That's great," she said brightly, shooting him a full watt smile.

"Yeah, I thought you'd be happy," he said uncertainly, like he wasn't sure she was being quite honest with him.

"Of course, it will be great to be able to sleep in my own bed, and curl up in my favorite rocking chair, and have all my stuff around me again," she said, keeping a big smile on her face. Fake it till you make it. Maybe if she pretended she was happy to return home when she got there tomorrow she would be happy.

She'd survived fourteen months alone in a cage in Mexico, she could survive staying in her own home.

It wasn't like she *needed* Ryder to be there to make her feel safe, she'd always felt safe in her home before, it was just a case of nerves. Everything would be okay.

"Hey, Abs?"

"Yeah?"

"You've been cooped up in the house the last couple of days so I thought you might like to have lunch outside today. At the beach."

"The beach?" She perked up at the idea, she'd grown up in California and always been a beach baby. She'd learned to swim basically the same time she learned to walk, she'd learned to surf when she eight, and spent any spare time away from the dance studio that she got at the beach. "I didn't know we were close to the beach here."

"Not just close, beachfront," Ryder told her, more relaxed now that she had relaxed, like some invisible thread linked their emotions. "I thought we could pack a picnic and spend the whole afternoon at the beach, if you're up for it you can go for a swim otherwise you can just lie in the sun and get some color back into you."

"It sounds like heaven," she said on a happy sigh. Sun, sand, surf was exactly the medicine she needed right now, and tomorrow she could worry about going back home alone. Today she was just going to relax and have fun.

* * *

11:08 A.M.

"Why don't you change and I'll pack some lunch," Spider told Abigail who had definitely perked up once he'd mentioned the beach. He'd thought she'd be excited when they got her blood work back and her vitals had stabilized, and she could go back home, but when he'd broken the news she'd looked ... worried ... no not quite worried ... scared ... she'd looked scared.

Which was the opposite of excited.

But she had been excited about the beach, and he wondered if he'd misinterpreted her feeling overwhelmed for scared. She had been gone for fourteen months, kept isolated in a small concrete cage, she hadn't interacted with anyone but him and the other SEAL team when they rescued her, no doubt the idea of assimilating back into society was overwhelming to her.

"Okay, I'll be down in about ten minutes," Abigail said, already walking toward the closet.

"Take your time," he told her as he grabbed a pair of board shorts and thongs.

As he headed down to the kitchen he could hear her coughing as she changed, but the coughs weren't the same whole body wracking, struggling to get enough air into her lungs coughs that she'd had out in the jungle. Now they sounded a lot more normal, and while he would like her to see her own doctor to get a medical professional's opinion, he was less worried about her physical well-being.

Her emotional and psychological well-being were still top of his list of concerns.

That and figuring out who had targeted Abigail, why, and if they were going to come back for her.

Right on the ten-minute mark Abigail came down the stairs, she was still moving slowly but if she continued to get plenty of rest and make sure she consumed plenty of calories, then she would continue to grow stronger each day.

Adding a couple of soda cans to the picnic basket, he picked it up and turned to face Abigail. "Ready to go?"

She stumbled for a moment, placing a hand on the wall to steady herself, her gaze fixed on his bare chest. Spider knew that he was good looking, and he worked out for several hours every day, women ogled him regularly, and often threw themselves at his feet. When he'd first become a SEAL, he'd loved the attention, loved the fawning women, loved fun, free, easy sex, but that all changed once he had Abigail that first time. After that every other woman paled in comparison. He didn't care if other women found him attractive or not but that Abigail found him attractive had his body responding to the heat in her eyes.

"Like what you see, honey?" he asked with an amused smile.

"I, uh, I, um …" she stammered as her gaze snapped from his chest to his face. Her cheeks were an adorable shade of pink, and while he wasn't used to seeing her shy and unsure of herself, he liked that she was obviously still attracted to him.

Walking over to her, he took her hand and winked at her. "Don't worry, honey, you look ridiculously sexy in that bikini."

The look she gave him said that she didn't believe him, and that was enough to put a damper on his libido. He didn't want his gorgeous, sexy, stunningly beautiful Abigail thinking that she wasn't attractive or that he wasn't wildly attracted to her.

Wrapping an arm around her waist, he dragged her up against him, close enough that she could feel how his body responded to her. "Don't ever doubt how beautiful you are. I know you're going through a lot, Abby, but I love you, and I'm not going anywhere, and when you're ready I'm going to tell you why I left and I'm going to do whatever it takes to get you back."

"Why can't you just …"

"Because I'm not going to burden you with that right now, but that doesn't mean I don't want to drag you into my arms and kiss you and touch you." Because he couldn't be this close to her and not kiss her, Spider whispered his lips across hers and then quickly released her before he could be tempted to do a whole lot more. "Let's go."

Leading through the house and out the front door, Abigail stopped short when she saw that they were right on the beachfront. "Wow," she murmured as she took in the white sand, blue skies, and rolling waves. "I almost forgot what it was like to be outside. I mean I remember us going through the jungle but it's all a little hazy, and that was different, that was us running for our lives, but this is …"

"Nature at its finest," he finished for her.

"Yeah," she agreed. She kicked off her flip flops, crossed the tiled patio, bypassed the pool, and moaned when her toes curled into the sand.

He remembered that moan.

Remembered it falling from her lips when they were in bed together.

"Uh, Abs, try not to make that sound."

"Huh?" When she looked behind her and saw that he was shifting uncomfortably she laughed and then took off at a run across the quiet beach.

Since he knew that his friends were all surveying the beach to keep watch for anything that might present a threat to Abigail he followed after her slowly. Until they knew more about Abigail's abduction, her safety was top priority which meant that she wouldn't be going anywhere on her own for the time being. But having his friends focusing on safety today meant he was free to focus on Abigail and making sure she had a good time.

Setting the towels and picnic basket down on the sand, he joined Abigail in the shallows. The bright pink bikini she was wearing hugged her slender curves but also served to remind him from her porcelain white pallor that she hadn't been in the sunshine for a long time.

"Did you put sunblock on?" he asked as he stood beside her. The small waves crashed around his ankles, the water delightfully cool against his skin, and just what he needed to try to get his head in the right place. This wasn't about pressuring Abigail into jumping into bed with him because his body felt like it was dying after three long years without her touch, this was about earning her trust back any way he could, and patching up the damage he had done to her heart.

"No," she said, never taking her eyes off the horizon where the blue water met the blue sky.

"Come on, we better do that now before you end up sunburned." Gently grasping her shoulder, he turned her around and led her back to their things. "I got it," he told her when she reached for the bottle of sunblock.

"Ryder," she warned, her gaze moving from his groin up his bare chest and settling on his face.

"Nothing sexual, babe, but I'd have to do your back for you anyway. Just relax, Abs, let me take care of you, you've been on your own for so long but I'm here now."

When she gave a small nod of permission, he opened the bottle and squeezed some sunblock onto his hand then knelt before her and began to rub it into first one and then the other of her legs. As he worked higher he could hear her breathing going shallow, and for once he knew it had nothing to do with pneumonia.

He moved onto her stomach, and when his fingers lightly brushed against the underside of her breasts Abigail inhaled sharply.

Spider smiled.

If it were up to her body he would already be back in her good graces. She was still attracted to him, and he was even sure that he already had her heart on board too because he believed that she still loved him, unfortunately the hardest nut to crack would be her mind. She was wary of him because he'd already let her down twice before, he would have to work hard to convince her mind to give him a third chance.

He stood and rubbed sunblock up her arms and then did her chest. As his hands moved to the v between the two triangles covering her breasts, he had to force his body to stand down. Being this close to her breasts and not being able to touch them, tease her nipples, take them into his mouth was the worst kind of torture. And he'd been tortured before.

"Turn around," he murmured.

She obeyed, and he covered her back before turning her around again.

Her eyes were glued to his, her breathing heavy, her pulse fluttering wildly in the hollow of her neck, she was as affected by his hands on her body as he was.

Carefully, he smoothed sunblock on her forehead, her temples, across her cheeks and down to her chin, his fingertips lingered at the corners of her mouth, how much he longed to press his lips to hers.

One little kiss couldn't hurt.

He'd already broken his own rule to keep things focused on her recovery by kissing her back in the house. What was one more kiss?

When Abigail's gaze dropped to his mouth Spider knew she wanted it too.

Happy to oblige, he stooped and brushed his lips over hers, just one little taste. It would never be enough, but it was enough to hold him over, keep him going.

"What do you want to do now?" he asked as he released her and set the sunblock back in the basket.

"Lie in the sun for a while, it feels so nice on my skin," she said with a delighted sigh. "Then maybe go for a swim before we eat lunch."

"Whatever my girl wants, she gets," he said as he spread out a towel for her. She didn't contradict him this time when he called her his girl, and unless he was mistaken the expression on her face when she looked at him was softer.

Progress.

CHAPTER 6

June 19th

2:17 P.M.

"Thanks, guys, for everything," Abigail said to the men standing around her. How could she ever properly thank them for saving her life? She knew it was their job, but that didn't mean that she didn't know every single one of them would have gone out there in their free time if they'd known she was there. And even if it had been just a job she still would have been eternally grateful.

"It was nothing," Matthew said, waving off her gratitude.

"No, it's not," she said firmly. "I would have died if you hadn't found me, hadn't come for me. I won't ever forget what you did."

Matthew ruffled her hair affectionately. "Seriously, Abs, no need for thanks."

"Well, you better get used to it because I'm going to keep saying thank—"

"Someone better tell her you're welcome or she's never going to stop," Ryder said with a laugh.

She shot him a glare. "Well, would you stop thanking the people who saved your life?"

"No, ma'am," he teased.

She rolled her eyes, but she could feel tears building up. Stubbornly she held them back and faked a smile she didn't feel. "I just want you guys to know …"

"You're welcome," Matthew said, giving her a hard hug.

Each of the other guys also hugged her and then it was time. She'd been procrastinating all morning, sleeping late, taking her time eating breakfast, and in the shower, and packing up the few belongings she had here. By the time she'd been done it was lunchtime so they'd all eaten together in the bright, airy kitchen, but now it was time to leave.

To go home.

The day at the beach yesterday had been wonderful, but constantly hovering at the back of her mind was the fact that she had to leave. It had haunted her dreams as well, and as much as she wished there was a way to put it off for longer there wasn't.

Which gave her only one option.

She had to face it.

"See, guys, I told you that saying you're welcome would stop her," Ryder teased her as he picked up her bag.

"We'll all do dinner together on the weekend if we're not called out on anything," Christopher told her.

"Sounds like fun," she said. It did, hanging out with the guys and their families was always fun but today was only Tuesday and the weekend felt a long way away.

"Night … uh, Eric, and the others should be back by then," Ryder told her.

"I know Eric's nickname," she reminded him. It should make her feel better that her big brother would be back soon, but since they'd never been close she didn't feel any comfort knowing he would soon be home. Eric hadn't approved of her relationship with Ryder either, maybe that had something to do with her lingering ill will toward her brother.

"Let's get going," Ryder said. The look he gave her suggested he knew something was going on with her, but she appreciated that he didn't push the issue.

"Bye, guys," she said as she reluctantly trailed after Ryder to the SUV parked in the driveway.

Neither of them talked during the fifteen-minute drive to her place. She appreciated that the guys had taken her to the gorgeous beach house when they brought her back. A hospital full of strangers would have freaked her out after so many months alone, and she hadn't been ready to go straight home.

She still wasn't.

"Home, sweet home," Ryder said when he parked in front of her building.

"Yeah," she said quietly, staring at the building that had once been her happy place. The building was only a ten-minute walk to the beach, she had her own little yard where she'd planted her own mini apple orchard and added flowers in boxes under the windows. She'd painted each room of the apartment, choosing the colors carefully to go with the feel she wanted, she'd sewn the lacy curtains herself, and spent months making the patchwork quilts both for her bedroom and the spare one. The paintings on the walls had been done by one of her best friends, and there were lots of framed photos of happy times with the people she loved.

This place had been her home, but now it felt as foreign to her as that cell in Mexico had when she'd first awakened in it.

"I'll grab the bags, you go open up," Ryder said as he opened her door for her and handed her the keys that had been in her purse the night she'd been abducted. Knowing that there was a chance someone had targeted her, taken her for a reason, didn't make coming back here any easier.

What if they came back for her?

No.

Ryder and the others wouldn't let her come back here alone if she was in danger.

Would they?

They were SEALs, not cops, it wasn't their job to keep her safe or find who had kidnapped her.

Taking the keys, she walked up the short path to her front door. Green apples hung from her trees, and it looked like the grass had recently been cut. The flowers at the windows were bright and colorful and she tried to let their cheeriness infuse a little cheerfulness inside her.

When she opened the door she knew immediately that Caroline hadn't just stopped by here to get her some clothes, she had come and cleaned to make sure everything was ready for her to come home. The floorboards sparkled, there was a stack of wood next to the fireplace, the frilly pillows on both of the sofas were arranged perfectly in the corners, the wooden dining table had been polished, and there wasn't a speck of dust anywhere. There was fruit in a bowl on the kitchen counter and cookies in her cookie jar, the fridge was fully stocked, and she was sure the carpet in the bedrooms had been vacuumed.

"Caroline cleaned and got food," she said when Ryder closed the front door and set her bags on the table.

"She wanted your home to be ready for you," he said.

"She's so sweet, I'll have to text her and thank her."

It was so overwhelming to be back here. She was happy

that she wasn't a prisoner anymore but felt out of place back in the real world.

Since she didn't want Ryder to know that she was struggling she pasted on a bright smile. "Thanks so much for everything you've done for me, Ryder, I can't ever thank you enough for saving my life and for bringing me home.

He cocked his head, studied her for a moment, then said, "Sounds like you're dismissing me."

"Not dismissing," she said quickly. "It's just there's no reason for you to hang around now, I'm sure you're dying to go back to your own place, or you have work to do back at the base, you've given up enough of your time for me." She wanted to beg him to stay, not to leave her alone, and the longer he was here the closer she came to caving and doing just that. She needed him to leave and the sooner the better.

Ryder closed the space between them in two strides, his hands curled around her shoulders, and he stooped so he was looking her in the eye. "You make it sound like you're a burden and that couldn't be further from the truth."

Why did he have to say such nice things?

They'd kissed a few times yesterday, and she couldn't deny that his touch affected her not just on a physical level. She was still attracted to him, she even still loved him, but she didn't trust him anymore and she had vowed to never give him another opportunity to hurt her. However, when his warm hands were on her shoulders, his strong body was before her, and he said sweet things it took all her self control not to throw herself into his arms, cling to him, and beg him not to go.

Instead, she kept her smile steady. "Thank you, I know that even though our history is rocky that you would never see me as a burden. I just have a lot to do, it's been a long time since I was here, and I just need some time to myself."

"Okay," he nodded, "but you'll call if you need anything."

"Sure," she said, knowing it would be a cold day in hell before she picked up a phone and called anyone for anything, especially Ryder, but if she didn't agree he wouldn't leave.

"Well, enjoy being back home." He kissed her forehead, then released her and walked to the door.

When it closed behind him her control snapped and she ran to it. Abigail was all set to throw it open and ask him to stay, but she stopped herself. She couldn't do that. If she begged him to stay then she'd be proving right everything her parents had ever thought about her.

She wasn't strong.

She wasn't tough.

She wasn't a survivor.

They were wrong.

She was all those things just not in the same way that they were.

Instead of opening the door, she moved to the window and watched as Ryder got in his car and drove away leaving her alone.

Again.

Pressing her fingers to her eyes she ruthlessly denied herself crying.

Crying wouldn't change anything.

She could cry all the tears in the world and she would still be standing alone in her apartment with no idea what to do next.

* * *

10:41 P.M.

Screams.

The sound snapped Spider out of his light sleep, and he was instantly awake and alert.

After dropping Abigail off at her place earlier in the afternoon he'd headed home, showered, changed, packed a bag, and then come back to her place. In an attempt to respect her privacy and support her attempts to rebuild her life he hadn't told her he was there, or that he intended to stay here until he was sure she was safe.

His plan had been to sleep on the sun lounge in her small yard at night, and spend as much time during the day with her as he could.

That changed when Abigail screamed.

He could hammer on her door, hope that the sound penetrated her dreams and woke her up, but that would draw more attention to them than her screams already had—which left either breaking down the door or picking the lock. Picking the lock would only work if she hadn't put a chain on.

Breaking down the door it was.

With one well-placed kick, the door splintered and he shoved it out of his way as he ran inside. He'd been to Abigail's place plenty of times and ran straight to her bedroom, bursting through the door just as she let out another ear-piercing scream.

PTSD.

She was already developing all the symptoms, while he wasn't surprised given the trauma she had just lived through, he hated watching her suffer. Post-traumatic stress disorder had the power to bring battle-hardened soldiers to their knees. What would it do to his sweet Abigail, who was a lot more vulnerable than she let people see?

He'd given her the name of a psychiatrist who he knew could help if Abigail would let her, but he was pretty sure that she never intended to make the call and reach out for help.

Which meant for now he was all she had.

She was thrashing wildly in the bed, her face twisted in pain, and he cursed the fact that dreams had the power to hurt you.

How many times as a kid had he been told that they were just dreams, that the only way they could hurt you was if you let them?

Too many to count.

Those words hadn't brought him any comfort as a ten-year-old child plagued by nightmares, and he wouldn't be saying them to Abigail.

Approaching the bed slowly, the last thing he wanted to do was startle her into waking up and finding a man standing over her, he stopped beside it. "Abigail, wake up," he said loudly enough that he hoped it might penetrate her dreams, but not so loud it would scare her more than she already was. He hoped.

Abigail whimpered and continued to fight off her dream attacker.

"Abby, wake up, you're dreaming, honey, you're safe at home." When she didn't wake he firmed his tone and took hold of her shoulders giving her a shake. "Abigail, wake up," he ordered.

She snapped awake on a strangled scream, her hands flinging out, fingers gouging at his eyes, where she actually managed to hook one fingernail across his skin. That was his girl, she always came out fighting, and he knew she had taken self-defense classes. It took a strong person to survive four-teen months of Hell and yet here she was, still fighting, working to reclaim her life.

Pulling her out from under the tangled covers, Spider set her between his legs, one arm gently pinning her arms to her sides because as proud as he was that she was a fighter, he wanted to keep both his eyes, his other hand stroked her hair as he whispered in her ear, "Its only me, Abs, Ryder. You're safe in your home, you were dreaming."

Her breathing was ragged, her skin cold to the touch, and she was shivering but she stilled. "Ryder?"

"At your service," he said, hoping to lighten the mood a little.

"I thought you left," she said, twisting to look up at him, and he loosened his hold on her.

"You thought I left? Why would you think I would leave you alone at a time like this?"

"Because I watched you get in your car and drive away."

"To change and pack a bag. And you weren't alone while I was gone, Kason was in his car across the street watching over you until I came back."

"I didn't see him."

"Because you weren't looking for him. Is this why you were freaked out yesterday and procrastinating coming back here this morning because you're afraid to be alone?"

"I wasn't scared to be alone." She huffed.

Okay, so Abigail was afraid to be alone, that made perfect sense given everything she had been through and he wasn't sure why she was trying to hide it.

Actually, he was.

Because she thought he would think she was weak if he knew that she was struggling. But even the strongest person in the world would be struggling after being abducted and held prisoner for over a year.

"I was sleeping in your yard, I would have preferred to be in here sleeping on the couch or in your spare room, but I thought you wanted time on your own to get your feet beneath you. Don't worry, honey, I won't make that mistake again."

"What does that mean?" she demanded.

"That you don't have to worry about being alone."

"I don't want you staying here out of pity," she snapped.

"I'm not here out of pity," he assured her.

"Then why are you here? Why is Mr. Always Walks Away still here?"

She tried to make the words come out angry but instead they were laced with pain. Her pain opened his own festering sores. "I'm here because I'm worried about your safety because we don't know who was behind your abduction."

"Oh," she said, disappointed, and she tried to wiggle out of his arms, he easily held onto her. "If you're just here to play bodyguard you can leave right now."

"Did I say that was the only reason I was here?"

"You didn't say it wasn't."

"Abby, I'm here because there is nowhere else in the world I would rather be. I'm here because I meant it when I told you that I intend to earn your trust back."

"So you can leave again?"

"No, I won't ever let you down like that again. I was an idiot to let you go," he said, letting his fingers trail up and down her bare arm.

"Then why did you?"

"Because I'm not good enough for you." Unfortunately, it was as simple as that. It didn't matter how many people he saved he could never make up for the one life he had taken that had eaten him up inside.

"I don't know what that means," she said, blowing out a frustrated breath.

"I know."

She waited a moment, clearly giving him an opportunity to explain, but he couldn't until he knew that she was on surer ground with her recovery. When he didn't say anything else she struggled in his hold again. "Let me up."

"One more moment," he whispered, pressing his lips to her temple and breathing in her sweet scent.

When he released her, she quickly darted up off the bed and put a little distance between them. It was written in every inch of her features that she didn't believe he wasn't going to hurt her all over again. That was his fault, a consequence of his actions, but he still wished she trusted him just a little.

Abigail coughed, pressing her hand to her mouth, and he was glad to see that her coughs no longer cut through her body. Then she shot him a frown when she saw he hadn't moved. "What are you doing now?"

"Getting some more sleep if you're going back to bed otherwise I'll stay up with you and we can hang out."

"You don't have to stay, I'll be fine on my own." She said it defiantly and straightened her spine, but he knew she was putting on an act. The last thing she wanted right now was to be alone. Spider wished he'd realized that this afternoon and he would have come right back in here when he got back to her place rather than hanging out in his car. Abigail was a good bluffer, but now he was hip to her game.

Standing, he crossed the room until he stood close enough in front of her that she had to crane her head back to meet his gaze. "Well, you're not on your own now so you better start getting used to that idea. I am not going anywhere. Not now when you're recovering from a traumatic ordeal, not after we find whoever took you, not ever. So you best just accept that and deal with it."

Spider leaned down, held his lips above hers, giving her a chance to pull away, when she didn't he kissed her lightly and then headed for the kitchen.

Calling over his shoulder, "Besides, I can't leave you here alone while you don't have a front door."

"Don't have a front door? Ryder Flynn, you better not be

telling me that you broke down my door," she sputtered, and he heard her come charging after him.

"No can do, babe," he said with a laugh. "Don't you know I would break down any barrier standing between us?" She stood at her broken door and looked over her shoulder at him, and he saw something shift in her gold and silver eyes. Comprehension dawned that he meant the barriers she had erected—rightfully—to protect herself from getting hurt by him again, and he realized that the first hurdle to winning her back had just been crossed.

CHAPTER 7

June 20th

9:20 A.M.

Abigail stretched and yawned as she blinked open heavy eyes. She didn't remember falling asleep, but since she was now waking up, obviously she had dozed off at some point.

The smell of smoke drew her attention and she immediately looked over to the fireplace to see a fire crackling away.

"I built you a fire," Ryder said, and she saw him standing in the kitchen cooking something.

"But it's warm out," she protested. The fireplace had been the thing that made her fall in love with this apartment. Even though this was California, and since they were by the coast it never got really cold here, most nights in winter she would light a fire then curl up and read or watch TV. There was something comforting about a fire, it soothed her and warmed her in more ways than just physically.

"You love fires," was all Ryder said as he continued with whatever he was doing.

She did, and when he was being all sweet like this it was hard not to remember all the reasons why she had loved him.

Why she *still* loved him.

He'd sat up with her last night when she didn't want to go back to bed after her nightmare. She couldn't even remember what it had been about, but she remembered the fear. That had been enough to curb her body's desire for sleep, at least temporarily since she had obviously ended up crashing.

Ryder had made her a sundae, and they'd watched some of her favorite movies, she had a bit of a Disney addiction and yet he hadn't complained about watching Cinderella, Tangled, and Beauty and the Beast.

He'd been good about it when they were together too.

He'd buy her Disney themed gifts for birthdays and Christmases, and they'd taken several trips to Disneyland while he'd been home.

If he was going to continue being this sweet she was in for a long couple of weeks or months or however long it took to find her abductors. Ryder's bags were sitting on the floor by the front door, a clear indication that he intended to follow through on his vow to stay here with her, either on the couch or in the spare bedroom.

Having Ryder here would definitely make her feel safer, and she'd missed him, but this had disaster written all over it.

Sighing, she removed the blanket Ryder must have spread over her once she fell asleep, folded it, and placed it over the back of the armchair, then went over to the kitchen. "What are you making?"

"Smoothies," Ryder replied, shooting her a grin. "If I remember correctly, someone is a little obsessed with them."

Did he have to be so considerate all the time? She hadn't really believed him when he'd said he wanted to win her trust back, had thought it was just something he'd said because they were out in the middle of the jungle, but now? Now she thought he was serious.

Why didn't she just kick him out now?

Right.

She knew the answer to that.

Because this was right where she wanted him to be.

"Do you have to remember everything from when we were together?" She huffed.

"I do," he said seriously, setting the knife down beside the partially chopped up mango.

"Do what?"

"Remember everything from when we were together. Abby, I know you don't believe me but being with you, those were the happiest days of my life."

Yeah.

They'd been the happiest days of her life too.

"I remember how you used to roll around in bed so much that you would end up with the covers tucked all around you and I'd be left with nothing," Ryder said as he returned to his task.

"You're a hot sleeper, you were always throwing the covers off anyway," she said with a reluctant smile.

"I remember how you used to have to listen to classical music to fall asleep. Do you still do that?"

"Yeah. I missed it when I was … you know … some nights I would sing myself to sleep." She cocked her head and studied him. "You were singing to me, humming, when we were in the cabin. I remember hearing it while I was in and out."

"I thought it would help," he said simply.

"It did."

"I'm glad." He smiled at her before scooping up all the fruit he had chopped and put it in the blender.

"I saw that there were lots of apples on my trees," she said, looking through the front window to her little yard. "We could pick some and I could make an apple pie later, I know you always loved my apple pie."

"I'd like that." Ryder's smile grew wider.

He turned the blender on, and they both stood and watched as the fruit got tossed around inside. Abigail felt a little like that fruit. Her whole world had been tossed upside down, she no longer knew which way to look to find stability, and with every passing second she was changing into something else. The scary part was that she didn't know what she would look like at the end of this.

Ryder turned the blender off, and she grabbed two glasses from the cupboard and set them on the counter. Once Ryder had filled both of them, they took them to the table in front of the window and sat down.

Her gaze fell on the empty hole where her front door should be. "I have to call someone about fixing my door," she said, shooting Ryder a reprimanding frown. Although it was a sweet idea for him to have slept in her yard, and although she had been grateful for his company last night, the facts were at some point she needed to get used to dealing with the nightmares on her own.

"Already taken care of," he told her. "Someone is also coming this morning to install a security system for you."

"That's not necessary." Right now she didn't have a job, when she disappeared the dance studio would have hired another ballet teacher. Maybe this was her chance to fulfill her dream and open her own studio, but she wasn't ready for that yet. The idea of being around people left her trembling just thinking about it. While she had enough money to tide her over for a few months, she couldn't be adding in any more big expenses and if she knew Ryder, and she did, he would have chosen the most expensive, top of the line system.

"It is," Ryder countered firmly. "Once we're back together I don't want to be worrying about you while I'm away on missions."

Abigail's mouth fell open.

How was it possible to be both this annoyed at Ryder's arrogance, and at the same time touched that he seriously did want to get back with her?

The fact that her feelings for Ryder were split down the middle between wanting him and wanting to get rid of him as quickly as possible only served to make her annoyed with herself.

Why was she allowing herself to get sucked into Ryder's world when she knew how this would end? She was tired of wanting what she couldn't have, she had to accept that it wouldn't work with her and Ryder, he always walked away and broke her heart. She should have learned her lesson by now.

"I don't think I can afford an expensive system right now," she said.

"Cost isn't a worry, Tex has it all worked out." The smile Ryder gave her was smug because he knew this backed her into a corner and wiped away all her excuses.

"Of course he does," she muttered. Tex would have set up the system so he could no doubt run it himself which meant she wouldn't have to pay him.

"Any more excuses?" Ryder asked.

"No."

"Good, so it's settled."

"You think you're pretty clever don't you?"

"Yep," Ryder agreed cheerfully.

"Why do you enjoy torturing me?" she groaned, but had to fight back a smile. One of the things she had loved the most about her relationship with Ryder was that it had been so fun and easygoing. They had teased each other, their arguments had never lasted long, they'd laughed and joked and had fun driving each other crazy.

"Because deep down you know you love it."

Abigail just harrumphed at that making Ryder laugh.

They sat in companionable silence while they drank their smoothies. Ryder hadn't just remembered that she liked smoothies, he had remembered exactly which were her favorite fruits and made it with mangoes, strawberries, and kiwi fruit.

Her resolve was weakening.

Both she and Ryder were older now, wiser, maybe they had reached a place where they could consider the idea of being together and actually make it work.

Was it stupid to hope that could be true?

Was she being naïve?

Was she being an idiot to even consider taking him back after he'd already broken her heart twice?

She wanted to ask him why he had left, maybe if she could understand then she would know what the future held for them, but she was already tired again.

"You're pretty cocky aren't you? So sure that I'll take you back," she said.

"No, I'm not," Ryder said simply.

Shocked, she stared at him, searching his eyes, which were now full of a vulnerability she had never seen Ryder Flynn show.

Maybe he really wasn't so sure that she would take him back. Somehow that made him harder to resist, it was one thing to push away the cocky SEAL who had broken her heart twice before, but another to push away the vulnerable man sitting at her table watching her like he needed her to live.

"Why don't we go and sit on the couch and you can rest," Ryder said, obviously picking up on the fact that she was exhausted again.

"I hate being so weak," she said, letting her head fall into her hands.

"I know, honey, but it's not for forever, your body just needs time to heal. Here, take your antibiotics and we'll watch another of your Disney movies." He set the pills on the table beside her, and when she lifted her head he gave her one of his winning smiles. "I'll even sweeten the deal."

"Yeah?"

"I'll give you a massage."

Abigail groaned. Ryder's massages were heaven. Another piece of the wall she'd erected to protect herself from him crumbled.

* * *

12:13 P.M.

If it was possible to freeze time just for a moment Spider would stop the world right now.

They were sitting on the sofa in Abigail's apartment, the heat from the fire was too much but he'd take it because Abigail was stretched out, her head propped up on a pillow, her legs draped across his lap. She'd fallen asleep halfway through his massage, and since he hadn't wanted to disturb her he'd been sitting here, The Little Mermaid playing in the background, enjoying being able to touch Abby again.

When they were together they often spent their evenings

like this, curled up together watching TV, usually whatever Abigail wanted since he wasn't much of a viewer. What he'd loved was the intimacy, the simple enjoyment of just being together, that had always been enough and the complete opposite of what his life had been growing up.

Abigail had saved him in a way he hadn't even known he'd needed saving. She'd healed his heart, something he hadn't thought could ever happen, and showed him what it was like to fall in love when he had been resigned to spending his life alone.

Someone knocked on the newly fitted front door, and he put his hand on his gun. The people installing the security system would be on their lunch break and wouldn't return for another forty-five minutes, and while he assumed it was his team he preferred to be cautious given the threat hanging over Abigail's head.

His cell buzzed with a text, and when he saw it was from Night he carefully eased out from under Abigail to open the door. Just because he had decided that he would fight for Abby didn't mean he wanted Night to know about them yet.

Especially given what happened last time.

"What are you doing?" Abigail asked sleepily as she stretched and sat up.

"Your brother is here," he told her as he opened the front door.

Night rushed through it and headed straight for his sister who he hauled up off the couch and into an awkward hug.

"Let me look at you," Night said, holding her at arm's length.

"I'm fine, Eric," Abigail said, brushing his hands off.

"Fine? You were gone for fourteen months. What did they do to you?" Night demanded.

"I thought Ryder would have filled you in," Abigail replied as she moved closer to him. He didn't know if she did it on purpose but when she was stressed or scared her subconscious mind sought him out.

"He said that you said no one hurt you, but you were gone for so long, Abs," Night ran his hands through his hair as he stalked around the apartment, freezing when he saw the bags sitting by the door. "What's this?"

"Ryder's bags," Abigail told him.

"And they're here because?" From the sudden tightness in his face and body, Spider knew that his friend already knew the answer to that question.

"Ryder and the guys thought that maybe something happened to me that I can't remember, and we think that maybe someone came after me on purpose," Abigail explained.

Night's gaze snapped to his, fear and horror on his face.

"Ryder is just staying here in case whoever it was comes back," Abigail added.

"So this is just what ... friends? I didn't know you two were so friendly." Night had inherited his father's silvery gray eyes which were now narrowed and focused like he was ready to pounce on them if he thought they were lying.

"Yes, friends," Abigail said firmly, but not before she snuck a quick look his way to see if he would contradict her.

It was now or never.

He could go along with what Abigail said and pretend he was here because he was solely concerned with her safety, or he could tell the truth.

For once he wanted to fight for what he wanted instead of letting someone dictate to him what his life should look like.

"No, not as friends," he said, looking his friend squarely in the eye. "I've already told Abigail that I want her back and that this time I'm not walking away from her. I don't want to lose your friendship, Eric," he said, addressing his friend by his given name because this went beyond the SEALs and the bond they shared because of it. "But I will if it means keeping Abigail. I'm in love with her, and I should never have walked away."

Both siblings gasped as they looked at him. Then Night began to pace the room, running his hands through his short dark hair.

Finally, he stopped and dropped into one of the armchairs, indicating that they should sit as well. "Look, Ryder, you're not going to lose my friendship if you want to date my sister."

"You know I do have a say in this as well," Abigail muttered as she curled up in the other armchair.

Spider just looked at Night and arched a brow in a silent question. Did his friend really mean it?

"Yeah, I do," Night said. "I shouldn't have meddled last time."

"Meddled?" Abigail straightened in her chair. "What do you mean meddled? What did you do, Eric?"

"No," Spider said quickly. "She's still recovering from what she went through, she doesn't need to hear this story now." Once Abigail knew, there would be no going back. Her view of him, her brother, and her parents would change forever, and not for the better.

"You don't get to spring this on me and then not follow through," Abigail warned her brother.

"It's time, Ryder," Night said with resignation.

"It changes everything," he warned. The last thing he wanted was for Abigail to be isolated from the only family she had at a time when she needed love and support the most.

"Tell me," Abigail demanded.

Sensing that Night would tell all regardless of whether it was a good idea or not, he resigned himself to the fact that he might be about to lose Abby before he had a chance to win her back.

"I'm waiting," Abigail said tensely.

"The night of your graduation when you and Ryder were together for the first time, someone saw you," Night started.

Abigail gasped. "You saw me and Ryder together?"

"No, not me, Dad."

"Dad? Dad walked in on me and Ryder in bed?"

"Yep," he confirmed when she looked to him.

"How did I not know this? And why do you know?" she asked her brother.

"Honey, your dad didn't approve of me dating his daughter," Spider said, breaking the news as gently as he could.

Her brow crinkled in confusion. "He told you to stay away from me?"

"Yeah, he did."

"That doesn't make any sense, my dad loved you, way more than he ever loved me. You were like a son to him. Wait …" she trailed off, pressing her fingers to her temples. "I get it now, he didn't think I was good enough for you."

That couldn't have been further from the truth.

"Dad loved you, Abs. How could you even think that?" Night demanded.

"How could I think that? Really? Did we grow up in the same house, Eric? Dad was disappointed in me my entire life. I wasn't strong enough, I wasn't tough enough, I didn't like shooting, I didn't like hunting, I didn't think it was fun to go traipsing through the woods carrying my bodyweight in supplies on my back. No, I liked to dance, I liked pretty things, I wanted to go shopping or get my nails done. I didn't fit in in our family and you know it. Of course Dad didn't think I would be good enough for his precious Ryder."

Tears swam in her eyes but she didn't let them fall. There was no way she would cry in front of him and her brother because she believed what she'd just said. Abigail believed that her parents hadn't loved her as much as her brother because she wasn't interested in the same things as the rest of them were.

He'd met Night when he was ten and he'd gone to live with his grandparents who lived next door to Eric and Abigail. He and Night had hit it off right away, his grandparents had been old, they'd loved him but they didn't keep good health and couldn't keep up with an active pre-teen boy. Night's parents had taken him under their wing, taking him along when they went camping or to the shooting range. They had become like a second set of parents to him, and he had loved them both dearly.

As much as he knew they had loved him back he wasn't their flesh and blood.

Abigail had been a tiny wisp of a girl, those magical eyes, her effervescent personality, her spirit, her love of life, her ability to see light where the rest of them saw darkness.

That made her special.

While her parents had been confused by her, unsure how to connect with a child who was so different than them, they had loved her.

"No, sweetheart, it wasn't that your dad thought you weren't good enough for me, it was that he didn't think I was good enough for you," Spider explained.

The worst part was, her father was probably right.

* * *

12:46 P.M.

"You're not good enough for me?" Abigail asked, confused. That didn't sound like something her dad would think, her whole life all she had heard was how wonderful Eric and Ryder were. They were so smart, so strong, so tough, they were going to make fabulous SEALs one day, and she was nothing but a ballerina.

Her dad had adored Ryder, loved him just as much as he had Eric. In fact Abigail had always believed that if he could, he would have changed DNA to make Ryder his son and her not his daughter.

Now Ryder was saying her dad had broken them up because he wasn't good enough for her.

No.

She didn't believe it.

None of this made any sense at all.

"I want to know what's going on, now," she said, giving both her brother and Ryder a sharp look. "Why would my dad think you weren't good enough for me, and why does this have anything to do with you?" she asked Eric. "Were you there with Dad as well that night?"

How had the most romantic night of her life turned into such a disaster?

It had been bad enough when the night had gone from special to awful when she woke up to find that Ryder was gone without so much as a goodbye, but now to know that her father and possibly her brother had seen them naked in bed together soured her stomach.

"Your dad came home about an hour after you fell asleep," Ryder began, looking resigned like he knew that her finally hearing this story was not going to end well. "I was lying awake, holding you in my arms and trying to figure out how a guy like me could have a girl like you fall in love with me and want to give me their virginity." He held up a hand when she went to ask what he meant by a guy like him. "The door to your bedroom was thrown open and your dad was there. He looked angry, and I didn't want you to be blamed for us running out on your graduation party so I snuck out of bed to talk to him in the living room."

"What did he say?"

"That I was never to touch his daughter again."

Massaging her temples, Abigail struggled to take all of this in. It still made no sense to her. "Why?"

Ryder hesitated for a moment, then said, "He told me that I wasn't good enough for you and that I should leave and never come back, then he collapsed."

"I know, he had a heart attack that night." Was that why Ryder had ended things with her, because he felt guilty that her dad had collapsed after seeing the two of them in bed together? It had to be because nothing else made sense. Ryder wouldn't just leave because her dad told him to. Sure, Ryder loved her father, but he had told her that night that he cared deeply about her. It wasn't the same as saying he loved her, but she'd known that he cared enough that it would turn into love one day if given a chance.

But that chance had been snatched away from them.

Because of her own father.

"Is that why you stayed away, Ryder, because of my dad's heart attack?" she asked. She knew there had to be more to this story than he was saying because the Ryder she knew would never just give up on her.

"When your dad collapsed I called Eric and your mom. They called an ambulance and he was rushed to the hospital."

"You'd already gone by then. I remember when my mom came into my room to wake me up and tell me about Dad, you were gone. We rushed to the hospital and I remember that Eric was in the room with him. He died before I got a chance to see him and say goodbye." Although she had spent most of her life feeling like an outsider in her own family she had loved her parents, she just hadn't been sure they loved her back. "What did Dad say to you?" she asked her brother.

Eric sighed and rubbed his hands over his face. "He told me that he found you and Ryder in bed and that he didn't want the two of you to be together. He knew he was dying and he made me promise that I would make sure Ryder stayed away from you."

Abigail gasped as all the pieces of the puzzle began to fall into place.

Her father had broken them up the first time, and her brother had broken them up the second time.

Tears burned her eyes and she shook her head, trying to erase what she was very afraid was true.

"Tell me you didn't," she begged her brother.

"Abby," he started, standing and moving toward her.

Abigail leaped out of her chair and backed away from him. "You broke us up the second time," she accused him.

He sighed and then nodded. "When you got back together I had to make a choice, let you two stay together or honor the promise I made to our dying father. At first I thought if I just waited that your relationship would run its course, you'd break up on your own and I wouldn't have to interfere."

"That wouldn't have happened, we were in love," she said.

"I know."

"So you told Ryder to leave me," she accused. Anger was quickly replacing the devastation that had come with learning the people who were supposed to love her had played God with her life with no concern to what she would feel and what she wanted.

"I'm sorry, Abby, you'll never know how sorry, I didn't want to, but I also didn't want to not fulfill the promise I made to Dad before he died."

She just shook her head, not even knowing what to say to that.

In all of this not a single person had cared about her.

No one.

Not her father who had ordered Ryder away from her, not her brother who had chosen their father over her, not her mother who must have known what was going on and chosen not to intervene, and not Ryder who was supposed to love her but had chosen her family over her.

This was too much.

She couldn't deal with all of this on top of her abduction and knowing someone might be after her.

"Get out," she said, walking over to the door and holding it open.

"Abby, please," Ryder entreated, cautiously closing the gap between them.

"No, I don't want to hear it, Ryder, I don't even want to look at either of you right now." She focused on the floor as she drew in a shuddering breath, she wouldn't cry in front of these two even if her heart felt like it was shattering into a thousand pieces.

Again.

She knew better than to let Ryder back in and yet that was exactly what she had been doing the last few days. Seeking comfort and reassurance from his presence, letting him edge his way back into her heart.

She was an idiot.

She deserved every ounce of heartache she got and more.

"I didn't want to leave you, Abby," Ryder implored.

"And yet you did."

"Because it was your dad's dying wish."

"And you care more about him and what he wanted than you do about me. You never loved me, Ryder. When you love someone you fight for them. I would have fought for you, if I'd known what my father was trying to do I wouldn't have let anyone tear us apart, but you just walked away. You didn't even say goodbye. Do you have any idea how much that hurt? How stupid I felt? And then I took you back, and you did it to me again and I felt like a fool. You loved my parents more than you loved me, and I'm not going to be stupid enough to fall for you a third time. Now leave."

"We haven't figured out who is after you yet," Ryder reminded her.

"The security system will be installed by the end of the day, Tex will be monitoring it so he can tell one of you if something happens."

Both Ryder and Eric made scoffing sounds at that.

"You are not going to be alone and that is final," Ryder said in his don't argue with me voice.

"Fine, whatever, if it makes you happy you can sit in your car in the driveway, but I don't want to see you again, Ryder. Or you," she added, nodding at her brother.

Reluctantly, Ryder gathered his bags and the two men left. Abigail slammed the door behind them, it was a little childish but she needed an outlet for the emotions which were smothering her.

Alone, she choked on a sob then ran to her bedroom, throwing herself on the bed. She wouldn't cry, it wasn't worth it, crying hadn't changed her fate in Mexico, and it wouldn't change anything now.

No tears.

Ever.

She wasn't going to cry over men who weren't worth it.

Her father, her brother, the man she had loved, none of them had thought very highly of her, they'd played with her and her emotions, left her alone, chosen their own needs over hers, and she was done with all of them.

In the end alone wasn't so bad, at least it was safe, and after fourteen months of living in constant fear for her life there was a lot to be said for safe.

She'd survived Mexico on her own, she could certainly rebuild her life on her own too.

CHAPTER 8

June 21ˢᵗ

10:33 A.M.

Night was keeping watch over Abigail when Spider parked his car in front of her building.

This was it.

Make it or break it time.

Abigail deserved to know the truth, the whole truth, and he was ready to give it to her.

Well actually, he wasn't, but he was doing it anyway.

It wasn't fair to her to expect her to make a decision about their future if she didn't have all the facts, so he intended to do just that.

"Hey," he greeted his friend as he got out of the car. "Anything?"

"Nope, no signs of anything and Tex has her system up

and running so if we get called away we'll know she's protected."

"Yeah," he agreed half-heartedly, knowing that he wouldn't feel like she was well enough protected when they were called out no matter how good the security system was. That was a new sensation for him. He had always loved Abby, always thought about her when he was away, but before she had gone missing he had never really considered the possibility of the darkness of the world curling itself around her and pulling her over to its side.

"You know she's probably just going to throw you out," Night said, nodding at the bouquet of flowers he'd gone to buy.

"So I should just give up on her?"

"No," Night said with a lingering look at Abigail's apartment that said he thought it was already too late for both of them to fix their relationships with her. "I just want you to be prepared."

"I think I have the advantage at least for the moment," he said as he squared his shoulders, feeling like he was about to walk into a battle. "Abby wants answers more than she wants to be angry."

Hoping he was right, Spider knocked on Abigail's door, the flowers held out before him like a peace offering. His eyes narrowed when she opened the door, there were dark circles under her eyes hinting she hadn't slept much last night.

"I asked you to leave," she said.

"I can't do that. I promised you that I wouldn't walk away from you again and I'm not."

"Ryder, what do you want?" she asked, exhaustion covered every word.

"To take you out on a date," he replied.

"Ryder ..."

"Look, don't decide yet, I want to tell you why your dad didn't think I was good enough for you." As much as he abhorred the idea of Abigail learning about his past, part of him wished he had done it back in the beginning. Maybe if there hadn't been any secrets between them then he wouldn't have felt like he had no choice but to leave.

Abigail studied him for a long moment, her expression not giving away any of what she was thinking, and Spider found himself holding his breath until she finally nodded and stepped back to allow him to enter.

Score one.

It was a small victory, but he'd take it.

"Did you sleep at all?" he asked as she closed the door behind them.

"Nightmares," she said shortly.

"Did you eat?"

"Not hungry."

"You have to eat, Abs, you have to keep your strength up."

"Why?" The toneless way she said it as she dropped down into one of the armchairs had his heart stuttering in his chest.

She sounded like she'd given up.

That was unacceptable.

That wasn't his Abby.

Knowing that it was because of what he and her brother had told her the day before that had pushed her to her limits had his guilt-meter ticking over to full.

"These are for you," he said as he held out the flowers.

"We're doing the flower thing again?"

"No, well kind of, it worked last time." He tried to joke, but when she arched a brow he set the flowers on the kitchen counter and sat down on the couch. "Abby, not fighting for you—for us—is my biggest regret, I can't take it back, can't undo what's been done, but I'm hoping that once you understand why that you might be willing to give me a second—or a third—chance."

She said nothing, just sat quietly with her legs folded beneath her and her hands in her lap, and waited for him to explain. She obviously wasn't going to make this easy for him, but he didn't deserve for it to be easy. He had messed up, big time, and now he had to try to clean up that mess.

"Did your mom ever tell you anything about my childhood before I went to live with my grandparents?" Spider asked.

"No. I know that you had a rough childhood, but I don't know any details."

"Your mom met me in juvenile court," he began.

Abigail's brow furrowed. "I can't imagine you doing anything that would have you in court."

He gave her a sad smile. "That's because you don't know the Ryder that existed before I met your family. As you know, your mom worked security at the court, she was there the day I had my court appearance. I had been getting into fights at school, it made me hate school, I was in foster care at the time and I snuck out, got some spray paint from one of the older kids, I went to the school and graffitied the buildings."

"What did the kids bully you for?" Abigail asked.

That she had zeroed in on the crux of what had led to him taking a spray can to the school made him smile. Although they had been like oil and water as kids a part of him had always known that she was special, that she got him. "I was a scrawny little thing as a child, tiny for my age, we didn't always have a lot to eat at my house."

"Were you abused, Ryder?" Abby asked, her voice soft and full of empathy, all traces of anger and hurt gone as she focused her entire attention on him and his story and not the bad blood between them.

"My dad was a drunk. A violent, mean drunk. He worked

in construction when he was sober enough to work, the rest of the time we went hungry. When he was drunk he used to beat my mom. As I got older he tried to come after me a few times, but my mom would always get in between us, offering up herself so long as he didn't put his hands on me."

Abigail slipped off her chair and joined him on the couch, gently covering his hands with her own. "I'm sorry, Ryder, that's awful. Your mom sounds like she was such a brave lady."

"Just like you," he said, cupping her cheek in his hand as his thumb stroked across the petal softness of her skin. "Do you know why my nickname is Spider?"

"No, I never really thought about it, and you never told me."

"One day when I was about six, I remember my dad was drunk and beating on my mom, and then this spider dropped from the ceiling and ran across his arm, he freaked out. The spider was a small one but he was terrified of it. The spider reminded me of myself. I was small, only no one was afraid of me, but it gave me comfort. If spiders were small and yet they could scare people then maybe the fact that I was small meant that I could be strong too, I could learn how to make people afraid of me so I didn't get beaten up. That fascination with them just kind of stuck."

"I remember you had a pet tarantula when you were a teenager." Abigail huffed, but her eyes sparkled. "I also remember the time you and Eric thought it would be funny to set it loose in my room to scare me. As I recall it did."

Spider laughed. "I'd forgotten about that."

"You and Eric loved to drive me crazy," she said with a reminiscent smile. "I remember I used to hate you so much. I used to feel like you stole my place in my family and left me out in the cold, but I remember the day that changed. I was twelve and my best friend Maria had a crush on a boy from her church. She lied to her mom and said all the kids from the church were going to hang out together but she and her boyfriend just wanted to make out. Her friend tried to kiss me, but I got this bad feeling about him so I told Maria I was going home. He followed me. He dragged me into my yard and tried to touch me and then all of a sudden you were there, pulling him off me. I think I fell in love with you that day."

He remembered that, remembered the look the boy had had on his face when he looked at Abby. It had reminded him of the look his father gave his mother before he beat her up. "I'm glad I was there."

"Me too. After that I hated that you just saw me as Eric's annoying little sister. I remember when you and Eric told us that you had made it, that you were SEALs, I cried for a month because I thought it meant that I could never have you. You drove me crazy, but I respected you, even when I didn't understand why you did what you did."

The smile she gave him touched him deeply, it said she didn't always get him in her head, but she did in her heart. It said they had a connection that nothing could sever.

At least he hoped so.

"I remember the day I fell for you. It was your eighteenth birthday, I hadn't seen you for almost eighteen months and all of a sudden you weren't a kid anymore, you were a woman. I remember you danced and you were amazing, I'd never seen you dance before but you were magical. I couldn't stop thinking about you, dreaming about you. When I saw you again a month later at your graduation I couldn't keep my hands off you."

"That night went from being the best of my life to the worst. Finally having you was everything that I dreamed of, I knew you didn't love me yet but I felt a connection to you, I knew that we could be happy together. But then you were gone, and my dad died, and everything fell apart after that. For four long years I missed you, I cried over you, I wondered what I had done that was wrong that made you go away."

"Aww, baby, you didn't do anything wrong," he said, putting his other hand on her other cheek and very softly touching his lips to hers.

"Then explain it to me, tell me why you left, tell me why you think you weren't good enough for me. I want to understand, I need to know. Please."

* * *

11:01 A.M.

It was going to be bad.

Abigail could see it in Ryder's deep blue eyes, feel it in the way his fingers lingered on her skin as though trying to memorize how it felt in case he never got to touch it again.

What was he going to say?

"Ryder?" she prompted, all thoughts of how angry she'd been at him for not loving her enough to fight for her faded away. She could feel his love as surely as she could feel his hands on her face, but then he sighed and his hands fell away, and she had to stamp down on the doubt and focus on what Ryder had to tell her.

"I was in foster care for a while because my parents died, my grandparents wanted to take me in, but they were old and not in great health, they weren't sure they could take me on," he started.

"But they did," she said, stating the obvious since they both knew he had come to live with his grandparents next door to her family.

"Because of your mom, because of your parents. My grandparents were there that day in court and your mom realized who I was. She spoke with them, found out what had happened to me and promised to help out with me if they would become my legal guardians. My grandparents happily accepted because they wanted me to come and live with them."

"So you felt like you owed my parents?" she asked, confused. "Is that why you let my dad talk you into walking away from me?"

"In part. I owed your parents a lot. Because of them, I got out of the foster system, I got counseling, I was loved by both my grandparents and by your family. If I had of stayed in the system I don't know what my life would have turned out like, but I know it wouldn't be this."

"Okay, well I see why you would be grateful to them, maybe even owe them something, but I still don't understand why you would think you weren't good enough for me. Because of the graffiti thing? I would have understood that, you were just a kid who had been abused and your parents had died." She paused as a thought occurred to her. "Did your mom die protecting you? Did she kill your dad to save you?" She reached out to cover Ryder's hands with her own, he shrugged her off, and she tried not to be hurt that he didn't want her comfort. It was her own fault, she had pushed him away when he said he wanted another chance with her because she was still hurt and focused on not letting him hurt her again.

But then she saw the tears shimmering in his eyes.

Ryder never cried.

Her heart clenched.

"No, sweetheart, my mom didn't kill my dad, I did. I killed him ... and her."

The way he said it made it clear that he blamed himself,

but she knew there had to be more to the story than he had just said. Scared that if she did anything at all to distract him he'd stop talking, she tried to sit completely still.

"Most of the time my mom protected me from him, but I guess I developed my protective streak early because by the time I was eight or nine I wanted to be the one to protect her. My dad had hit me a few times, usually when my mom wasn't around, but this night when he went after her I stepped in. It was bad, he told me if I wanted to act like a man he'd treat me like a man and he started hitting me. I was almost to the point of blacking out when I remember my mom shoving me out of the way. He started punching her, and she threw me something. I was on the floor, and I remember it bouncing on the tiles before coming to a stop beside me. It was a gun. She screamed at me to shoot him. I lifted the gun, tried to aim it but I was only ten and I had never held a gun before, I didn't know we even owned one. I fired it, but the bullet went through my mom into my dad. It killed them both."

The expression on Ryder's face hit her deep. So much guilt, so much pain, so much regret. Abigail knew there were no words that would comfort him right now so she did the only thing she could. She climbed onto his lap, threw her arms around his neck, and held onto him as tightly as she could.

"She had bought the gun," Ryder said quietly. He didn't move to hold onto her, but he also didn't shove her away. "She'd had enough of him, she had been planning on killing him the next time he came after her, there was a history of domestic violence she would have claimed self-defense and it wouldn't have been a lie, sooner or later he would have killed her. And me. If I hadn't interfered that night we could have finally been free, instead I lost her. I killed her."

He sounded so broken that she tightened her hold,

pressing her face against his neck. "Your mom got what she wanted," she whispered, "you were safe after that."

A groan shuddered through his body and then his arms came around her, holding her in a grip that was almost crushing, but she made no move to ask him to loosen his hold. She didn't want him to.

"Did my dad threaten you with this?" she asked softly, trying to control her anger at her father.

"He was trying to protect you."

"Don't defend him, Ryder. I hate him for doing that to you," she said harshly, wishing that her dad was here so she could rip into him for being so cruel.

"I didn't tell you so you would hate him, I told you because I wanted you to understand. I felt vulnerable, I was ashamed of what I'd done, I didn't want you to know, I was afraid that you would see me differently. That you'd leave me."

Frustrated, she pushed at his chest until he released her, then she stood up and paced the room. "I hate my father for doing that to you, and I'm so angry with you for going along with it. No one cared about me, no one gave me any credit for knowing what my heart told me. I wish you'd told me this sooner, I would have been there for you, I would have told you as many times as I had to that you didn't do anything wrong, that you were just a little boy and so brave."

Ryder stood and tentatively came toward her. "I'm sorry. I should have told you the truth, I shouldn't have let your dad or your brother dictate my decisions. If he hadn't died that night then everything might have turned out differently, but I can't go back and fix it, Abby, I wish I could but I can't. All I can do now is give you the future you deserve."

Abigail studied him carefully, her brain still told her not to trust that Ryder wouldn't walk away again, but her heart knew that this was the only man she would ever love, just like it had known that when she was twelve. Stepping forward, she wrapped her arms around his waist and pressed her ear to his chest. "Yes."

"Yes?"

"Yes, I'll go on a date with you."

His hands on her shoulders eased her back, and his eyes said he wasn't quite sure she'd really said that. "Yes?"

"I can't magically undo the hurt or wipe away the pain of you leaving me without an explanation, but now that I know why I can understand. I'm willing to work on things, it will take time to get back to where we were before. But, Ryder, you can't ever walk away from me again. I can't take you back a fourth time." She knew in her heart that was true. Giving him a chance now was one thing because she finally knew the truth, but if he did it again it would be over between them no matter how much she loved him.

Ryder's arm scooped under her bottom, lifting her up so they were eye to eye, and she wrapped her legs around his waist. "Abigail, I promise you that I will *never* walk away again. I can't. I don't want to lose you. I understand that you need to take things slow, that we need to rebuild trust, I won't rush you. You are in control of what happens and when. I'd wait for you for all eternity."

Satisfied that they were finally starting out in a place where they might be able to make it this time, she asked, "What did Eric do when he found out about us?"

"He punched me." Ryder grinned when she sputtered. "I deserved it, you don't sleep with your best friend's little sister."

"Did he know?"

"About my past? No, not when your dad told me to leave you, and not when he made the promise on your dad's deathbed."

"Did he know when he told you to leave me?"

"No, he found out after it was already done, after I'd left you again, he asked, and I told him. He hated himself when he found out, Abby, try not to be too hard on him."

"I think I hate him, Ryder, my dad. What he did to you … I don't think I can forgive him for that."

"He did what he thought was best for his little girl."

"He was wrong. I was in love with you, you would never have laid a hand on me, you would have protected me with your dying breath."

"We all make mistakes. If your dad had lived he would have come around. He didn't know you loved me, all he saw was a man who had killed his parents in bed with his eighteen-year-old daughter."

"How can you be so forgiving?"

"Because all that is important to me right now is that I'm holding you in my arms, I have another chance with you, and I know I'm not going to mess it up this time. This time is forever."

"Kiss me, Ryder," she said with a smile. When his lips touched hers the broken pieces of her heart clicked back into place. This was where she belonged, in the arms of the man she had never stopped loving.

5:55 P.M.

Spider stroked Abigail's hair as she slept with her head in his lap.

After their talk and their kiss they'd curled up on the couch together just like they had the day before and watched some of Abby's favorite Disney movies. It hadn't taken her long to fall asleep, and while he'd kept the movie running for background noise, all he'd done was sit and look at her and try to believe that he really had another chance with her.

A chance he was determined not to blow.

Thankfully Abigail had slept well, no nightmares, and he hoped that maybe she was starting to turn the corner. It was probably wildly naïve of him to think that, she'd only been back a few days, and it wasn't like his love could magically cure her, but he wasn't used to this side of things. Usually, he and his team did the rescuing and then they handed the victim off to family and friends and professionals, but this time he was the friend, the family, he was the one who had to support her through this, and he felt woefully inadequate for the task.

What did he know about helping people heal from trauma?

"If you keep doing that I'm never going to get up," Abigail murmured with a content moan.

"Then don't get up," he said simply, continuing to let his fingers glide through her silky locks.

"I can't just sleep forever," she protested but made no move to get up.

"Your body needs sleep right now to recover," he reminded her, although he was in no hurry to encourage her to move out of his arms.

"I know, but I hate just lying around, it feels … lazy … like I'm … I don't even know," she said, sitting up, climbing into his lap, and curling into him like she needed him to surround her.

Happy to oblige, he wrapped his arms around her and pulled her closer. "You're not lazy, sweetheart, you're healing, and as much as you don't like it, it's going to take some time. You're not just recovering from pneumonia you're recovering from fourteen months of terror. Your body isn't supposed to live like that, loaded with adrenalin."

"I know, I guess I'm just feeling a little sorry for myself."

"You're entitled."

"No, I think I wasted enough of my life feeling sorry for myself. I might have felt out of place in my family but at least I went to bed fed every night and safe. What happened to you …" she trailed off, and her hands slipped under the hem of his t-shirt, her fingertips tracing over his bare skin. "I wish I could make it go away, I hate that you were hurt like that."

"That's the same way I feel about your pain, I wish I could take it away."

"I wish my dad and my brother hadn't stolen so much time from us."

"We have the whole rest of our lives to spend together," he reminded her. He wished he hadn't been a coward, wished he hadn't been ashamed of what he'd done, afraid to have Abigail find out. He wished he hadn't doubted her love for him or her strength, but she'd been only eighteen back then, and he hadn't been sure she could handle it.

His mistake, but unfortunately they had both paid the price.

"Yeah, we do," Abigail agreed, touching her lips to his jaw.

Her lips on him made him start to grow hard, it had been so long since he'd been able to hold her and kiss her and he captured her lips and began to kiss her properly. Abigail's hands came up to clasp his shoulders, and she twisted on his lap so she was straddling him.

He pulled her closer, kissing her like a starving man. This woman was his heart and soul, and living his life without her in it—even if it had been his own doing—had been living with a part of himself dead. His hands spanned her waist as he plundered her mouth, growing harder as the heat of her body seeped into him.

"I'm sorry, Ryder," she said, pulling away from him. "I'm not ready for more yet."

They were both breathing heavily and he could see the arousal in her eyes, but he meant what he'd said earlier, they had the rest of their lives to spend together, there was no need to rush anything. "It's no problem, Abs," he told her.

She was breathing heavily—as was he—and her gaze dipped to the tent in his pants. "If you want—"

Spider touched a finger to her lips, silencing her. "I don't want," he assured her. "The only thing I want in the world right now is your happiness."

Abigail gave him a sweet smile. "I missed you."

"I missed you too, babe. I wish I hadn't cost—"

This time Abigail silenced him with a finger against his lips. "No more wishing. We can't change the past. My dad did what he did, my brother did what he did, and you did what you did, now I just want to focus on the future."

He kissed her fingertip. "The future it is. And speaking of the future, you slept through lunch, you must be hungry, I'll cook us dinner."

"I'll help."

"No, you'll rest." Lifting her easily, he stood her in front of him then scooped her up into his arms and laid her down on the couch. Fluffing up some pillows, he put them behind her and then grabbed the throw and spread it out over her. "What?" he asked when he saw her watching him with a bemused smile.

"You're such a mother hen. It always makes me smile, you're such a big guy, so tough, so strong, and yet you're so sweet and gentle when you want to be, I just like it, it makes me feel safe."

"Because you are safe with me," he said, stooping to touch his lips to her forehead. "I would do anything to keep you safe, Abby, including giving my life for yours or killing anyone who is a threat to you."

Abby shivered at his deadly tone but she didn't break eye

contact. "Does it make me a bad person that when you say that I only feel safer?"

"No, because you know I would only kill someone who deserved it. We will find who kidnapped you, Abby, and if he comes after you again I won't hesitate to take him out." Taking out Abigail's abductor would give him more pleasure than it should, but unlike Abby, he wasn't worried about whether that made him a bad person or not. "Spaghetti and meatballs okay for dinner?"

"Sure," Abigail agreed, settling back against the couch.

Leaving her to rest, Spider went to the kitchen and set a pot of water on the stove to boil while he grabbed a packet of spaghetti from the cupboard and frozen meatballs from the freezer. While they'd been in the safehouse he'd given Caroline a list of some of Abigail's favorite foods and asked her to stock up the place. Abby could be a picky eater, but he knew pasta was one of her favorites so he'd made sure there was plenty there to keep her going for a while. The less she was out and about right now the better, as they had no idea if her kidnapper was keeping track of her.

Once the pasta was in the pot and the meatballs were heating on the stove, he set the table and filled two glasses with sparkling apple cider, another of Abigail's favorites. Using the good china, he went all out, lighting candles and setting the flowers he'd brought her in a vase.

"What are you doing?"

"It's our first date, it has to be special," he replied.

"I'm wearing yoga pants and a t-shirt," Abigail said, making a face. "That isn't really date attire. Plus my hair is a mess and I'm not wearing any makeup."

"You look perfect, I don't care what you're wearing and you're so pretty you don't need makeup," he told her completely honestly.

Abigail rolled her eyes but her cheeks turned pink, and he knew that she was pleased with the compliment.

Ridiculously pleased to have made her happy with a few simple words, Spider returned to the kitchen and busied himself with dishing up the meal. When he turned around to carry the plates to the table and ask Abby if she needed help getting up he found her standing by the table. She must have slipped quickly through to her bedroom because the t-shirt and yoga pants were gone, in their place was a pretty purple sundress, and she had taken her hair out of the messy bun and twisted it up with a sparkly clip.

"Should I take it from your expression that you approve?" she asked with a sweet smile.

"Yeah, you should," he said, viciously stamping down his libido before it could ruin the evening. She'd said she wasn't ready and he respected that. Not only had she just been saved after more than a year as a captive, but she had just learned some heavy stuff about him and her family, she needed time to process everything.

"Good," she said, seemingly satisfied, and he wondered if her self-confidence had taken a battering with everything she'd been through.

"Let's eat," he said, carrying the food to the table then holding out her chair for her.

She smiled, and he couldn't help but stare at her lips, she had obviously put on a little gloss because they shimmered seductively.

How could he look at those lips and not kiss them?

Picking up a piece of spaghetti he held out one end to her. Abigail frowned in confusion before breaking into a grin.

"Lady and the Tramp." She giggled.

He just grinned back, knowing her penchant for all things Disney he knew it was a surefire way to bring a smile to her face.

Abigail put one end of the piece of spaghetti in her mouth and he took the other. His eyes met hers and didn't break the connection as their mouths slowly came to meet each other in the middle. When they kissed, another open wound from his messed up childhood scarred over.

CHAPTER 9

June 22nd

2:40 P.M.

"I have a surprise for you."

Abigail looked up from her book to see Ryder smiling down at her. He'd been busy this morning, making phone calls, and she assumed it had something to do with her abduction although he hadn't specifically mentioned it. He hadn't taken a break for lunch so she'd made sandwiches and given him one then taken a nap after she'd eaten. Now she was reading and hoping that Ryder would be done soon because she missed him.

It was silly because he was only in her living room, and yet she missed him. They'd lost so much time and while she was trying not to be too angry with her father—especially since she couldn't get any resolution by being able to yell at him—it was hard. Her anger toward Ryder had mostly gone when she learned of his awful past and the heavy burden he had carried all these years, and now she just wanted to move forward.

"A surprise?" she asked, setting her book on her nightstand.

"Yep. Let's go." He reached for her hand and pulled her off the bed, towing her behind him toward the door.

"I'm wearing sweats," she protested, trying to pull against him which was like trying to pull against a truck.

"It's fine," he assured her as he led her through the apartment and out the front door. Ryder nodded to Eric who was in his car on the street outside her place as he bundled her quickly into his car.

She hadn't spoken to her brother yet, wasn't sure she was ready too, their father might be gone but Eric was still here, and she was worried if she talked to him now she'd be doing a lot more yelling than actual discussion. She hated what Eric had done both to her and to his supposed best friend, and she wasn't sure she was ready to forgive him just yet.

"So, where are we going?" Abigail asked as she looked away from Eric's car.

"You'll see when we get there."

"I guess in the time we've been apart you forgot that I hate surprises," she grumbled, but she was actually a little excited. This was the first time she had gone out since returning home, and while she was nervous about large crowds it was nice to get out and do something normal. And she knew that wherever Ryder was taking her would be safe, he was as concerned about her safety as she was, perhaps even more.

"Trust me, you'll like this one," he promised.

As he drove he reached out and rested a hand on her thigh. She liked the weight of it and the warmth, both made her feel safe and she rested her hand on top of his, hooking her thumb around his.

The last few days she had been so focused on learning about her relationship with Ryder and what had torn them apart, then learning about Ryder's past, and slowly finding their way back to one another that thoughts of her abduction had been pushed to the backburner. Abigail doubted that could last long, but it was nice to think about something else, even if not all of those thoughts had been pleasant.

Now she felt like she was starting to get her life back, she had a long way to go to get back to normal, but at least she was moving forward instead of being trapped in the same place for so long.

Lost in thought, when she realized the car had stopped driving and looked out the window to see where they were, she gasped.

"The dance studio," she said, turning to look at Ryder. Had he brought her back here to try to get her to remember the night she had been taken?

"Nope," he said, reading the question in her eyes. "I brought you here to dance."

"To dance?"

"You love dancing, it's how you express yourself, how you deal with your emotions. I thought this might be what you needed right now."

Fumbling with her seatbelt, Abigail scrambled across the center console and into Ryder's lap. "This is wonderful, perfect," she gushed, "I mean, I'm a little nervous that some bad memories might come back, but you're here, and that makes me not so scared, and it's been so long since I danced, this is just what I need right now." She planted a kiss on Ryder's mouth and then hugged him hard.

Ryder's shoulders loosened, and she knew he'd been worried that bringing her here would be a mistake. "I parked around the back so you wouldn't have to go through the parking lot."

"I'm not worried about it," she assured him. "Is Veronica here?"

"No, I thought it might be best not to overwhelm you all at once since this is the first time you've been out since you came home. But ..." he reached around her to pull out something from the glove compartment. "This is your new phone, we transferred all your old data across so you have all your contacts and apps and everything. I'm sure V would love to hear from you when you're ready."

Tears filled her eyes and she brushed them away. "You think of everything, you're so good to me."

"I love you, baby," he said. Taking her face in his hands, he kissed her deeply, and she rethought her not ready for sex stance.

Breaking the kiss, Ryder opened the car door and climbed out, still holding onto her, then set her on her feet. Hand in hand they slipped into the building through the back door. Abigail braced herself for bad memories to come rushing back but all she felt was the same peace she always did when she was in a dance studio.

"For you," Ryder said, holding out a pink sparkly gift bag.

"A gift? You've done enough for me."

"Open it," was all he said.

She took the bag and opened it to find a pair of pink tights and a pink leotard with a skirt. She loved her leotards with skirts and loved the way the skirt flared and twirled when she was doing turns. At the bottom of the bag was a pair of ballet slippers. "You didn't have to do that, I have leotards at my place."

"I wanted you to have something new," Ryder said. The love shining from his eyes filled up her soul which had had a hole drilled in it when he left her, and the light had been slowly dripping out of her life ever since. In that one look her soul was patched and refilled and she threw herself at him.

"I love you so much, Ryder."

"I love you too, Abby, more than you can ever know. Dance for me, sweetheart." Ryder set her on her feet and nudged her toward the studio.

Abigail walked into the room she had spent so many years in. A lot of students had come and gone in that time, most hadn't pursued dancing as a career but a few had gone on to dance professionally.

Slipping off her sweats, she changed into her dance clothes unable to wipe the smile off her face as she put on her pointe shoes and walked into the middle of the room.

It had been a long time since she'd danced and she was still recovering from being sick. The first few turns she tried she wobbled and nearly lost her balance.

Before she could get frustrated she saw Ryder watching her, the smile on his face made her want to dance beautifully for him, thank him for everything he'd done for her.

Focusing, she tried again, and before she knew it, she was spinning just like she had been doing since she was a little girl.

When she set both feet on the ground again she found herself scooped up into Ryder's arms, his mouth descending on hers.

"I love watching you dance," he said against her lips.

"It's what I was born to do."

He looked down at her, expression both wary and curious. "Why did you come back from New York, Abby? You were talented enough to make it as a professional dancer. Why did you give that up?"

When she'd been sixteen she was offered a partial scholarship to a ballet school in New York. Her parents hadn't wanted her to go, hadn't thought that dancing was a legitimate profession and had told her that if she went she would be on her own, responsible for paying her own bills.

Abigail had gladly accepted those conditions.

She'd gone, gotten a job at a convenience store working the late shift after her classes and schoolwork were done for the day, shared an apartment with several other girls, and had the time of her life.

Until it all came crashing down around her.

"You know what happened, I didn't make the cut," she said softly, unable to meet his gaze.

"I know that's what you said, I just don't think that's all there is to it."

She didn't want to tell him, but he had opened up to her, shared his darkest secrets and if they were having a third go at this relationship then this time they should go in with no secrets. "You know my parents didn't want me to go, they wouldn't support me so I had to get a job. I worked nights at a convenience store, one night some kid high on something came in to rob the place. I panicked, was too slow getting him the cash from the register, so he hit me, knocked me unconscious, I had a concussion and unfortunately there was permanent damage that left me with balance issues that ruined my career."

"Oh, sweetheart." Ryder's arms tightened around her and he clutched her close against his chest. "I'm so sorry."

"It is what it is," she said nonchalantly. It had hurt a lot at the time but she'd been seventeen then and was twenty-six now, meaning she'd had nine years to come to terms with it. "Sometimes life doesn't turn out the way we want it to, but that doesn't mean we have to be unhappy. I love teaching children to dance, and now I have you back in my life, and I can honestly say that I don't care that I won't ever be a professional ballerina because I have everything that I could ever want right here."

It was true.

She might have mourned the loss of her career at one point, but now she was dreaming of opening her own studio, and being held in the arms of the man she loved made her heart overflow with happiness.

CHAPTER 10

June 23rd

9:27 P.M.

"We should go to bed," Spider said as he kissed the top of Abigail's head. She was curled up on his lap, and she tilted her head back to look up at him, it was the first night she'd managed not to fall asleep early, but they'd had a long day and she needed rest.

"I thought for sure that I would have been asleep hours ago after all that fresh air and walking, but it's nearly half-past nine and I'm still awake. I know it's silly, but I feel so much more like a normal person going to bed at a normal hour," Abigail told him.

"You are a normal person, Abby, it will just take a little while for your life to go back to normal."

"Today helped a lot, the last few days have," she amended.

163

"But today's picnic and walking along the beach, the waves and the sand, the more time I spend at the beach the better I seem to feel."

"Then we can go there every day," he told her. He loved the beach as well so it certainly wasn't any hardship to take Abigail there every day, but he knew at some point she would have to confront her emotions over what she'd been through instead of just avoiding them.

"At least until you get called out," she said, and he saw the anxiety in her eyes. She was dreading that. If he was honest he was too. Spider had always loved his job, loved the adrenalin rush, loved saving lives and capturing terrorists, but now for the first time the idea of leaving filled him with dread. Abigail wasn't ready to be alone yet, but if his team was called up, he would have to go whether he liked it or not.

"Let's not worry about that just now," he said.

"Besides, if you get called away you won't have to watch any more Disney movies with me, see there's a bright side to everything," she said with a laugh.

"Hey, true love is watching Disney movies with your girl if that's what she wants to do," he told her, his smile mirroring hers.

"You mean that don't you?" Her face grew serious, contemplative.

"Honey, I would watch Disney movies with you every day for the rest of our lives if it made you happy. All I care about is being with you." Spider meant it too. Disney definitely wasn't his thing, but it was important to Abigail, and that made it important to him too.

Abigail moved on his lap so she was straddling him. "I'm ready."

"Ready?"

"For you, for this," she said as she began to undo his jeans.

"Abs," he warned. He wasn't sure she was ready to take the

next step in their fledgling relationship, but if she kept that up it would be hard to say no and do the right thing.

"I want this, Ryder, I'm ready, I knew it yesterday in the dance studio, but I wanted to be sure that I wasn't just getting caught up in the moment. All day today when I held your hand as we walked through the waves all I could think about was your hands on my body. I don't want to wait any longer, I love you, you love me, we've lost so much time already. Why should we waste more?" Her mouth caught his and she kissed him with enough confidence and passion that he was convinced that she knew what she wanted.

Breaking the kiss, Spider stood, holding Abigail in his arms, and carried her to the bedroom. "If we're doing this then we're doing it right, not hard and fast in a chair."

"I'm not averse to hard and fast right about now," Abigail said as she wrapped her legs around his waist.

"I am. Do you know how long I've waited to touch your body, to taste you, to bury myself so deep inside you that it feels like we've become one person?"

Abigail shivered and kissed him again. "Okay, I guess hard and fast can wait."

"Sweetheart, we'll be doing slow and sweet, and hard and fast, and everything in between."

In her bedroom, Spider set Abigail on her feet and took a moment to look at her. Her bronze hair hung loosely around her shoulders. After a couple of days outdoors her pale skin had a little color to it, and although she wasn't eating a lot she was starting to put back on some of the weight she'd lost while she'd been held captive. Her eyes watched him, and the heat and desire in them brought him to his knees. Literally.

Spider knelt before her and opened her jeans, sliding them slowly down her legs, letting his fingers trace along her skin as he did so. She wasn't wearing any shoes so he lifted each foot and removed her jeans.

His hands caressed each inch of her legs as they made their way to her backside where they curled around her cheeks and pulled her forward so he could press his nose to her and breath in her scent.

Abigail shivered, her hands curling into his hair, and while he longed to give her what she wanted he hadn't finished his exploration of her body yet.

Taking hold of the hem of her t-shirt, he pushed it up, and she slipped both arms out and then pulled it over her head and tossed it on the floor. His lips kissed their way up her stomach between her breasts before taking one of her nipples into his mouth. Abigail moaned, her hands on his shoulders using them for leverage as her knees weakened.

He grinned up at her. "I forgot how much you like that."

"Your tongue could be put to much better uses than talking," she murmured.

Spider just laughed and touched the tip of his tongue to her other nipple then blew on it making her shiver again.

Hooking his thumbs into the waistband of her panties, he eased them down her legs. As soon as he had them off he nudged her legs apart then pressed his lips to her center in the gentlest of kisses.

Standing up, Spider guided Abigail backward to the bed, then spread her out on it and drank in her body with his eyes as he stripped off his own clothes.

When he stretched out over her, Abigail began her own exploration of his body as she traced every inch of his abs and his chest while they kissed. Balancing his weight with one hand, his other moved between her legs plunging inside her to stroke her deep, stretching her to prepare her for him.

"Now, Ryder," she begged against his lips.

"Okay, baby." Ripping open the condom he'd pulled out of his jeans pocket, he slid it over his length then positioned himself at her entrance. A sliver of doubt crept through him.

She claimed no one had touched her while she'd been gone, but she obviously didn't remember some of that time, and she had refused to see a doctor. Was she really ready for this?

Then he met her gaze.

Love.

That was all he saw looking back at him.

Yes, there was passion and desire, but what stood out was the love.

Because she loved him, she trusted him, and from her heavy breathing and impatient lifting of her hips she wanted this every bit as much as he did.

She gasped as he started to enter her and he moved slowly, reclaiming her lips as he eased his way inside her hot, tight body.

"That's perfect, I feel whole," Abigail whispered as her hands curled around his bottom pulling him deeper.

"Me too, sweetheart," he said.

As he started to move he reached between them touching her where their bodies joined because he wanted them to come at the same time and he knew that Abigail needed both external and internal stimulation to orgasm during sex.

He felt it building, harder, faster, stronger than anything he had ever felt before. Spider held back, he wasn't coming until Abigail had. Her breathing had quickened, and her fingers clawed at his back, her lips never leaving his.

Then it hit her, her internal muscles clamping around him as she came on a scream that was swallowed by his mouth.

Letting himself find his own release, Spider continued to thrust into her, drawing out both their pleasure as white dots danced in front of his closed eyes and he felt like he had traveled to a whole different dimension.

"You know how we talked about going several rounds? I don't think I'm going to be able to move for about a day, that orgasm touched every part of my body," Abigail said with a contented sigh.

"Uh-uh, baby, no way I'm waiting to do this," he said as he moved down her body, closing his lips around her sensitive bud, making her gasp and then moan as her hips came off the bed. She was going to come on his tongue, and his fingers, before he entered again, then they would fall asleep in each other's arms.

CHAPTER 11

June 24th

10:12 A.M.

Abigail yawned and turned over in bed, then froze.

She was alone.

The sheets smelled like Ryder, but they and the pillow beside hers were cold, it was clear he had left her bed some time ago.

But where had he gone?

Panic gripped her hard. Had he gone? Left her again?

"Hey, Abs, you're awake and just in time to get ready to meet everyone for lunch."

She spun around at the sound of Ryder's voice and sagged in relief when she saw him standing in the bedroom doorway. He hadn't left, hadn't abandoned her again, he must have just woken up a while back and decided to let her get some more rest while he got up.

"I didn't leave, Abby," he said, quickly covering the hurt that flashed through his eyes. "You were just so peaceful, and I know how tired you've been, I wanted to let you sleep while I went for a run." He pointed at his sweaty t-shirt and shorts as though she might need more convincing.

"I'm sorry," she said, already feeling bad for having doubted him. "I shouldn't have thought that you would leave, not after how wonderful you've been the last few days and what we shared last night."

"It's okay," he assured her.

"It's not," she countered.

"No, it is, my past behavior has given you no reason to expect anything but me leaving you. I guess we both just have to accept it will take time for you to trust me again." Ryder crossed the room and sat down on the bed beside her, curling an arm around her shoulders and pulling her against his chest.

"I don't mean to not trust you, it wasn't a conscious decision to believe you'd left, I just woke up and you weren't there, and I panicked," she explained.

"We'll get there, it will just take—"

"Time," she said for him. "Yeah I know, I just don't like it."

Ryder kissed her forehead. "Well, we have lunch with our friends to look forward to today, so why don't you grab a shower, get dressed, and we can head to the beach."

Shoving away her frustrations, Abigail kissed him and then stood up. "It won't take me long to get ready."

"Take as long as you need, I'll shower when you're done."

"If you hadn't let me sleep so long we could have showered together." She winked, then headed for the bathroom.

"Oh, we'll be doing that tonight," Ryder called after her,

and she heard his groan which she knew meant his body did not want to wait until tonight.

Less than an hour later, they were both showered, dressed, and piling into the car along with the couple of apple pies they had made the day before after their walk along the beach. Ryder's SEAL team would be there today, along with the team who had saved her life, and she wasn't sure if any other teams were coming as well. She'd wanted to bake more pies but Ryder had said two was enough, he hadn't wanted her to wear herself out. Although she was getting stronger each day she did tire easily, which is why she hadn't fought him on it, but she was anxious to get her life back.

Today was the next step.

She had Ryder back, she and her friend Veronica had talked about her starting her own studio, and now she was going to do something completely normal and hang out with her friends.

Practically as soon as Ryder parked the car, her door was thrown open, and she was being pulled out and wrapped up in the arms of her friends. Matthew's wife Caroline was there, and Christopher's wife Alabama, there was Hunter's wife Fiona who had been through something a little like what she had, and Summer, Cheyenne, and Jessyka. All of these women had become her friends when they'd joined the SEAL team family, a family she had been born into and then continued to be a part of because of her brother. A lot of these men were like surrogate big brothers to her, and although they didn't always spend a lot of time together, she knew that if she needed help any one of them would be there for her.

They had been there for her.

If it wasn't for them she would still be lost in Mexico, stuck in that concrete prison.

"Are you okay? Let me look at you," Caroline said, holding her at arm's length. "You've lost too much weight," she tutted unhappily.

"My captors weren't real big on feeding me," she said wryly.

"Is Ryder taking good care of you?" Alabama asked, her tone making it clear he would be in trouble if he wasn't.

"He is," she assured her, looking over her shoulder to find Ryder watching her with that dreamy smile she'd missed so much since they broke up.

A big smile broke out on Summer's face. "Are you two back together?"

"Yes," she acknowledged, then wondered if maybe she shouldn't have said that. Did Ryder want his friends to know they were together again? She assumed he'd been as open with them as he had with her so she thought he probably wouldn't mind.

"That's great." Caroline beamed.

"Thank you so much for everything you did. Sending clothes for me to wear while I was in the safehouse, and cleaning my apartment, filling the fridge, it made coming home so much easier," she told Caroline.

Caroline waved off her thanks. "Of course, you would have done the same for any one of us. Come on, let's go get you something to eat and then we can talk. You have lots to get caught up on."

Allowing Caroline to take her arm and lead her across the parking lot and onto the beach, she saw where everyone had gathered. There were a couple of tables full of food, towels scattered about, some kids were building sandcastles, and there had to be at least three dozen adults standing around talking and laughing.

Panic settled in her stomach.

So many people.

More people than she had been around since she'd come home.

Had it really been only ten days since Ryder found her?

Abigail stumbled over her feet as she tried to force them to keep moving instead of digging in and refusing to go any closer to all those people than they already were.

"You okay, Abby?" Caroline asked, concerned brown eyes giving her a onceover.

"Yeah, I, uh, I skipped breakfast, guess I'm a little lightheaded," she lied. She hated to lie but what was the alternative? Tell her friend that it suddenly felt like she was losing her mind? That the idea of hanging around with a group of people she knew suddenly made her feel like she was facing down her abductors.

"Then let's get you some lunch."

Caroline continued walking, the other women chattering around them. Abigail had no idea if one of them was speaking to her because all she could hear was the thumping of her pulse echoing in her ears.

She was about to freak out.

Melt down.

She'd tried so hard to keep her emotions under control, not even allowing herself the luxury of crying because she was worried once she started she wouldn't be able to stop. Now it felt like all her hard work was about to unravel.

They were just a few yards away from the group now, and all of a sudden it seemed like everyone noticed her arrival.

Dozens of pairs of eyes all focused on her.

She couldn't breathe.

She couldn't think.

She couldn't move.

And then all of a sudden she was moving.

Running.

Away from the eyes, away from the people, away from the

questions and the pity and understanding that didn't feel like understanding at all because how could they understand what it felt like to be held prisoner for fourteen long months?

How could anyone understand that?

All of a sudden, Abigail felt very alone in the world.

She was running across the sand, but there were people everywhere she looked. Her gaze landed on the water. Out there, in the middle of the sea, that was where she could be alone again, where she could find peace and maybe even sanity.

Veering sideways, she splashed into the water and began to swim toward the horizon.

She had to get away.

She'd spent too many months alone, and now it was the only place she could think of to escape to.

She had to be alone.

She had to get away from everyone.

Abigail swam frantically, splashing through the water, the horizon seemed further and further away with each stroke she made.

A sob was building inside her, it felt like a bomb, ticking down toward detonation with each passing second. The fuse had already been lit, tears were now inevitable no matter how much she loathed the idea of breaking down.

* * *

12:22 P.M.

One moment Abigail was walking toward where they'd set up with some of the girls chattering around her, and then the next all the color drained from her face, and she was running in the opposite direction as though her life depended on it.

Spider dropped the pies he and Abigail had baked the day before and took off after her.

She was fast, and whatever had set off her panic attack was obviously lending her extra speed, and before he could catch up to her, she had veered off and thrown herself into the water, swimming as far away from the shore as she could get.

Water was obviously his thing since he was a Navy SEAL, and even with her desperate strokes it didn't take long for him to reach her.

As soon as his arm curled around her a sob tore free.

"Shh, sweetheart, it's me, Ryder," he said, worried she'd thought that someone was after her. He wasn't sure what had set off the breakdown, she'd been excited about today, told him that it felt like doing something normal, and that made her feel like she was part of the real world again instead of removed from it like she'd felt for the last year.

Abigail didn't answer just cried, but when he turned her so she was facing him she didn't try to get out of his grip just wrapped her arms around him and buried her face against his neck and wept. Her whole body shook from the force of her sobbing, and they were too far out for him to stand, so he trod water and took her weight, letting her get out all the emotions she'd been bottling up.

He'd seen this coming.

Known it was inevitable.

No one could go through what Abigail had and expect to be able to lock down their emotions and never have to deal with them.

It just wasn't realistic, and as much as he hated to see Abby in pain, he was relieved that she'd broken down now when he was here to support her because his job meant he could be called away at any time, and he hated to think of her going through this alone.

"Honey, I'm just going to swim us to shore, okay?" he said, his lips against her ear so she could hear him through her tears. She was still shaking, and he was worried that if she spent too long in the cold water it would push her further into shock.

She didn't answer, but she also didn't fight against him as he eased her onto her back and held her close against him with an arm across her chest as he used his other arm to swim them to shore. As soon as he was close enough that his feet could touch the bottom, he swung her around so she was cradled against his chest as he walked through the shallows.

The dozen SEALs waiting for them all wore identical concerned expressions as someone passed him a towel which he immediately wrapped around Abigail, who had steadfastly pressed her face into his chest and refused to lift it. What gutted him the most was that while every man and woman before him was tough and strong and had lived through at least one horrific ordeal, Abigail would cast herself in a different light. She'd say she wasn't strong, wasn't tough, because her parents had drilled into her head that only those in the military deserved those titles.

Spider had loved Eric "Rock" McNamara Senior, and Stephanie "Stevie" McNamara, but that didn't blind him to their faults. While he didn't think they had deliberately given Abigail that idea nonetheless, their attitudes and behavior had led her there anyway.

Zeroing in on one face in particular, Spider said, "Fiona, could you give me five minutes and then come see if she'll talk to you?" Of all of them, Fiona Knox, Hunter "Cookie" Knox's wife, had lived through something the most similar to what Abigail had, and he wondered if Fiona might be able to say something that would reassure Abigail that what she was going through was completely normal.

Cookie tensed, and he could tell from the look on the

man's face he was going to protest that he didn't want his wife having to talk about her ordeal, but Fiona set a hand on his arm to stop him. "Of course."

"Thanks." With a nod at her, he started walking further down the beach, finding a quiet little spot away from the other beachgoers and sat down, holding Abigail in his lap, the towel wrapped tightly around her. "We're alone now, Abby."

"I couldn't stop it," she cried in a tortured whisper.

"Stop what, honey?" His hand rubbed circles on her back in an attempt to soothe her and he curled his body around her as much as he could to make her feel like she was cocooned in a bubble of safety.

"This," she said, finally lifting her tear-stained face and gesturing at the teardrops that continued to stream down her cheeks.

"You never could."

"I tried to, I didn't let myself cry."

"Why, sweetheart?" He knew she wanted to prove that she was every bit as strong and tough as any Navy SEAL, but not allowing herself to feel her emotions wasn't the way to go about doing that.

"Because of that." She waved a hand in the direction of their friends. "Because I was scared that once I started crying that I wouldn't be able to stop. Because crying about it—acknowledging it—makes it so much more real. Because I don't want anyone to think that I'm weak. Because I don't want *you* to think I'm weak," she finished softly, letting her head drop so her forehead rested on his shoulder.

"Think you're weak?" he echoed, dismayed she would ever think that. "Abby, look at me."

She shook her head.

"Abs, I need you to look at me so you can see my eyes when I say this, so you know I'm not lying, not just telling you what you need to hear." Spider waited until she reluctantly lifted her head and even more reluctantly made eye contact. "I think you are the strongest woman I have ever met. What happened to you would break most people and yet here you are making plans to rebuild your life."

"It did break me," she whispered. "For fourteen long months all I thought about, all I prayed for, all I waited for was someone to come, to not be alone anymore, and now that I'm back home the idea of being around people freaks me out."

"Of course," he said, moving a lock of wet hair that was plastered against her cheek and tucking it behind her ear. "You adapted, survived, now it's going to take time to readjust. You're okay in small groups so this big gathering was too much right now. We can work with that, keep things to what you're comfortable with until you're ready for more."

"What if I'm never ready?"

"Then we'll cross that bridge when we come to it."

"We?"

"Do you honestly think I would leave you alone to deal with this?"

Doubt crept into her stunning eyes. "If you're just here because you feel sorry for me then I'd prefer you weren't here at all."

Instead of answering that with words, Spider cupped the back of her head in his hand and touched his lips to hers. The kiss was soft and gentle, sweet, he wanted to infuse every drop of love for her he had in his heart into this one moment so she knew that he was here by her side for one reason and one reason only, because he loved her.

"H-hmm."

They both looked up at the sound of the throat clearing and saw Fiona standing beside them.

"Do you guys need more time?" she asked.

"I thought that since you and Fiona went through something a little similar, if she was willing, it might help you to talk to her," he explained.

"I couldn't ask her to do that," Abigail protested.

"It's okay, I want to," Fiona said, dropping down beside them.

"You want me to go?" Spider asked Abigail.

"No," she said, grabbing onto a fistful of his wet t-shirt.

"I'm sorry for freaking out," Abigail said to Fiona, the first hint of color returning to her face as her cheeks heated.

"You don't need to be sorry about that. Trust me."

Abigail straightened a little. "You freaked out after you came back home?"

"Oh yeah, big time. Way worse than running away and trying to swim out into the middle of nowhere," Fiona said. "It's hard to come back home after months of your life spent as someone's prisoner and then assimilate back into the real world."

"I thought I could do it, I tried," Abigail said softly.

"But you can't. I tried too, it doesn't work. I ended up freaking out and thinking that the men who had kidnapped me had found me that they were trying to get to me again. I ran off, tried to hide, I was so terrified, it was like one part of my brain knew it wasn't real but the other part was utterly petrified that it was and that those men were going to find me and take me back. Thankfully, Tex was able to find me and keep checking in with me until Hunter could come and get me. Hunter, and my friends, were like a lifeline keeping me tethered to reality while my brain struggled to process things that it isn't designed to have to cope with. Kind of like your brain is trying to do right now. People aren't supposed to be kidnapped and locked away from the world with no one to talk to for over a year, your brain has no natural coping mechanism for that, all you can do is take one day at a time and let the people who love you and care about you be there for you."

Abigail turned to look at him and he pressed a kiss to her forehead. "I am here for you without question because I love you, and this is where I want to be. Nothing is more important to me than you are."

"You know what else helped?" Fiona asked.

"What?"

"Talking to someone, Dr. Hancock has been amazing."

"Is that the doctor who's number you gave me?" Abigail asked him. "I, uh, I never looked at the card because I didn't intend to call. Sorry."

"Yes, and don't be sorry, you weren't ready then, but maybe you are now," he said hopefully. He knew that his love alone wasn't enough to get Abigail through this, she needed professional help as well.

Abigail looked from him to Fiona, then past Fiona's shoulder to where they could see their friends, then she looked back to him, her eyes meeting his directly and holding his gaze. "Yeah, I'm ready to accept that maybe I don't have this as under control as I would like to think I do. I'll call Dr. Hancock and make an appointment."

"I'm so proud of you, Abby." Spider crushed her against him, hugging her tight, there wasn't anything he wouldn't do for this woman, including admit he couldn't handle this on his own and make her get the help she needed. "You got this, Abs."

"What if I don't?" her scared voice asked.

"Then I'll hold you safe in my arms until you realize your own strength."

CHAPTER 12

June 25th

8:53 A.M.

"Would you just say whatever it is you want to say? You're making me nervous," Abigail said as she passed Ryder her plate. He'd been quiet all morning and that was a sure sign that he had something he had to tell her, but didn't want to tell her. Normally she would wait him out, but her nerves were already about as frayed as they could get without snapping, so she just wanted to find out how bad whatever he was afraid to tell her was.

"I don't mean to make you nervous," he said, setting her plate into the dishwasher then leaning against the counter and drawing her between his knees.

"Well, you are," she told him, resting her hands on his chest.

"It's not bad news."

"But it's something you think I won't like or you would have just told me already."

Ryder acknowledged that with a smile. "Night and the others are coming by this morning."

"Here? Why?" A mixture of panic and embarrassment filled her. After her freak out at the beach the day before she didn't want to see any of the SEAL guys or their families ever again let alone so soon after breaking down for all of them to see.

"Abby, no one thinks less of you because of yesterday, you know that," Ryder said firmly.

"I'm not ready to see them yet," she protested. After talking with Fiona yesterday she and Ryder had slipped quietly away, and her plan had been to basically never see any of them again. Okay, so that wasn't really her plan, but today? She couldn't face them when she still felt like her entire world was spinning out of control no matter how much she tried to contain it.

"Honey, you know the guys love you, and they've all dealt with some heavy stuff."

"You too, huh?"

"Yeah, babe, me too."

"I don't like to think of your job getting you hurt," she said, lifting her hands to his cheeks. The idea of anyone hurting Ryder made her feel sick inside.

"Same way I feel about you, all those months you were gone it was like being trapped in Hell. No matter how hard we looked for you we couldn't find you." Ryder leaned over to touch his forehead to hers.

"But you did find me," she reminded him.

"By accident."

The way he said it made it sound like that made a difference, but in the end she didn't care if they'd known she was there or found her by accident because in the end the outcome was the same, she got to come home. "It doesn't matter, Ryder. You found me, you saved my life, and you got me safely through the jungle and back home. That's what matters. This is what matters." Standing on her tiptoes, she touched her lips to his. That first second of contact always felt like the stars aligning, the world falling into place, the missing pieces of her heart clicking back together.

The sound of the doorbell had them reluctantly pulling apart.

"Your decision, Abby, you want me to tell them you're not ready to see anyone yet and I'll send them away."

With the ball in her court she felt like a little of her control returned, and she nodded, may as well get that first awkward out of the way now. "They can stay."

"I'm proud of you, Abs, don't ever doubt your own strength." Ryder gave her another quick kiss then went to answer the door while she gathered her courage.

When she heard voices, she turned to face the room. There was no point in hiding, yes they'd seen her lose it, but it was done, she couldn't change it, so she just had to do her best to put it behind her.

Pasting on a smile, she walked into the living room to face her fear straight on. "Hey, guys."

"Hey, Abs," Owen "Fox" LeGrand said, coming to wrap her in a tight hug.

"It's so good to see you back where you belong," Charlie "King" Voss told her, taking his turn hugging her.

"It wasn't the same around here without you," Logan "Shark" Kirk added as he gave her a hug.

"It really wasn't," Grayson "Chaos" Simpson agreed as he ruffled her hair and kissed her cheek.

"I missed you guys too," she said as the four men took seats, their presence dominating her cozy little apartment.

Abigail noted that Eric was the only one who hadn't come to say hi and give her a hug, and she hated the distance between them. They might not be close, but he was the only family she had, and she didn't want this. Walking over, she wrapped her arms around his waist and rested her head against his chest. "I'm still angry with you, Eric, for what you did, but I love you."

She felt relief shudder through his big body and his arms came around her, holding her just a little too tight, not that she would tell him that because she sensed he needed this even more than she did. "I'm sorry, Abby, I never should have gotten involved, I should have let you and Spider be happy, but please believe me when I tell you I regret it, you have no idea how much."

"It's okay, we can work past it," she assured him.

After another squeeze he released her, and they both joined the others in the sitting area of the living room. The guys had taken over the couch and pulled over chairs from the table leaving both armchairs free, Eric took one, and she took the other, Ryder perched on the arm of her chair, his arm around her shoulders.

They were all looking at her.

It was then that she realized this wasn't a social call.

Darting her gaze up to Ryder, she asked, "Why did you invite them over? It wasn't just to hang out was it?"

Ryder exchanged a glance with the others then shook his head. "They did want to see you, but no they aren't just here to hang out. I would prefer to wait until you have your feet back underneath you, but I'm not sure that we can wait."

"Because we think that someone targeted me and we're worried that they might come back," she said. They'd discussed this already back at the safehouse. "But I already told you everything that I remember."

"You've told us everything your conscious mind remembers," Ryder corrected gently.

"What do you mean?"

"You know you talk in your sleep," he started slowly.

"Yeah, it's embarrassed me more than once over the years," she said. When they were kids Eric and Ryder had loved sneaking into her room at night to see what she would say in her sleep and then tease her about it the next day. "I'm guessing I said something in my sleep that makes you think my subconscious remembers more."

"It started when we were hiding out in the shack on Perez's compound," Ryder explained. "Your fever spiked, you were delirious, hallucinating, and you were terrified that someone was in the room with us, that they were going to take us back, you begged me to kill you rather than let them take you again."

"I don't remember saying that," she said. If her conscious mind was blocking out what had happened to her then she didn't want to remember. Abigail lifted her hand and looked at the fingers that were a little crooked. If someone had tortured her did she really want to know?

"One night in the safehouse you talked about not knowing anything," Ryder continued.

Okay, so that pretty much confirmed it.

She *had* been tortured.

"We've been trying to figure out why Perez had taken you and then kept you for so long. We wondered if maybe he wanted to keep you and he was working on breaking you, or if he thought you had seen something you shouldn't have."

"But now you have a different theory," she said. It was written all over Ryder's face and on the faces of the other men on his team.

"Unfortunately, we do," Eric said.

"Last night you started talking in your sleep again," Ryder

said, sounding troubled, almost guilty. "In your nightmares someone was asking you questions, you kept saying over and over that you didn't know anything."

"Yeah, you said I dreamed that already." There was obviously more happening than they had let on yet, and the longer they took to just say it the more her anxiety amped up. "Would someone just say what you guys came here to ask me about?"

Ryder opened his mouth, then let it fall closed, his blue eyes tormented.

Since it was obvious Ryder couldn't say whatever it was that needed to be said, Eric leaned over and rested a hand on her knee. "Abby, you mentioned our names; whoever was questioning you was questioning you about us."

She didn't understand

She didn't *want* to understand.

"Questioning me about you guys?"

"Abby, honey, whoever organized your abduction targeted you because of us, because Eric is your brother, because you and I dated, they took you because of us," Ryder finished, his face tortured.

Someone had taken her because of her association with the SEAL team?

They'd obviously wanted information on the team that she hadn't been able to provide which meant that Ryder, and her brother, and the others were in danger because they were the real targets.

And she still couldn't remember a thing about her abduction.

* * *

12:43 P.M.

. . .

186

Spider watched the color drain from Abigail's face as the ramifications of what they'd just told her sunk in.

There was disbelief, then shock, then horror, then finally guilt.

"I don't remember, you guys are in danger and I can't remember," she said dismally, and he could see the panic building in her eyes.

Pulling her against him he held her tight. "It's not us we're worried about, we can take anyone who comes for us, it's you we're concerned about, Abs."

"But if they took me to try to get to you then I have to remember or you won't be safe," she continued, clearly not paying attention to what he'd just said. Before Spider could try to reassure her again, Shark stepped in.

"Abby, you're not going to remember if you work yourself into hysterics," Shark said calmly. The man was unflappable. Spider didn't think he'd ever seen the man get worked up, angry, or emotional. It didn't matter what situations they found themselves in, what the odds against them were, how many guns were being fired at them, Shark just calmly went about doing what had to be done with that blank look in his eyes, just like his namesake.

Now, however, his friend's words earned him a scowl, Abigail was already upset about her breakdown in front of everyone yesterday, she didn't need Shark throwing around the word hysterics like that.

Shark simply ignored the glower. "If you want to remember then you need to calm down and focus," he continued.

Abigail nodded and drew in a long, slow breath like she was counting in her head, then she nodded at Shark.

Shark nodded back approvingly. "We're not going to focus on the things you've already told us instead I want you to look at your hand." He waited until Abigail had lifted her left hand and then continued, "I want you to relax your body and your mind, just like if Spider here was giving you a massage." Shark winked at him and Abigail gave a small laugh, while Night frowned; nobody wanted to picture their little sister with a man.

Abigail relaxed back against the armchair but clutched Ryder's hand with her right one, and he let his thumb brush backward and forward across her knuckles to help calm her.

"Once you feel relaxed I want you to look at your hand, but not try to force your memories to come back," Shark instructed. "It's okay if it takes a few minutes, or longer, we're not in any hurry here. The more you try to force it the less likely your memories are to return."

"When did you get to be such a shrink?" Abigail asked as she did as Shark directed.

"Mom was a shrink," Shark replied, and while no emotion flickered on his face, and his tone didn't change, Spider sensed there was a story there if anyone was able to drag it out of him. Which he suspected no one could. Shark held his cards close to his chest, and of all the men on his team, Spider felt like he knew Shark the least.

Instead of keeping the pressure on Abigail with them all sitting watching her waiting to see if she could remember what had happened to her, Shark started a conversation with Fox, and soon all the guys were chattering away quietly.

Spider kept his focus on Abigail, she was still tense despite her attempts to relax, and he could see on her face that she was still trying too hard to remember. Prying his hand out of hers, when Abby shot him a panicked look he kissed her temple. "Not going anywhere, babe, just going to give you that massage Shark was talking about."

"That's what I'm talking about." Shark threw them a grin. "I knew Spider there had magic hands."

Night made a low growling noise, and the other guys

laughed as Spider angled Abigail in her chair so he could rub her shoulders. Starting at the base of her neck he worked her tight muscles, kneading them until he felt her start to relax.

Several minutes passed while he massaged and the others talked, then all of a sudden, Abigail gasped.

"I-I didn't wake up in th-the cage," she stammered, her panicked face turning to meet his.

"Where did you wake up?" Shark asked before he could offer reassurances.

Turning her attention to Shark she said, "In a room. It was dark, there weren't any windows, I was in a chair, my arms were tied to the arms of the chair with rope, I remember it cutting into my skin when I tried to pull against it. My legs were tied to the chair too, and ..." All the color drained from her face, and Spider felt his gut churning with anxiety.

"And what, honey?" he prompted, keeping his hands on her shoulders, lightly working her muscles.

"And I was naked," she finished.

That shouldn't have surprised him, she was naked when he found her, but her being naked and alone in a cage was one thing, her being naked and tied to a chair in a room with other people was quite another.

"Did they touch you, Abby?" Shark asked, his voice gentle.

"I don't think so, I don't remember. I remember a man, I can't see his face but he's standing in front of me, and he's asking me questions about you guys. He's asking where you are and what you're doing, and when I tell him I don't know and that I haven't seen any of you in months he gets angry."

"What does he do when he gets angry?" Shark asked, and Spider had to fight against his instincts to tell his friend to shut up and not put Abigail through this.

His protective instincts to shield her from pain had to be pushed aside because as long as her abductor was out there then she wasn't safe. They had to find out all they could about her kidnapping so that she would be safe.

"He tells one of the other men there to hit me," Abigail answered.

"Where did he hit you?" Shark asked.

One of her hands lifted to touch her face. "My cheeks, my head, my jaw. I remember telling him that even if I knew where you guys were I wouldn't tell him anyway. He got mad, he told one of the men to take my hand and when he asked me if I had changed my mind and I said no, he told his man to break my finger. I remember the pain," she said, her voice hitching, "I think I might have thrown up."

"Shark," Spider started, this was enough. She'd confirmed that she'd been tortured and that whoever had taken her had really been after them. There was no point in putting her through this any longer if she didn't know who had taken her.

Shark just waved him off. "What happened next, Abby?"

"I remember the men were still there when I woke up, I remember him laughing at me, calling me a little girl, saying I wasn't strong enough to survive what he would do, that sooner or later I would crack, that I would still serve my purpose even when I broke."

"Did he say what that purpose was?" Shark asked.

"No, he just had one of his men break another of my fingers. I don't remember anything after that, and when I woke up I was in that cage where Ryder found me. My whole body hurt so they must have beaten me some more before they left me there."

Tears spilled down Abigail's cheeks and he lifted her, taking her place in the armchair and settling her on his lap. He tucked her head under his chin and wrapped her up in his arms, cocooning her in a bubble of safety. A kind of rage he'd never felt before filled Spider, he'd been angry with his father, hated the man for what he did to him and his mom, but this was different. Abigail had been targeted because of them, and unlike his mom who had known that her husband had both an anger and a drinking problem even before she married him, Abigail was completely innocent. She'd been dragged into this against her will.

A glance at his friends had him seeing his own anger reflected on each of their faces. Not just anger, protectiveness too, as SEALs they were protectors by nature but this was personal for each and every one of them. As the daughter of a SEAL and Night's baby sister she was family, and no one messed with their family and got away with it.

From the protectiveness and anger that filled the room Spider was sure of one thing. Whoever had targeted Abigail, abducting her and interrogating her, would pay for what they had done.

Pay with their life.

CHAPTER 13

June 26th

2:19 A.M.

Fingers.

For some reason Abigail couldn't seem to stop staring at her fingers.

As she looked her left pinkie began to change. It started to bend sideways, just a little at first then more and more until it was at a ninety-degree angle.

Turning her head in the direction that her finger pointed she saw the dance studio. It was dark, all the lights were turned off, and when she looked around she realized she was standing in the parking lot.

When she looked for her car she found it parked in the back corner she always used. And beside it was the black SUV.

Although she wanted to run in the opposite direction, get as far away from the car and the abduction she knew was coming, her feet began to move toward it.

Step by step she got closer.

And then she saw him.

A man.

The shadows hid his face, but he was walking steadily toward her.

Run, her brain screamed, but her feet refused to cooperate.

"Who are you?" she asked.

"You know who I am," the man replied, his voice was familiar but she couldn't place it.

"Tell me your name," she demanded as he continued to come closer.

"You know it."

"I don't," she screamed, frustrated.

"You know me."

"Tell me who you are," she begged. Tears streamed down her cheeks, and somewhere in the distance she heard a voice call her name.

"You know who I am, and now you need to come with me."

"I'm not going anywhere with you."

"You have to, they're hurt, they need you."

"Who's hurt? Who needs me?"

"Abigail," the other voice called.

She ignored it. "Tell me please, who are you?"

The man reached her and leaned down, his face just inches from her own, and she finally realized who he was.

Abigail screamed.

The man reached for her, grabbed her, began to shake her as he dragged her toward his car.

She fought him with everything that she had.

"Abigail, it's me."

"No, no, I don't want to go with you, I don't want to go back

there," she pleaded for her life as she fought against her abductor's hold.

"Abigail, it's me, it's Ryder." A slap to her cheek hard enough to sting accompanied the words, and her eyes popped open to find herself lying on the floor of her bedroom with Ryder on top of her.

Dreaming.

It had just been a dream.

Forcing her brain to accept, she fought to slow her wildly beating heart.

Ryder leaned in close, his eyes searching hers for confirmation she was awake. "Sorry, I hit you," he said as his fingertips stroked across her still stinging cheek. "I couldn't get you to wake up, you were screaming and crying."

Her cheeks felt wet so the tears of her nightmare must have turned into real tears.

The terror hadn't left her yet, and neither had the shock of realizing who was behind her abduction. It didn't make any sense, but she knew the man who had taken her, she just didn't know why he'd done it.

"Honey, are you all right?" Ryder asked. The concern in his voice was evident and she wanted to answer, but she couldn't seem to get her control back.

For so long she'd thought her abduction had been random, then she'd been rescued and learned she was probably targeted. Then yesterday remembering that whoever had taken her had done so because they wanted to know about her brother and Ryder had shaken her, but this ...

"Sweetheart, you're scaring me." Ryder moved off her and gently untangled her from the covers before wrapping them around her and gathering her into his arms. "In your dream you were fighting me so hard you fell off the bed. I had to hold you down, I was afraid you were going to hurt yourself," he said as he carried her out of the bedroom and through to the living room where he settled them both in the armchair. "What did you dream about, Abby?"

Ryder's warm body helped to warm her own freezing one, and she rested her cheek against his bare chest letting the steady beating of his heart try to calm hers. "I saw him. The man who took me."

"You remembered your abduction?"

Not just that, now that she had seen his face she remembered everything. "I know him," she said softly.

Ryder's body stiffened beneath her. "Who is he?" The tone of his voice said he was debating depositing her someplace safe and going immediately to the man's house.

"You know him too."

"Who is it, Abby?"

"It was Alex, Ryder. Alex Irwin, one of the SEALs on your team."

A low growl rumbled through his chest frightening her. That meant something to Ryder although what, she had no idea.

"Ryder, what is it? You're scaring me," she said, twisting so she could see his face.

"I need to call the guys," was all he said as he went to move her off his lap.

"No, Ryder, wait, tell me what's going on. I have to be wrong, right? Because why would Alex kidnap me? And why would he be asking me questions about you guys when you're on the same team?" None of it made sense, and she had to wonder if maybe her mind had just conjured up Alex's face because she needed answers.

For a moment it looked like he would refuse to tell her, but then he sighed and drew her close, holding her in an almost crushing grip. "Alex got kicked out of the SEALs about six months before you disappeared."

"Why? What happened?" Abigail asked already knowing it wouldn't be good.

"Alex had an anger problem, beat up his girlfriend. Once she realized she was safe she told us that Alex had been working as hired muscle for a local drug dealer. The drug dealer had ties to Luis Perez, the man who owned the compound where you were being held. When we found out about what Alex had been doing he went AWOL. We haven't heard from him since."

"He was there the night I was leaving the studio. It was his car parked beside mine, I remember him coming across the parking lot as I was leaving. I recognized him even though I hadn't seen him in a while, and I didn't know that he'd been kicked off the team. He told me something had happened to you and Eric. Ryder, I went with him willingly." Now looking back she knew she should never have gotten into that car, she'd always had a bad feeling about Alex, that kind of sixth sense that said he wasn't safe, but she'd gotten into the car because despite her anger toward Ryder she had still loved him, and Eric was her brother, she'd thought they'd been seriously injured and wanted to be there for them.

"You had no reason to doubt him, Abby," Ryder reminded her.

"What does he want?"

"My guess, revenge," Ryder answered simply. "We were the ones who found his girlfriend. Alex didn't turn up for PT, and when we went looking for him we found his girlfriend passed out and the apartment trashed. Once she told us about Alex's extra job we reported him to the cops and to our commander, and that made Alex a wanted man both with law enforcement and the military. He went AWOL, had to give up his whole life or come back and face the consequences."

"So he went after me to try to get to you guys." Abigail

shivered. Now that her memories had come back she could recall every single second of pain and terror she'd undergone at Alex Irwin's hands as though she were back in that room with him.

"I'm so sorry, Abby, that you were hurt because of us." The torment in Ryder's voice ate at her. She didn't want him blaming himself, she didn't want what Alex Irwin had done to come between them but she had no idea how to stop that from happening.

"It's not your fault, it's Alex's. Do you think he's going to come back?" They had thought it was a possibility her abductor would return for her if she was targeted specifically, but now that they had a name to the kidnapper she didn't know if that increased or decreased the chances of that happening.

"Yes. He'll be back," Ryder said with such fierceness that it made her shiver.

That answered that.

But there was one more thing she needed to know. It was one thing to know that her own life was in danger, she'd come to terms with that having spent the last fourteen months living on borrowed time, hovering on the edge of the precipice between this world and the next, but it was another thing to worry about the people she loved.

"Is he coming back for me or for you?"

* * *

5:52 A.M.

"What are we doing here at this ungodly hour?" King groused as Spider opened the front door of Abigail's house to let his team in. Of all of them, King was the only one who hated early mornings. Actually, the man hated late nights too, King's favorite place to be was in bed, sleeping or having sex, Spider had a sneaking suspicion that if it was possible the man would all but live in his bed.

"Abigail remembered everything," Spider replied as he closed the door behind them.

"Everything?" Fox asked.

"Everything," he echoed.

His team immediately sobered and snapped into work mode as they took seats around the kitchen table and Spider passed out cups of coffee.

"So put us out of our misery. Who abducted her?" Chaos asked.

"Alex," he said.

Five shocked faces looked back at him.

"Our Alex? Who used to be on our team?" Shark finally asked.

"The one and only," he confirmed. Of all the people who could possibly have been involved in Abigail's kidnapping and imprisonment, Alex Irwin wouldn't have even been on his list. The man had only met Abby a handful of times, and she had nothing to do with him being kicked out of the teams, going AWOL, or being on the cops' radar. Obviously, he'd gone after her because he'd thought she might have inside information on them, something that he could use to bring them down. Or he'd taken her intending her to be bait to lure them into a trap. If they hadn't been out of the country when she was taken they might have been able to follow the trail and track down where she had been taken.

"Where is Abby?" Night asked, looking around the apartment.

"Cookie and Fiona picked her up because I didn't want her here while we discussed this. They're taking her back to their place for breakfast and then to her appointment." To say that he was worried about Abigail was an understatement. She'd been upset to remember that she had been tortured and shocked when she remembered who had abducted her, but he knew she was holding back, still trying to keep a lid on her emotions, still trying to pretend they didn't exist, still trying to pretend that she was strong enough to handle everything.

And she was strong.

Spider knew that without a shadow of a doubt.

She'd already survived months of isolation which was its own form of torture and enough to break most people, but she needed to start dealing with her emotions, her fears, and concerns instead of acting like she had everything under control. She had already had one breakdown and the longer she put off dealing with things the bigger the second breakdown would be when it eventually came.

Just like he had known the first one was coming, he knew another one would hit her sooner or later.

He missed her, he wanted her back, every inch of her, he wanted her to trust him, he wanted her to never doubt him again, he wanted to see her laugh and be able to let go and let her guard down, and yeah he wanted to be intimate with her. They hadn't done anything more than kiss since her breakdown at the beach, and although he was prepared to wait as long as it took he was worried about her, worried about the effects of everything she'd been through, he wouldn't be making any demands of her, when she was ready she could let him know.

"She went to see Dr. Hancock?" Fox asked.

"Yes, she agreed to see the doc," he said.

"That's good, she needs to talk to someone." Fox nodded as though pleased by this.

"Yeah, she does," Spider agreed.

"What about you?" Fox eyed him closely.

"What about me?" he asked, confused. The only thing he cared about right now was ensuring that Abigail was safe, both physically and psychologically. He would be there for her, support her however she needed him to, and make sure that she knew he was here for her.

Something which she still wasn't convinced about.

The fear and doubt in her eyes the morning after they'd slept together when she'd woken to find he was no longer in the bed was etched into his mind's eye. He hated that he had no one else to blame but himself for that doubt. She still didn't completely trust him, but he would earn her trust back if it was the last thing he ever did.

"That," Fox said, waving a hand at him.

"What do you mean that?"

"You're distracted, you're worried about her, your focus is on Abby," Fox replied.

"And it shouldn't be?" Spider growled. He'd let Abby down enough over the years he wasn't going to do it again.

"No, it should be, but how are you going to deal when we get called out?" Fox asked.

"Same as I always have."

Fox shook his head. "This is different. What she went through changes everything. You need to speak with someone too."

"A shrink? I don't need to see a shrink," Spider said adamantly. He'd had enough of that after his parents' deaths. All he needed was for Alex Irwin to pay for what he'd done to Abigail.

"You telling me you don't feel guilty about what happened to her?" Fox demanded.

Spider opened his mouth to deny it but then snapped it closed and glared. Of course he couldn't say that, he blamed himself for what she'd gone through, if it wasn't for them then Alex would never have set his sights on her.

"Thought so," Fox said. "Look, I get it, I feel guilty about what happened to her and I'm not in love with her, but if we're going to bring Alex down then we all need to be able to focus one hundred percent."

"I won't do anything that will get anyone hurt," he vowed. "But we need to figure out a plan. Abby asked me earlier if I thought Alex would come back for her or for us.'"

"What did you tell her?" King asked.

"I didn't answer because I didn't want to worry her more, but he's coming back for her. He took her to get to us, nothing has changed. Alex is a coward, he knows that if he comes up against one of us he's going to lose, the only way to get to us is to lead us into a trap, and the only way for him to do that is to get his hands on Abby again and then dangle her out in front of us as a lure." Knowing that Abigail was in danger because of him was a special kind of torture. It made him want to pack up his bags and get as far away from her as he could while at the same time wrap her up in cotton wool and handcuff her to him so that he could keep her in his line of sight at all times.

"We need to use every contact that we have to try to find Alex before he can make another play for Abby," Chaos said.

"We know he worked for one of Luis Perez's men here in California, and that he had her on Perez's compound, that means his connections go all the way to the top," Shark said.

"He's probably working as Perez's top enforcer," Chaos said.

"We need to find out everything we can about the cartel," King said. "I'll call Tex, see what he can find on them, we need to know all of their houses in the area, and how many men they have in each location, see if we can plan a take-down before he even comes close to getting to Abby."

"There's one good thing about us being the target and not Abby," Night said, speaking up for the first time.

"Yeah?" Spider asked, he couldn't see a single good thing about this entire situation, but he'd take a bright spot right about now.

"If our team is a target then we're not likely to be sent out on any missions until this situation with Alex is resolved. And if we're not sent out on any missions, then we don't have to worry about leaving Abby alone and unprotected. If Alex wants her, he'll have to go through us to get her, and he's too much of a coward to take us on, he'd rather use an innocent woman as bait."

Spider couldn't argue with that. The most terrifying part of this was that Abby was in danger, he didn't care about himself, he and his team were more than capable of taking on the likes of Alex. Alex had a sadistic streak that he'd managed to hide for a while, but none of them had ever completely trusted the man and now he knew why.

He had failed Abby before, he'd let her down, not been there when she needed him, but now he had her back he wouldn't let anyone take her away from him again. So long as he stayed here with her in her apartment he could keep her safe, and he and his team *would* find Alex. It wasn't a matter of if, simply of when.

* * *

7:26 A.M.

"You guys can just drop me off," Abigail offered as Hunter pulled to a stop outside of Dr. Hancock's building.

"Spider would freak if he found out I didn't watch your back," Hunter protested.

"Yeah, well, Ryder isn't the boss of my life," she muttered, but secretly she was grateful that Fiona and Hunter had come with her, she wasn't sure she could do this on her own. If left to her own devices she probably would have bailed on the appointment because she wasn't sure she was ready to talk about it yet.

Or ever.

She just wanted to put it behind her, forget about it, pretend like it never happened. She'd remembered her abductor, told Ryder everything she knew so he and his team could be prepared, now she wanted to just move on. Even though she knew avoidance was only going to lead to more breakdowns, she still just wanted to shove her emotions down and pretend they didn't exist.

"Spider bosses because he loves you," Hunter said, making her sigh.

"Yeah, I know he does, I just don't want to be here."

Fiona twisted in her seat to hold out a hand, and Abigail took it and squeezed. "That's why we're here with you, moral support as much as making sure you're safe, right, Hunter?"

"Sure," her husband grinned. "But I'm on bodyguard duty, and you're the one here for moral support."

That elicited a small chuckle from Abigail, and she opened her car door, if she had to do this, she wanted to just get it done, it was nice of the doctor to have scheduled this early morning appointment for her.

"Wait for me before you get out," Hunter reminded her.

Although she didn't like it, she certainly didn't want to end up back in Alex's clutches so she waited until Hunter got out and rounded the car before they walked inside together.

"Thanks for coming," she said when they reached the door to the doctor's office.

"Of course," Fiona said, and Hunter ruffled her hair. "You got this, Abby. And there are no rules in there, you can say as much or as little as you want, this is for you, for you to start dealing with what happened to you. Dr. Hancock is a great doctor, you can trust her, Abs, and Hunter and I will be right out here waiting for you when you're done."

Because she knew she didn't have a choice, Abigail offered them both a smile she hoped conveyed how grateful she was for their support, then faced her fears with as much courage as she could muster.

Inside the room, the doctor was sitting waiting for her and gave her a big smile. "Morning, Abigail, how are you today?"

"Okay, I guess," she said, closing the door behind her even though she wanted to beg Fiona and Hunter to come in with her.

"You want to ease into this or jump straight in?" Dr. Hancock asked, leaving her desk to come and sit down on a loveseat, indicating Abigail should take a seat on the other loveseat.

"I'm a jump straight in kind of girl," she said as she sat.

"I like that, I am too," Dr. Hancock said with a smile. "So this session is for you. What do you want to talk about?"

"Nothing," she replied quickly. "I want to forget, not bring all those memories back up."

The doctor nodded knowingly. "You were gone for a long time, fourteen months I was told, and you were kept isolated for most of it. What did you do to pass the time so you didn't have to focus on your emotions?"

Abigail shrugged. "Anything that made me feel like I wasn't losing my mind and my sanity. I'm a dancer so I would dance, try to see how many old routines I could remember. I'd work out, try to keep my strength up in case I ever got a chance to try to escape. Do math problems, try to remember song lyrics, talk to myself, imagine my parents were there and tell them all the things I was too much of a coward to say to them while they were still alive."

"Your parents are dead?"

"My dad had two massive heart attacks the night of my high school graduation, the second one killed him. My mom died a year later in a single-car accident; supposedly she fell asleep at the wheel."

"Supposedly?"

"Well, that's the official cause of death, but …"

"You suspected something different."

"I thought she did it on purpose only if she was alive she would deny that vehemently, only *weak* people commit suicide. My parents weren't very understanding, they weren't really big on empathy or sympathy, and they thought anyone who wasn't as strong as them was weak. They were both retired military, my dad was a SEAL, so it was hard not to be as strong as they expected me to be. My brother is a SEAL too, and so is my …" What were she and Ryder calling what they had going? She assumed they were dating although they hadn't officially put a title on it. "So is my boyfriend."

"You feel inadequate?"

"Only my whole life." Abigail sank back against the sofa, she couldn't remember ever feeling like she had lived up to their expectations. Dragging her bottom lip between her teeth, she began to chew on it. She didn't want to open up, but what was the point of being here if she wasn't going to be honest? It wasn't like she had anything to lose. "I'm … this is … hard. I … it's … I'm struggling," she finally admitted.

"That's hard for you to say."

"My parents made admitting that you weren't in control of something sound like a weakness, and I guess I learned to think it was, but it's true, I don't have anything under control right now, I'm holding on by a thread, a thread that could snap at any second. What scares me the most is Ryder."

"Has he done anything to hurt you?"

"Not this time. At least not yet. Ryder and I go way back. All the way to childhood. He and my brother used to tease me mercilessly, then I fell in love with him, we had one amazing night of sex, then he disappeared. He came back, worked really hard at earning my trust back then left me again. I just learned the truth of why he left and I can blame my dad for that. Now I have him back, but …"

"You're waiting for him to leave again."

"He's been perfect, and I know it's not fair, but I keep worrying that he's with me because he feels guilty, especially now we know why I was taken." Not sure if she was supposed to talk about that, she stuck with vague, and the doctor didn't press her for details.

"You believe he doesn't really love you?"

"No, I know he does, and that makes me feel so bad for doubting him. I don't want him to know that I'm struggling, I don't want him to blame himself, and I'm afraid that if I fall apart that when he gets called away he'll be worried and distracted and he'll be hurt because of it."

"You really love him."

"More than anything. Enough to get past him leaving, and to let him explain. He's been through so much, and he's not only survived but he's thrived. He's smart, and strong, and brave, and he dedicated his whole life to protecting others. I want him to think I'm strong too. I don't want him to know how much I'm struggling, I don't want him to know I might not be able to make it through this, I don't want him to see me as a victim who needs saving I just want him to be with me because he loves me."

"You're torn between thinking he's with you because he loves you and because of guilt."

"He hasn't touched me since I had a meltdown the other day," she admitted. "We slept together for the first time the day before that, but these last couple of days he's barely touched me. It's like he's afraid to. It … uh … it makes me feel insecure. Like I'm not good enough for him anymore and he knows it. He just doesn't want to say it out loud."

"Or," Dr. Hancock said slowly and Abigail perked up, ready to hear the doctor's take. "He loves you and is understandably concerned about you because of what you endured, and he wants to let you be in charge for a change."

"What do you mean?"

"While you were held captive you didn't have any control over your own life, now you're home, but you're battling the inevitable fall out from such a trauma, he doesn't want to add to that, doesn't want to make you do anything you're not ready for, so he's leaving the ball in your court. Have you told him you need physical intimacy right now?"

"No."

"It's my experience most people aren't mind readers," the doctor said with a grin.

Abigail huffed a laugh. "Yeah you're right. So I should tell him?"

"Absolutely. What you need as you try to work through your feelings and come to terms with everything are support and love, it sounds like you have a man who wants to give that to you but you need to be honest with him. Tell him that you're struggling, tell him what you need and when you need it. Do you know what real strength looks like?"

She shook her head, Abigail had always known that her parents' perception of strength wasn't correct, but she'd never stopped to think about what was the correct definition of strength.

"It's admitting that you're not superhuman. It's facing the things that scare you and allowing others to support you when you need it. It's knowing that your strength comes from those around you who love you just as much as it comes from inside you, and it's realizing that you're stronger together than you are on your own. You survived hell on your own, now to survive this new challenge you need to reach out to your support system."

The idea of not being able to do this on her own terrified her almost as much as seeing Alex again did, but Dr. Hancock was right. She couldn't do this on her own, and she did have a support system she could reach out to. If she wanted to get her life back then now was the time to prove to herself that she was strong. She would be honest with Ryder, she would face each and every one of her fears head-on and when she felt like she couldn't she would come and let Dr. Hancock remind her.

She could do this.

She and Ryder would do it together.

Because the doctor was right, she was stronger when she was with Ryder than she was on her own.

* * *

3:38 P.M.

Spider tried to pay attention to what his team was saying, but he couldn't seem to stop staring at the door. Abigail had texted around three to say that Cookie and Fiona were bringing her home, but it had been closer to forty minutes now and they still weren't here even though it shouldn't have taken more than thirty minutes to get here.

He was being paranoid, Spider knew that. Abigail was perfectly safe with Cookie, the man was a fellow SEAL, and was perfectly capable of eliminating any threats. Since Alex Irwin had waited until Abby was alone before going after her he didn't think the man would try anything until he could get her alone again.

Which wasn't happening.

Until they had Alex in custody, Abigail would have someone with her twenty-four hours a day. Taking chances with her safety wasn't an option, not only was she still recovering from the physical ramifications of her imprisonment but the psychological ones as well.

"Spider?"

"Yeah?" He didn't even bother turning to look at Fox.

"What do you think about ..."

The front door opened and he didn't even pretend that he cared about whatever Fox was saying he just walked over to Abigail, and dragged her into his arms.

She laughed—a real, light, happy laugh—and hugged him back. "I take it you're happy to see me."

"I missed you."

"I was only gone what, like nine hours," she said, eyes twinkling.

"You saying you didn't miss me?"

"Nope."

Spider couldn't take his eyes off her, Abigail looked different, there was color to her cheeks and her eyes looked alive; she seemed more relaxed. He knew that one session with a therapist wasn't enough to help her get over what she'd been through, but it seemed like it had been a good first step.

Fox cleared his throat. "We'll leave you two love birds alone."

Night made a groaning sound and Abigail frowned at him. "We're together, big brother, you better get used to it. Ryder and I have sex and we're going to keep having sex, so make your peace with it now."

The others laughed and even Night cracked a smile. "I'll do my best, little sister. Spider, I'm sure it goes without saying you break my sister's heart and I break you."

Ignoring the irony that Night was partly responsible for

the previous breaking of Abigail's heart, Spider knew it was time to let the past stay in the past and focus on the future. A future he was determined not to mess up this time. "I won't be breaking any hearts here, if anyone ends this it won't be me." May as well declare his intentions with an audience and make sure everyone knew that Abby was it for him.

"I won't be ending anything, I love you, Ryder."

As he captured her lips and kissed her whoops, whistles, and cheers sounded around them, and when he ended the kiss and slung an arm around Abigail's shoulders he couldn't help but laugh.

"We'll meet up again tomorrow morning," Fox said as everyone collected their things and headed to the door. "Hopefully we'll have something to work with by then. Tex is doing everything he can to dig up anything out there about Alex, Perez, and the cartel."

Once they were alone, Spider drew her close but she pushed him away. "We need to talk."

Spider would worry that it was bad news, but she'd just declared in front of her brother and his entire team that she loved him so he knew it wasn't that. Taking her hand, he led her to the couch and sat her down. Sitting beside her, he held her hands and waited for her to speak, it was clear from the expression on her face that this wasn't easy for her.

"Ryder, I'm ..." she paused, her gaze darting around the room before steadfastly meeting his. "I'm not okay." When he opened his mouth to say something she shook her head and continued. "I'm scared all the time, the idea of going anywhere where there will be a lot of people terrifies me, and so does the idea of being alone. I get this panicky feeling inside me like one wrong move or word is going to release the plug holding my emotions in check, and they're going to come flooding out and crush me. I ... I'm scared I won't be able to keep the plug in forever."

"You don't have to, sweetheart," he said, tucking a lock of hair behind her ear. "No one expects you to."

"I have to," she insisted.

"Why?" He was glad she was opening up, glad she'd finally spoken with someone who could help her, and he wanted to understand everything so he knew how best to support her.

"Because I'm scared."

"Of what?"

"You getting hurt," she admitted, finally dropping her gaze.

"Me getting hurt? What do you mean?"

"You love me."

"And that's a problem?" Spider had no idea where she was going with this.

Abigail gave a half-smile. "No, it's not a problem, but you love me and you worry about me, and when you get called away—which we know you will at some point—if I fall apart you're going to be thinking about me and not your mission. What if you get hurt?"

From the look in her eyes Spider knew she was legitimately concerned about this, and he didn't really know what to say to reassure her. If he told her that he wouldn't worry about her it would be a lie and she would know it, but if he told her he would worry about her while he was away then she'd continue to feel like she had to hold everything in.

"Honey, I don't want you to worry about that." His hand cradled her cheek and he let his fingers stroke along her smooth skin.

"How can I not? How would I cope if, because of me, you or one of your team got hurt or killed?" she demanded, and her eyes shimmered with unshed tears.

"Sweetheart, I can love you and worry about you and do my job at the same time. Know why?"

Abigail shook her head.

"Because I have the best reason in the world to come home safely. You. Yeah, I am going to worry about you whether you were dealing with all of this or not, but I'm also going to do what I've been trained to do because I want to make it home to you."

She took that in, her face conveying she hadn't considered that yet. "Dr. Hancock said that I should be honest with you, that I shouldn't try to keep things from you, that I should let you worry about me because I need to feel like I'm not alone right now. Ryder, I feel so disconnected from the real world." The devastation on her face had him folding her into an embrace. "You, you're the only thing that makes me feel like I'm still part of the world, the only thing connecting me to humanity."

"I'm not going anywhere, Abby, I'm right here, with you, and I'm never going anywhere. Don't fight it anymore, don't try to hold it in, don't try to put me above what you need."

"And if I break?"

"Then I'll help you pick up the pieces?"

"If I fall?"

"I'll catch you."

"And you won't think I'm weak?"

His grip on her tightened. "I already know you're strong, and crying or raging about what happened to you isn't going to change that." He prayed that she believed that it was true, but her hang-ups about strength ran deep and it would take time for her to overcome them.

"Ryder?"

"Yeah?"

"There's something else Dr. Hancock said I should talk to you about."

"What?"

"You haven't touched me since I had that breakdown at

the beach and I ... well, I understand if it's because you see me as a victim, but ..."

Spider cut off her words by crushing his mouth against hers and hauling her onto his lap. "I didn't want you to feel pressured to do anything you weren't ready for."

"I don't feel pressured." One of her hands curled around his shoulder, the other touched her stomach. "The only pressure I feel is here, it's need, I need you, Ryder, I need you to treat me the same way you would if I hadn't been kidnapped, I need to feel normal. I know you keep telling me everything I'm going through is normal but I don't feel it, and I need to feel it, Ryder, please make me feel normal again."

Her pleas left him with no doubt that Abigail knew exactly what she needed and more than happy to oblige, he pulled her tank top over her head baring her beautiful breasts. As he took one nipple into his mouth, one of his hands held onto her hip while his other slid inside the waistband of her capris.

A whimper fell from her lips as he began to touch her, and her moan when he pushed a finger inside her had him so hard he was almost coming in his pants like he was still a teenager.

"Ryder, more, please," she begged.

Adding another finger, he stroked deep then curled them around so he could touch that magic spot inside her that would have her seeing stars. Keeping steady pressure with his thumb he worked her inside and out, and it wasn't long before her entire body went taut before it began to shake as her internal muscles clamped around his fingers.

Eyes glazed with pleasure, cheeks flushed, pink lips plump, breathing heavily as she sagged down against him, Ryder thought his woman had never looked more beautiful in her life.

CHAPTER 14

June 27th

8:28 A.M.

She could stay like this forever.

When she was curled up on Ryder's lap, his arms around her, his lips on hers, just kissing and touching each other like they were a normal couple and there wasn't a crazy ex-SEAL out there who wanted to abduct her and use her as bait to lure in Ryder and his team, the whole rest of the world faded away.

Abigail never wanted this to end.

She hated that they had lost so much time, but she had decided she wouldn't dwell on it anymore, what was done was done and she couldn't change it, but she could make sure that no one messed with their future.

Which meant she knew what she had to do.

Ryder—and Eric, too—weren't going to like her decision, but as far as she could see it was the only way to end this once and for all. Once Alex was caught then they would be free and clear to make the future they wanted a reality.

"I could kiss you forever, you taste so good," Ryder murmured against her mouth.

"Then why did you stop?" she asked with a laugh.

"Because I want to taste every inch of you," he said as his lips touched her jaw then trailed a line of kisses down her neck to her collarbone, making her shiver in delightful anticipation. "Baby, you're going to do more than shiver like that, you're going to come all over my face, so hard you can't even remember your own name."

"Ryder," she moaned as heat immediately flooded her system, and she shifted restlessly on his lap.

His head lifted, his dark hair messy from her curling her fingers in it and his blue eyes dark with desire, his smile did things to her insides that no other man could do. Even though he had broken her heart and she had believed that they were finished for good, no other man had ever been able to affect her like Ryder had, to the point she had almost given up on being able to move on.

Now she knew why.

Ryder was her soul mate, and although fate had tried its best to keep them apart it had failed.

"You have way too many clothes on," he said as he slipped a hand up under the pale pink sundress she was wearing. "You're naked under there." He groaned as his fingers whispered across her aching center.

"Took you long enough to realize," she said, sucking in a breath as he found her swollen bud and began to roll it between his fingertips.

"I was a little busy with that delectable mouth of yours,"

he said as he plunged a finger inside her making her gasp and then moan in delight as he started to stroke her.

Not wanting to just sit back and take, Abigail slipped her hand inside Ryder's shorts and grasped his already hard length, smiling as she felt it jerk in her hold.

"Sweetheart, that does not help my getting you naked so I can taste you plan," Ryder said tightly, like he was holding back.

She didn't want him to hold back.

She wanted him to let go and give her every single inch of himself.

"I want to touch you, I like touching you. Are you going to deny me that?" she asked, arching a brow.

His fingers stroked deeper, and his thumb pressed firmly against that sensitive bundle of nerves making her insides clench in anticipation. "Baby, I couldn't deny you anything."

Satisfied, her free hand cupped the back of his neck as she drew his mouth back to hers while she continued to stroke him and he continued to plunge in and out of her.

He was close, she knew he was, but still holding back. "Let go, Ryder," she begged.

"Can't, you have to come first," he said tightly.

"No, you'll come first this time. I … I need to know I can still make you come," she admitted.

With a growl he claimed her mouth again.

A knock at the door had them both stopping what they were doing as disappointment washed over her.

"They can wait," Ryder said.

Maybe it should make her uncomfortable to be touching the man she loved while her brother and the rest of Ryder's team waited outside her door, but it didn't. She was too far gone, too desperate to feel her man come in her hand to care about anything else.

Moving her hand faster, a heartbeat later she was

rewarded by his orgasm, and his pleasure became her own as she found her release. It shuddered through her with the power of a tsunami and continued to roll over her in wave after wave as Ryder refused to stop touching her until he had wrung out every last little drop of pleasure.

"Is it just me, or does that get better every time we do it?" she asked, drawing lazy circles on his abs.

"It's not just you," Ryder said with a quick kiss. "And I wish we could do that again, I wish I could take you to bed and spend all day there with you, but unfortunately I can't."

She groaned, imagining how wonderful an uninterrupted day in bed with Ryder would be and reluctantly climbed off his lap. "We better wash up," she said as another knock sounded at the door.

They both washed their hands in the bathroom while Ryder changed his shorts, and she slipped on a pair of pink panties that she was already picturing Ryder pulling off, then while he went to the door she headed for the kitchen to make coffee.

"Don't think we don't know what you were doing in there," Charlie said as soon as Ryder opened the door.

"Don't think we care," Ryder shot back, making Abby laugh.

Eric just growled, and she laughed again, for breaking them up he deserved a lot more than to know his best friend and little sister had been making out on the other side of the door while he'd stood there and no doubt had no choice but to listen to them.

The laugh died on her lips as she thought about what she was about to say, and how badly Ryder would react to it. She knew he wouldn't like it but logic said this was how it had to be, it was what Alex wanted, and so it was the only thing that would achieve their goal.

While the guys chattered and took seats at the table, she

ferried cups over and then brought over a pot of coffee. Ryder pushed his chair back and patted his lap, and she sat down on it, praying he didn't shove her off when he heard what she had to say.

"Uh, guys?" she said, interrupting them. Dr. Hancock had told her that the best policy was just to be honest about what she was feeling and what she needed, and she figured that was a good policy for everything not just dealing with Ryder.

"What's up, Abs?" Owen asked.

"I want to play bait," she blurted out before she could second guess herself and let her fear stop her from doing what had to be done.

"No," Ryder said like it was that simple.

"I second that," Eric quickly added.

The other guys exchanged glances like they had already floated this possibility when Ryder and Eric weren't around.

"I wasn't asking for your permission, Ryder, or yours either, Eric," she said. She wasn't a child and if she wanted to do this—and she did as much as it terrified her—then no one would stop her.

"This is insane. Do you remember what he did to you last time?" Eric roared.

"Yes. I can't forget," she said softly. "I remember the pain each time one of Alex's men hit me, I remember the fear that I was going to die, I remember the crushing loneliness that I thought would drive me insane. I see it, I hear it, I feel it, it's imprinted on my soul, and I won't ever be able to get it off."

"You are not doing this, I won't let you." Ryder said it as though that made it so, but she was sitting on his lap and she could feel the panic coursing through his body. "You know what he's like, you know what he'll do to you."

"I also know that this is the only way to guarantee we find him. This is what he wants, this is his plan, this will work, and we all know it. I can't just sit back and wait, you're asking me to give up more of my life, Ryder. How long should I wait? Days? Weeks? Months? What if you can never find him? I spent fourteen months of my life trapped in a cell, I'm not going to spend anymore being trapped in my home, my life on hold. You told me earlier you couldn't deny me anything," she said, knowing she was playing dirty by using Ryder's words, said while they were being intimate and not intended in this context, against him. "You know that it has to be this way, don't fight me, support me, keep me safe, make this happen."

* * *

9:03 A.M.

"Why isn't anyone saying anything?" Spider demanded tightly. His panic was a thick, dark thing, smothering him. How was he supposed to be okay with handing Abigail over to a dangerous and highly trained killer on a silver platter?

"I'm saying something, absolutely not," Night said firmly.

Fire shot from Abigail's gold and silver eyes. "You're not the boss of me, Eric."

"Real mature, comeback, Abby," Night said with a glower.

"I'm not five years old anymore, you don't get to tell me what I can and cannot do," she said through clenched teeth, glaring at her brother.

"Abby, Alex is dangerous, not the kind of man you play games with," Spider said hesitantly not sure of the best way to go about convincing her this was a bad idea.

"Are we back to that weak argument, Ryder?" she turned to face him. "Of course I know he's dangerous. *I'm* the one he beat and tortured and kept locked in a shack in the middle of the jungle for over a year. But if it wasn't me we were talking about you would agree that this is the best plan we have."

"But it is *you* we're talking about," he shot back.

"So you didn't mean it when you said you couldn't deny me anything." Her eyes searched his looking for something, but he wasn't sure what.

Spider growled, she knew what he'd meant when he'd said that. How was this even a discussion? "That was sex talk and you know it. This isn't happening so get that out of your pretty head. Now, why don't you go and read or watch TV or something so we can figure out a real plan?" He knew he was being a jerk, dismissing her like she wasn't needed—wasn't valuable—but he couldn't look at her without seeing her thin, deathly pale face when he'd found her in that cell. Abigail knew he loved her. How could she ask him to put her straight back into the same situation she had only escaped by accident?

Abigail shoved off his lap. "You're being a jerk, Ryder, and it's very unattractive. If you and Eric can't handle this then maybe you should leave," she said with a scathing glare. Then she turned her attention to the rest of his team. "You guys have brains that aren't clogged by stupid alpha male protectiveness, so you agree this is our best plan of action, right?"

Fox, Shark, King, and Chaos exchanged glances, and Ryder knew his friends were about to betray him.

"We did discuss this as a possibility," Fox acknowledged.

"See," Abigail said, throwing a frown his way then went to lean against the wall since there were no spare chairs left, and she obviously wasn't going to come back and sit on his lap. "Then let's make this happen. He has to be watching me so all he needs is a chance to come for me, which means that Ryder needs to leave so I'm alone, he's not coming so long as he knows I'm protected."

"If you think I'm leaving you you're crazy," he exclaimed.

There was no way he was leaving Abigail alone while some psychopath had her in his sights.

"Did you just call me crazy?" Abigail fumed.

"Lovebirds, you can fight later," Fox said firmly. "Sorry, man, I think this is our best play, I wouldn't have suggested it but if Abby is up for it then I think we should do it."

"I'm up for it," Abigail said firmly, shooting him a look that dared him to disagree again.

"Spider, I get that you don't want to do this because it's Abby, but you can't deny if it was anyone else we would be discussing this plan and finding a way to make it work," Chaos said.

"We'd have a tracker on her," King added.

"Alex will expect that," he said.

"Right, we're not trying to trick him, this is Alex's plan, he wants to lure us out of the country where he thinks he'll have the upper hand so we go along with that. Let him take Abby, follow him, and then take him out," Shark said.

If only it were that simple.

Unfortunately, he could think of a dozen things off the top of his head that could go wrong with this operation.

But his team was correct about one thing. If this operation was about anyone else except Abigail then he would agree that this plan had the highest chance of getting them their guy and getting him quickly.

Abigail was right, she was a big girl and didn't need his permission to do this, so if she was doing this with or without him, he didn't really have a choice.

Ignoring his instincts that were screaming that this was a mistake, he pushed back his chair and held out his hand to Abigail, who simply stood where she was and arched a brow.

"Is this your way of apologizing for being a controlling jerk?" Abigail asked.

"This is my way of saying I shouldn't have tried to tell you what you can and can't do, and that if you're convinced this is the route you want to take then I'll support you," he said.

Abigail smiled triumphantly. "I forgive you for being a controlling jerk," she said as she came to sit on his lap.

"I didn't say I was a controlling jerk," he reminded her.

"Not in so many words." She grinned and then gave him a quick kiss. "Thank you for supporting me, I feel much safer doing this knowing that you're going to be there to watch my back."

"So that's it?" Night demanded, shoving his chair back and stalking around the room. "You're all just going to let her do this? I thought you loved my sister." Night stormed toward him.

Because he knew his friend was saying that purely out of fear Spider let it slide. This time. "Watch it, Night," he warned. "You know I love her, but I can either send her off to face a killer alone—a killer who only targeted her because of us—or I can make sure she comes out of this alive and in one piece."

"Okay, let's work this out then," Abigail said as she looked around the table. Although he heard the confidence infused into her voice he could feel the small tremors wracking through her body, and knew that the idea of doing this terrified her. If he hadn't already thought Abby was the bravest, strongest woman he'd ever known then he did now. Despite her fears, she was doing this anyway because she wanted to keep him safe. His love for her swelled.

For the next several hours they talked through every detail of the plan, every scenario that might arise, every problem that could possibly go wrong. Through it all Abigail kept a cool head, asking for clarification if she needed it and asking questions when she was unsure of something. After they worked everything out, they started on self-defense drills. Moving all of her furniture to one side of the room they took turns demonstrating how to get out of various holds, and what to do if she had to defend herself.

By the time dusk arrived, Spider realized that it was time to leave. He had to turn his back and walk away from Abigail and pray that they'd be able to get to her before Alex put his hands on her.

"It will be okay, Ryder, I trust you and your team," Abigail said as she slipped an arm around his waist and rested against him.

"What if he hurts you?" he asked, drawing her closer.

"I can take it if he does. Ryder, I don't care, I just want him caught, I don't want to live my life knowing that someone is after you."

"I can take care of myself, Abby."

"I know you can, but Alex needs to be caught, I need him to be caught."

The desperation in her tone had him clutching her to him. "Okay, baby. We'll make this work, the guys and I will be watching your house tonight, and you have the trackers on you. I don't think he'll try anything tonight, but tomorrow you're going to have to go out, maybe go for a walk along the beach or something. He'll no doubt wait until you're alone before he makes his move."

"We went through all this, Ryder, I know what to do," she said with a smile, then stood on her tiptoes, took his face between her hands, and kissed him.

"I hate walking away."

"I know. I wish you didn't have to, but he has to think you guys are gone. I ... I wish you could be here tonight, I'm scared to go to sleep without you here," she admitted.

Spider very nearly ended the mission before it began, but he managed to hold onto his control simply because the only way to make sure Abigail stayed safe was to remove the threat against her. "If you need me, honey, you call me, okay? I can assure you I won't be sleeping."

"It's time, guys," Chaos told them.

"Abs, kiss Spider goodbye on the doorstep in case Alex is watching. We want him to know that you two are together and you're still a good piece of bait to dangle in front of us to lure us in," King added.

Spider tried to memorize every single thing about that kiss, the way the lingering light made her hair shimmer like bronze, the look of complete and utter trust in her amazing silver and gold eyes. The way she nibbled on her bottom lip indicating she was nervous and the light taste of lemon and lime from her soda when he kissed her. Her soft skin that was beginning to get some color to it and the way she fit so perfectly against him like she was literally made for him.

He was all too aware that this could be the last time he ever kissed her.

CHAPTER 15

June 28th

10:10 A.M.

It was now or never.

And after how hard she had fought to make this a reality she could hardly back out now.

Abigail put on some sunblock then pulled her hair back into a ponytail before scrutinizing herself in the bathroom mirror. She was wearing jeans, a t-shirt, and sneakers, not what she would usually have put on to go for a walk along the beach but she had to think ahead. Once Alex took her he would spirit her back to Mexico so she had to be prepared for anything, and wearing a pretty dress and flip-flops would put her at a disadvantage.

The trackers—one on the bottom of her left foot, the other just under her hairline behind her ear—would ensure that Ryder and the others could follow her, but for this to work they had to let Alex get her out of the country and back to Mexico. They had to know what they were walking into so that they didn't walk into the trap Alex thought he was setting which meant that she would be with Alex for a few hours at least. There was no telling what he would do to her in that time.

Since she knew that Ryder would be watching her for as long as he could the t-shirt she'd put on was one of his. It was way too big for her, more like a dress than a t-shirt, but it smelled like Ryder and wearing it made her feel like he was by her side, his arms wrapped around her, rather than her facing this alone. Besides that she'd thought it was a nice added touch to let Alex know she was still a viable way to get to Ryder and his team if he hadn't been there to see the kiss last night.

That kiss.

She could still feel it lingering on her lips, she'd gone to sleep last night reliving it, dreamt about it, and now it was the only thing fueling her. It shoved away the fear because if she wanted more kisses like that then they needed to get Alex out of the picture.

This was the only thing that would accomplish that even if Ryder didn't like it.

She didn't like it either, she just had to do it to keep Ryder and his team safe.

So she metaphorically pulled up her big girl panties, grabbed her cell phone and purse, and walked out her front door. Although she set the alarm, and there was a load of laundry in the dryer waiting to be folded, and dinner in the slow cooker, Abigail's gut told her she wasn't coming back here after her walk.

Alex had been waiting too long to do this, he wouldn't pass up any opportunity to grab her.

Although her stomach was churning, and her hands had been shaking all morning, Abigail resolutely walked to her car. She fought the urge to look around and see if she could spot Ryder or his team, who she knew were somewhere watching her, or Alex and his men who she was sure were out there too.

When she climbed into her car, she realized this would be the first time she had driven in over fourteen months. It felt weird to turn the engine on, snap her seatbelt into place, and put her hands on the steering wheel.

For a moment Abigail wondered if she would even remember how to drive after so long, but as soon as she pulled out of her driveway it all came back to her. The journey to her favorite little secluded beach only took ten minutes, and although she spent the whole time looking in her rear vision mirror trying to spot the vehicles she knew were following her she was unable to.

Parking her car when she reached her destination, she couldn't help but stop and draw the fresh air into her lungs. The feel of the sun on her skin didn't just warm it but warmed her soul as well. She had always taken something as simple as sun on her skin for granted, just like she had taken so many things for granted, but she was determined that she wouldn't squander this second chance. She would live her life to the fullest, she would let go of old hurts, she would embrace love and accept that her insecurities would soon fade rather than dwell on them, and she would chase her dreams.

Her abduction would always be a part of her, and the wounds were still raw, they would take time to heal, but she had time. She had all the time in the world.

After Alex was taken care of.

With a glance around the quiet street, when she didn't see anyone she wondered whether they had all made a mistake.

Had Alex moved on? Was he no longer interested in getting revenge on his team? He had kept her a long time, well after it became apparent that his ploy to use her as bait hadn't worked so maybe something had changed.

Shrugging off the sudden bout of insecurity, Abigail headed for the small path through the trees that led to the beach. It was usually quiet down here, away from the more popular beaches, and she let out a sigh of relief when she came out from the trees and stepped onto the sand to find that there wasn't anyone else in sight. The last thing she wanted was for some innocent person to get caught up in this scheme if they should witness her kidnapping, or to put Alex off if he didn't want any witnesses.

Kidnapping.

Was she really about to allow herself to be kidnapped again, knowing there were no guarantees that this would work out the way they wanted?

Panicked terror hit her so hard her knees buckled, and she hit the sand hard.

She couldn't do this.

She couldn't.

Air wheezed in and out of her chest.

The world dimmed around her.

Great, she was hyperventilating.

What had she been thinking believing that she could play bait for a man who had tortured her then left her locked in a cage for over a year?

Of course she couldn't do this.

Why hadn't she listened to Ryder?

If she had, she would be back in her apartment right now, curled up on his lap, kissing, making up for lost time, instead of out here alone ready to make what would no doubt be the biggest mistake of her life.

Was it too late to back out?

Would Ryder be disappointed in her if she admitted she was too scared to follow through?

Abigail wrapped her arms around her waist, rocking backward and forward. Tears streamed down her cheeks, and she was still struggling to breathe, but when her fingers curled into the soft material of Ryder's t-shirt she felt his strength seep into her suddenly chilled skin. She could imagine him sitting down beside her, his bright blue eyes catching hers and holding them, his mouth setting into that stubborn line. His tone would be firm when he told her that she was strong enough to handle anything and that she wasn't doing this alone. He was right there with her. Even if he couldn't be physically by her side he was still there, in her mind and her heart, if she felt alone all she had to do was picture his intimidating form standing beside her. No, Ryder would always stand in front of her in the face of any danger, always the protector.

Feeling stronger now, Abigail brushed at her wet cheeks, then concentrated on getting her breathing under control. Ryder and his team were watching her, they would follow wherever Alex took her, and as soon as they knew what his trap looked like they would take out his men and then they would get Alex.

She hoped they killed him.

No, what she wished for him was that someone would throw him in a cage and leave him there for a year just like he had done to her, see how he liked it.

Looking out at the ocean she let the gentle rolling of the waves soothe her, and when a shadow suddenly fell over her she looked up, startled.

A man stood above her.

Memories flashed through her mind, this man standing before her, his hand circling her wrist, his other hand taking hold of her pinkie finger, the sadistic smile on his face as he yanked on her appendage, snapping it like it was a twig.

"Hello, Abigail," he said, his eyes roaming her body making her feel like she was naked instead of fully dressed. "Alex is waiting for you."

Before she could react he swung an arm at her, something sharp pierced the skin on her upper arm, and then a moment later the world faded around her.

Her last conscious thought was to pray Ryder got to her in time.

* * *

11:15 A.M.

"Relax, man, she's okay," Chaos said, a hand on his shoulder.

"She's crying," Spider said sharply. Actually, Abigail looked like she was falling apart. She had dropped down onto the sand like she no longer had the strength to remain upright, her arms were wrapped around her middle and she was rocking. Even through the scope of his rifle he could see that she was crying and hyperventilating.

This was too much for her.

He should never have gone along with this.

"You have to hold it together," King said.

"Hold it together?" he demanded. He could barely breathe knowing the woman he loved was deliberately dangling herself in front of a dangerous killer because she was scared for him.

Scared for him.

It was all so backward, she wasn't supposed to put herself in danger for him it was supposed to be the other way around.

"Yes, hold it together, just like she is doing," King said, gesturing to the beach where Abigail was curled up losing it while he wasn't there to tell her that everything was going to be okay.

"Look, man," Chaos added when he didn't put his eye back to the scope.

Reluctantly he complied, and when he looked at Abigail again he saw that she had managed to regain her composure, she now appeared to be staring out at the ocean, she wasn't crying, and she was no longer rocking herself.

Any relief he might have felt at knowing that she was holding it together was fleeting because a man appeared on the beach and began to walk toward her.

"Spider," Chaos warned and he realized his finger was on the trigger of his weapon.

Forcing himself not to shoot, when he looked closer he saw the man heading straight for Abigail wasn't Alex. Of course this couldn't have gone easy, he'd been hoping Alex would be the one to come for Abigail so they could finish this now without having to let her get spirited out of the country.

But Alex wasn't that stupid.

He knew that the only way he even stood a chance at taking out the team was to lure them into a trap.

Coward.

The man stopped beside Abigail, and when she realized he was standing over her and looked up at him the expression on her face—raw terror—had him shoving to his feet.

This wasn't happening.

Couldn't happen.

There was no way he could risk her life like this.

Hands clamped on his shoulders before he even realized that he was about to jump into the water and try to swim to shore in time to stop the abduction from happening.

"You'll never make it in time," King reminded him.

He knew that.

He wasn't stupid.

But he also wasn't letting Alex Irwin put his hands on Abigail a second time.

"This is what she wanted to do," Chaos reminded him.

"She's putting herself in danger," he muttered, trying to break free of his friends' hold. They didn't understand. How could they? Neither of them had ever been in love and it wasn't their heart that was about to be snatched away with no guarantees it would be returned. Or at least returned in one piece.

"She's doing it because she trusts you," Chaos said. "Because she believes in you."

Those words should probably comfort him, but instead, they cut through him like a knife.

When his mother had believed in him, trusted him to save her, he hadn't. Instead he had ended her life.

It didn't matter how many times someone told him it was just an accident, that he was just a little boy, that his mother wouldn't have blamed him, he didn't think any of those things had sunk in. He had failed his mother and the idea that he would fail Abigail too nearly paralyzed him.

"What if I fail her?" he murmured, more to himself than Chaos and King.

The hand on his shoulder squeezed reassuringly. "You won't," Chaos said.

"You can't know that," Spider said, suddenly weary, he'd been carrying the burden of his mother's death for so long and some days it felt like too much. Today was one of those days. He needed Abigail, needed to hold her, to feel her heart beating against him, her warm breath on his skin, he needed her love and her support, but Abigail wasn't here and he felt perilously close to losing it.

"I can know it," Chaos said firmly, fiercely. "You won't allow yourself to fail."

Those words startled him out of his growing melancholy and bout of self-pity. They were true. He *couldn't* allow himself to fail. Failure meant Abigail suffered and there was no way he would be responsible for that.

With a nod at Chaos to say he wouldn't jump out of the boat and attempt the swim to shore, he looked over at King. "What's going on?"

"The guy drugged her," King replied. "He's picking her up and carrying her off the beach."

"Then it's time for us to move," Spider said, making no move to check his own scope to see what was happening. There was no way he could cope with watching Abigail's abduction so he wasn't going to torture himself.

Since Abigail was wearing a tracker they didn't need to follow the kidnapper to see where he was going. While they assumed that Alex was having Abigail taken back to Mexico, there was no way to be certain. They had a helicopter standing by ready to transport them, and they had every other SEAL team standing by should they find they needed backup once they got to wherever Alex had set up his trap.

Everything was in place, they were as prepared as it was possible to be, and yet none of that eased his anxiety.

He wanted this case closed, he wanted Alex Irwin dead, he wanted Abigail safe, he wanted the chance at happiness he had been too scared to fight for last time.

As they drove the boat back to shore where they would meet up with Night, Fox, and Shark, Spider kept his attention focused on following the tracker. Part of him was comforted by the knowledge that for the moment at least, Abigail was unconscious, as long as she was asleep she couldn't be hurt. While he would love it if she remained drugged until the op was over, he knew that wasn't what Alex had planned.

233

Hurting Abigail was just another way to hurt him and Night, and by extension the rest of the team, and it seemed like hurting them was at the top of Alex's to-do list.

"Looks like they're headed for the airport," Fox said as they joined the others, climbing into the car and heading for their own airstrip.

"That's what we thought," Shark added. "He's heading back to Perez's compound. He wants this to go down on his home turf, and if he's working with Perez then that means Alex has an army at his beck and call."

"What's in it for Perez?" King asked thoughtfully. "Luis Perez is a vicious man, he thrives on money and power, he kills anyone who gets in his way, he'll deal in anything so long as it makes him money, and has zero regard for human life."

"Maybe that's it," Chaos said. "Money. Abigail is drop dead gorgeous." That comment earned him a growl from both Spider and Night, and Chaos laughed and held up his hands. "Hey, I'm just stating facts here."

"He's right," Fox said. "And we discussed that as a possibility before we even knew about Alex. Maybe that's why Alex kept her alive even though his plan to use her as bait didn't work. Alex gets Perez's help to get his revenge, and then Perez gets Abigail, he'd get a small fortune selling her, or he can keep her for himself, I'm sure he'd be the envy of his cohorts owning such a beautiful woman."

The idea of Abigail belonging to a man like Perez made him nauseous. She wasn't an object to be used and abused and he took hold of his fury and harnessed it. It didn't matter how many of Perez's men Alex had access to, it didn't matter that the trap he was laying was on his home turf, they were SEALs, the best of the best, and they weren't just fighting to save anyone, this was a woman who they all cared about.

Hold on, Abby, he said, praying that she could feel his words even though they weren't together and he knew she was drugged unconscious. Although he knew it wasn't possible he could swear his hand could feel the phantom caress of her hand closing around it. Spider felt her trust in him, her belief that she was safe because he would come for her, and he knew he would not let her down. He had tried to save his mother and he had failed, he couldn't let that happen again.

He would save Abigail or he would die trying, but one way or the other she was going home alive.

* * *

4:32 P.M.

Everything was proceeding just how he'd planned.

Alex couldn't be happier.

Well, that wasn't quite true; he *could* be happier if the woman in front of him would finally wake up and open her eyes.

At least he was pretty sure she was still out cold from the drugs his men had given her to transport her back to Mexico, but there was always the chance that she was faking, just pretending to be unconscious to keep the inevitable from happening for as long as possible.

Abigail McNamara was a strong woman.

Strong enough that she intrigued him and not many women did. His ex certainly hadn't, all she'd done was nag, and whine, and complain, and somehow manage to mess everything up. Carly could find a way to turn the simplest of tasks into an ordeal, she was stupid, and ugly, and to be honest not good in bed. But Abigail on the other hand was a stunner.

He'd had her here on the compound for over a year, and he still hadn't managed to break the woman. That had been his goal, by the time her useless brother and boyfriend had finally managed to track her down he'd been hoping she would be nothing but a shell of the former feisty woman they had previously known.

Unfortunately, that hadn't happened, but now he had her back, and he knew that his old team was on her heels, this time he would crush her before selling her off to Perez as payment for the use of some of his men.

Or perhaps he would keep Abigail for himself. He could always pay off Perez some other way.

Deciding he had waited long enough for Abigail to wake up, the drugs should have worked their way out of her system by now, and she should have regained consciousness, Alex walked over to where she lay on the floor of the cell and delivered a swift kick to her ribs.

Abigail grunted and rolled over, pressing her chest toward the cold, stone floor since her arms were tied behind her back and she was unable to use them to protect herself, confirming his suspicions that she had only been pretending to be out cold.

"Open your eyes, Abby, I don't like games," Alex said as he pressed a foot down on her back between her shoulder blades, causing her to hiss in a pained breath.

"No?" she gritted out as he pressed harder against her back. "Isn't that the whole reason you kidnapped me—twice —because you wanted to play games with your old team?"

Alex tossed back his head and laughed, got to love a woman with spunk and Abigail had it in spades. "Touché, Abs, touché."

Removing his foot, he strolled across the cell and dropped

down into a chair, studying the woman before him. Although her wrists were bound behind her back, and her ankles were also bound, she managed to wriggle herself over onto her back then up into a sitting position. Alex knew she had to be hurting, but when her eyes met his they practically shot sparks of fire at him.

"You going to tell me you don't know why I'm here?" he asked.

"What would be the point in that? You know that I told Ryder and Eric that you're the one who kidnapped me, and you know that they told me about how you got kicked out of the SEALs for beating up your girlfriend and working as hired muscle for a drug cartel. We know you took me as bait and you know that the guys are going to follow me here."

"Want to know what I'm going to do to them when they get here?" he asked excitedly. He'd never been a patient man and waiting nearly two years to get his revenge had been hard. Hard but necessary. If he'd gone after the men on American soil he would never have achieved his goal, so he'd been forced to learn patience, but now that his time had almost come he was bubbling with excitement like a soda someone had shaken up.

"You're going to kill them," Abigail said, shifting slightly to rest against the wall and wincing at the movement.

"Eventually," he agreed, "but not before I make them suffer. I'll let them watch as my men beat you, torture you a little, and then when you can't scream anymore I'll slit their throats."

"Ryder will kill you first," she said.

"Will he now?" Alex stretched back in his chair, crossing his legs and folding his hands in his lap, watching as confusion warred with distrust on her pale face.

"You know he will," Abigail said.

"But will it be because he and his team are angry I got out

of the country, or because of you?"

Her brow furrowed. "What do you mean?"

"I know the story," he said conversationally. "He took your virginity when you were only eighteen then left you. Came back when you were finished college but only lasted a year before leaving you again. Don't you find it odd that when he had something to gain from sticking close to you, he came crawling back?"

Her eyes widened, but then promptly narrowed. "Ryder explained why he left."

"Maybe. But not why he came back."

"He didn't even know you were behind my abduction until my memories came back."

"So he says."

Abigail opened her mouth and then snapped it closed again. "Why would he do that? If he knew it was you he could have gone after you, there was no need to suck up to me to do it."

"Actually, there was."

She arched a brow.

"Suck up to you, get it?" Alex laughed at his own joke. "Sex, Abigail, maybe he was just using you for sex while knowing all along you were going to lead him straight to me."

"Ryder wouldn't do that." She huffed, but he saw the glimmer of doubt hidden deep in her amazing eyes.

"He's a man, isn't he? And you're smoking hot, trust me, darling, there isn't much a man like him wouldn't do to get in the pants of a woman like you."

"What do you mean a man like Ryder? Ryder is a good man."

"He's a SEAL, and SEALs like women. *Lots* of women," he added.

"Is that why you became a SEAL, to sleep with lots of

women?" Abigail looked disgusted by the possibility and that sent anger flaring through him.

"You think your boyfriend is any better?" he sneered, stalking over to stand above her. "He dumped you didn't he? Twice. But when it suited him he made nice to get in your pants. I'll tell you what I don't understand, I don't understand why when I was going down on you all you did was cry, and yet when he does it you scream in ecstasy. Okay, so I dosed you up with Rohypnol because I wanted you to think that you were in that cage the whole time, needed to isolate you to break you, but there was no way I could stay away from this body."

Alex crouched in front of her and ran a hand down her chest. She shied away from him, and he could see the terror in her eyes, the tears threatening to spill out. He'd just dropped a bombshell on her, and the fear on her face had him growing hard.

"I didn't have sex with you before because I wanted to make more money off you when I sold you to Perez, but you know what?"

Wide eyes just stared up at him.

He swung a fist, connected with her jaw. "I asked you a question. You know sometimes that stubborn streak of yours is just plain annoying. This time I'm not holding back, this time, I'm going to take what I want from you and if Perez doesn't like it then maybe I'll kill him too. Women, power, and money, it's all a guy really needs anyway." Grasping her chin between his thumb and forefinger, hard enough to make her flinch, Alex leaned in close. "Maybe I'll wait until your boyfriend and the team get here before taking you. I bet Spider would love to watch me do his girl."

Alex leaned in, intending to kiss her, but she slammed her bound legs up, connecting with his manhood.

Screaming in pain he tumbled sideways, clamping his

thighs together in an effort to ease the pounding agony.

"That's what I think of that, Alex," Abigail snarled. "Ryder loves me, and when he and my brother and the rest of the guys get here it's going to be you who's sorry. You're a sorry excuse for a SEAL, a sorry excuse for a man, a sorry excuse for a human being."

Anger shoved aside the pain and Alex staggered to his feet. "You aren't going to like the consequences of your actions, *little girl*," he sneered.

* * *

5:00 P.M.

Okay, so taunting the man who had orchestrated her abduction twice, and currently had her tied up and in what she thought was the same cell where he had previously tortured her probably wasn't her smartest move, but it felt so good.

Abigail knew that until Ryder and his team showed up she was stuck here, but she wasn't going to lie down and take whatever Alex dished out without fighting back. She hadn't done that last time, and she wouldn't be doing it this time. The first time Alex had wanted something from her, information on each of the team, did they have girlfriends, hobbies, anything that could be used against him, and his anger had stemmed from her refusal to answer.

This time all he wanted was her pain.

And she had no way of stopping him from taking it.

Already her ribs throbbed with each breath she took, and she hadn't needed his warning that she wasn't going to like the consequences of kicking him and goading him because she already knew it.

But Ryder would have been proud of her for fighting

back, executing one of the moves he'd taught her. A move that had she not been locked in a cell might have resulted in her earning herself enough time to make a run for it.

Now she watched warily as Alex walked to the bars of the cell and called out to his men. A moment later the door to her cell clanked open, and two other men strode in. She remembered one of them, he was the one who had broken her fingers, who had snatched her off the beach, but the other man she didn't recognize.

Fear laced her blood, but she didn't let it show, she wouldn't cower in terror at Alex's feet, she would take whatever he did to her and never shed a tear, she would show her parents that she was strong, she had survived him once she could do it again.

"Our guest here needs to learn a little lesson in manners," Alex drawled, but she could see how he moved gingerly, and she took pride knowing she was the cause.

"Once you finish off teaching me a lesson," she would have used air quotes for that but her hands were tied behind her back, "maybe you ought to teach Alex some self-defense moves. Hit by a girl, a *bound* girl, what a pathetic SEAL."

Alex glowered at her, then nodded at his men. One of them backhanded her sending her head slamming backward into the stone wall, while the other slammed his foot into her stomach so hard she gagged.

Abigail bit back a scream, no way was she giving Alex even an ounce of satisfaction. Ryder was coming, she didn't know how long she'd been out, but she knew that the team would have followed her here. They would be forming a plan right this very second, she only had to hold out a little longer.

She could do that.

Women, money, and power, Alex had said it himself, that was all he cared about, he hadn't joined the SEALs to save lives, he cared nothing about honor and integrity, he'd easily traded in fighting for his country to working for a powerful drug lord.

"Why did you even become a SEAL?" Abigail asked once she could draw a breath again. "Scrap that question, how did you even pass whatever psychological screening they do?"

"You think you're so funny, don't you, Abigail?" He squatted before her, his face inches from her own, his eye ticking as he attempted to reign in his rage, he wanted her alive when his old team arrived.

"No, I don't see anything amusing about any of this," she answered honestly. "I didn't think being abducted was funny, I didn't think what you did to me while you kept me prisoner was funny, and I don't think you trying to kill six good men is in any way funny."

"What makes you think they're good?"

The question caught her by surprise. "Of course they're good men."

"Because they're *SEALs*?" he sneered.

"Because they put themselves in danger to keep others safe."

"How many men do you think your *boyfriend* has killed?"

"I don't know, as many as he had to, to complete his missions and come home alive and not a single one more. Where are you going with this?" Abigail knew that everything Alex did he did for a reason, but what reason was there for trying to tear down the SEALs? Blaming them for him losing his job and having to flee the country was one thing but tearing them down, was there something she was missing?

"Just thinking you put an awful lot of trust in men who didn't save you the first time around. What makes you think that they'll save you this time?"

"Last time they didn't know where I was," she reminded

him. He seemed to be awfully interested in trying to convince her to turn her back on the SEALs. Did he have a more personal reason for targeting her specifically out of all the family members of the men on his team he could have gone after?

"So they say." The anger had gone from his voice, now he sounded like they were just sitting around chatting like old friends. "Maybe they just didn't care."

"Stop," she said firmly. She wouldn't doubt Ryder, or her brother, or the rest of the team. They were coming, she had the trackers on, they knew where she was, all they needed to do was figure out a way to foil whatever trap Alex thought he had put in place.

"I'm not going to stop, sweetheart, I'm going to beat you so badly that by the time your boyfriend gets here he won't even recognize you."

A hint of a memory whispered at the back of her mind.

Shortly after Ryder had left her the second time, she'd been out at a bar with some friends when Alex had shown up. He'd asked her out but she'd turned him down.

He *had* chosen her for a reason, he wanted revenge on her too.

Abigail huffed a laugh. "You can beat me, you can kill Ryder, you can even drug me and have sex with me over and over again, but you know what, Alex, I am never going to want you."

His eyes narrowed. "I don't know about that. When I had you in that cell, you were begging for someone to talk to you, begging not to be left alone. That changed, sweetheart? I bet if I toss you back into that cell, let you watch your boyfriend die a long, slow death, I bet I can break you enough that you'll be begging me to touch you any way I want."

"Won't happen," she said simply. "Ryder is my heart, my soul, no matter what you say I love him, and I know he loves

243

me. He's coming, and even if he wasn't I still would never beg for anything from you because you're nothing but a sellout. You sold out your own team, your brothers, the men who are supposed to have your back, so you could go and work for a drug cartel."

Alex's face turned red, and he stood and clenched his fingers into fists. "Hit her," he ordered his men.

"Too pathetic to do your own dirty work?" she pushed, just as a shoe connected with her ribs again.

Agony sliced through her but she wouldn't cry.

She wasn't going to scream.

Another strike got her in the stomach and then one in the head as she slumped over onto her side. Pain exploded behind her closed eyelids but she could do nothing to protect her head and vital organs restrained as she was. The best she could do was attempt to curl herself into a ball.

The blows continued, one after the other until her entire body burned and throbbed. Her teeth were clamped into her bottom lip to keep from screaming, and she held back her tears with every drop of strength that she could muster.

She felt Ryder's presence surround her. He might not be here in person, but she was still wearing his t-shirt, and just like at the beach when she had broken down she felt him here with her. Abigail felt his hand curl around one of hers, and that feeling of no longer facing her ordeal on her own meant that she took each and every blow with a strength she had spent a lifetime fearing she didn't possess.

Ribs, abdomen, back, head, the two men kicked and punched her, while Alex stood watching, a delighted smirk on his face. But the last thing she saw as unconsciousness finally claimed her wasn't his face but Ryder's, standing over her like her own personal sentinel.

Peace overrode the pain and the fear, and she floated off into the blackness.

* * *

11:34 P.M.

It was time.

After hours of excruciating waiting, planning, and evalu-ating, it was finally time to go in and get his girl.

Relief filled Spider, he could be a patient man, but that was when the life of the woman he loved wasn't hanging in the balance. Abigail had been with Alex for twelve hours now, there was a lot that could be done to a person in twelve hours. For now he had to keep that fear shoved to the back of his mind because if he dwelled on it then he wouldn't be able to function.

Since they knew that they were walking into a trap they had to plan out this mission differently than they normally would. It was always a possibility of course, and there had been times when he and his team walked into an ambush, but this time they knew for sure that was what Alex had planned, and they had the added concern that Alex had trained with them, worked with them, he knew how they operated and what they would be likely to do.

Quietly, Spider and his team approached the building where Abigail's tracker said she was being held. They didn't have a floor plan for the building so they were going in blind, but Abigail was in there, and they weren't leaving without her.

They had split up into two teams, himself, Chaos, and King in one, and Night, Fox, and Shark in the other. The other team was providing cover for them as they approached the building. From their observations, it appeared that there were four groups of two-man teams guarding the building. They circled in a counter-clockwise manner around the structure so that one team was monitoring one side of the square building at all times.

The men were of course armed, but they weren't as highly trained as his SEAL team and they were able to easily eliminate all eight guards and enter the building.

It was old but looked like it was in the process of being restored, and Spider wondered whether this was Alex's personal home. It was on the far end of the Perez compound, the opposite end to the one where he and Abigail had hidden out when he'd rescued her the first time.

Since they were still on the Perez compound there was a chance that Alex could call up more men if he felt like he needed them, but they knew Alex had been planning this for over a year and Spider assumed that whoever he had here was who he thought he needed to best them.

There were no lights on in the house, and it was quiet, no more guards, no voices talking, nothing.

It was like the place was empty.

Only they knew it wasn't.

Abigail was in here somewhere.

The house was large but not exceedingly so, around thirty rooms spread out over three floors. They cleared the first floor without finding any signs of life, then moved on to the second and then the third; both other floors were similarly empty. It was obvious that someone lived in the house, there was food in the kitchen, tools and building materials in several rooms, furniture strewn haphazardly about in a couple of the rooms, and a few of the bedrooms had clothes in them and toiletries in the bathrooms.

Finding no one waiting for them they headed to the one place they hadn't looked yet.

The basement.

Taking the lead, the three of them made their way back down to the first floor and started searching for a door that would lead to a basement. There was nothing obvious, and it wasn't until they started checking out all the walls that a portion of the kitchen wall popped open, revealing a set of stairs leading down to a dimly lit space.

Abigail was down there, he could feel it, she was there, and she was waiting for him to come for her.

They made their way down a long staircase until they had to be deep underground, the air was chilled and smelled musty, and there was the unmistakable metallic smell of blood.

At the bottom of the stairs they found themselves at one end of a long passageway, on either side of the passage were cells. The cells were all empty until they came to one about halfway down and on the left. Inside there was a chair, and a small figure huddled in the corner.

Abby.

Leaving King and Chaos to finish checking the cells, Spider curled his hands around the bars, desperate to get to Abigail to check her out and see how badly she was injured. That she was injured was a given, she hadn't responded to his presence, she just lay there, unmoving, and he prayed that she was still alive.

No.

Of course she would still be alive.

Alex wanted them to suffer, which meant he wanted them to watch while he tortured Abigail.

"We're clear," King said, returning to his side.

"I don't like it," Chaos muttered. "Why have the guards on the outside of the building but no one in here except Abs?"

Right now he didn't care why. All he cared about was getting to Abby.

"There were a set of keys hanging down on the wall at the other end, I'm guessing they open the cells," King said, handing them over.

Spider's hands were shaking as he took them and inserted the first one into the lock on Abigail's cell's door. He had to go through five keys before one finally gave him the clink he had been waiting for.

Wrestling the door open, he ran to Abby, dropping onto his knees at her side as he pressed his fingertips to her throat.

Not only was he rewarded by the thumping of her pulse but she moaned at his touch and tried to curl in on herself.

"It's okay, Abby, it's me," he said softly, wanting to reassure her, but he couldn't shake the feeling that they were still playing into Alex's hands, giving him exactly what he wanted.

"Ryder?" she croaked weakly.

"Here, babe. I'm going to have to move you, sorry," he said, wincing, already knowing this would hurt her. Still, he couldn't stop a gasp escaping when he rolled her as carefully as he could onto her back so he could get a better look at her injuries.

"That bad huh?" she asked, one corner of her mouth quirking up. "I would say it's not as bad as it looks, but it really is."

"I'm so sorry, sweetheart." Tears burned the backs of his eyes. She had endured all of this because of them, because Alex blamed them for his own choices.

"Not your fault," she murmured as her swollen eyes fluttered closed.

There was no point in arguing with her. Of course this was their fault, they were the ones that Alex was after. Needing to check her injuries before they moved her in case there was anything life-threatening that had to be dealt with, he bypassed the obviously broken cheekbone and bruising on her face, and ran his hands over her body. She sucked in a pained breath when he touched her ribcage and when he pulled up the t-shirt she wore he saw her entire front was already covered in a mottled array of black and blue bruises.

He swore under his breath as he clamped one hand on her shoulder and the other on her hip and carefully rolled her onto her side so he could examine her back. It was likewise bruised, and he prayed that none of her organs had been badly damaged. Internal bleeding wasn't something they could deal with in the middle of an extraction.

"How bad?" Chaos called from the door of the cell.

"Bad," he muttered as he eased her back down.

"I don't like that Alex still hasn't shown himself," King said. "The guys say there's no sign of him approaching the building. I thought he would have waited until we were all but trapped down here with only one entry and exit point before storming in, but so far nothing."

"Why lead us all the way out here only to let us get Abby and leave?" Chaos asked.

"Maybe he's waiting to get us on the way back to the helicopter," King suggested. "Surround us and gun us down out in the jungle."

"Abby, did he say anything about his plan?" Spider asked as he gently pulled her shaking body into his arms.

"Just that he hates you guys, was angry I turned him down, and how he can't wait to make you watch him rape me," she whispered, tears leaking from her closed eyes. "Ryder, he said when I was here before he would drug me with Rohypnol and..."

She didn't finish her sentence but she didn't have to.

His entire body clenched with a fury so deep it rocked him to his core.

Alex Irwin was a dead man.

"Come on, honey, let's get you out of here," he whispered, preparing to stand with Abigail in his arms, just as the basement erupted into yelling and gunfire.

CHAPTER 16

June 29th

12:01 A.M.

The sudden gunfire made Abigail flinch, and Ryder's arms tightened around her.

"It's all right, babe," he whispered in her ear before setting her down on the floor, tucking her into the corner, and standing between her and whoever was shooting.

But it wasn't all right.

He was here, his team was here, Alex was here, they'd played into his hands, given him what he wanted, and now it was time to see if they walked out of this alive. It wasn't that she didn't trust Ryder and his team it was just that she had no idea what they had planned, and at the moment whatever it was didn't seem promising.

"Better late to the party than never," Alex's voice boomed.

"Weapons down, men, I think it's safe to say we hold the advantage."

To her surprise, Ryder set down his weapon. She wanted to ask him why he was doing that, but she was so weak, and she wasn't sure she had the energy to speak.

"Kick them over here," Alex instructed, "then all three of you into the cell with Abigail."

Three?

Where were the others?

Was this why Ryder was doing as Alex instructed because he knew that the rest of his team would soon be here?

The sound of the cell door clunking shut filled her with dread. They were trapped. Locked in. Alex had them. He had Ryder, who had just given up his weapon.

No.

Wait.

Ryder wouldn't just have one gun on him.

Maybe that was the plan, wait until Alex came in here to do whatever it was he had planned next, and then they would jump him.

That hope quickly fled.

"All weapons," Alex said cheerfully. "I know you guys are still armed and I want everything. You're outnumbered, you're on my home turf, and if you try anything stupid then it will be Abigail who suffers the consequences. I know you're all gentlemen and wouldn't want that."

Although he wasn't touching her, Abigail felt Ryder's whole body go tense at the threat against her. While she knew that Ryder could take Alex armed or not, right now they were trapped in a cell, unarmed, while Alex's men still clutched their weapons, all of which were currently pointed at her.

"A bullet through the knee is pretty painful I'm told," Alex added when Ryder and the others didn't make a move to do as he requested. "Actually, I don't just need to be told I've heard the screams of men who have experienced it."

Ryder growled low in his throat but complied and threw the last of his weapons out of the cell.

"There, that wasn't so hard was it?" Alex asked. "Now, where are the others? I know the three of you didn't come alone. Where are Night, Shark, and Fox?"

So it was Charlie and Grayson who were trapped in here with her and Ryder. At least the others were somewhere close by, and she hoped that whatever they had planned they were going to do soon. Alex had waited too long for this, he wouldn't drag it out, he would rape her and beat her some more before killing the others, then he would either take her to this Luis Perez guy or he would keep her for himself. Either way she wasn't dying today along with the others.

"Not going to answer?" Alex asked, all cheerfulness gone from his tone, now he sounded just plain angry. "She decided it was a good idea not to answer my questions, I think you know what that achieved."

"You lay a hand on her, you die," Ryder warned.

"I don't think you're in any position to be making demands, Spider," Alex growled. "Did you get a chance to chat with your girl? Did she tell you how she and I used to have a little fun while she was my guest?"

If Alex thought goading Ryder was a good idea then he was sorely mistaken.

All he would achieve by making Ryder angry was ensuring that they made him suffer before they killed him.

"You lay a hand on her again, and I'll rip your head off," Ryder said, his voice all the more threatening by how quiet it was.

Alex threw back his head and laughed. "I'd like to see you try. Did you miss the part where you're locked in a cell—

unarmed—while my men have weapons trained on your girl?"

"Why go to all this trouble, Alex?" Charlie asked. "You really think what happened to you was our fault?"

"You're the one who decided to become an enforcer for a drug cartel. You're the one who chose to beat up your girlfriend and who threw away your life. What did that have to do with us?" Grayson asked.

"Being a SEAL was fun, I liked the women who threw themselves at me, I liked the killing, but the money sucked," Alex replied.

"Money?" Grayson asked. "This all boils down to money?"

"Most things in the world do," Alex said. "I had it all, the SEALs, family, a girlfriend who knew her place, and the money from working for Perez, and you ruined that. I don't like people messing with my life, never did. Now all I have left is the money, and I'm going to be swimming in it if I decide to sell that pretty piece of meat lying on the floor. After I do her," he added.

Ryder lunged, but Charlie and Grayson grabbed hold of him. "He's trying to provoke you, don't let him," Charlie muttered.

Alex laughed. "King ain't wrong, but I *am* going to do her. Pick her up, Spider, and bring her to me, not sure she can walk after the beating we gave her. Not sure she'll be able to walk when I'm through with her either."

Abigail couldn't help but shudder at what was coming next. There didn't seem to be any way to stop it but she wasn't going to scream, wasn't going to cry. She wouldn't beg or do anything that would make this worse for Ryder.

"Pick her up, Spider. If you don't I'll shoot her in the knee and use her blood for lube when I take her," Alex threatened.

The growl that came out of Ryder was inhuman and

deadly lethal, but he stooped at her side and scooped her carefully up.

"Don't watch, Ryder," she pleaded. Then she whispered so no one else would hear, "Ryder, there's a secret tunnel that leads out into the jungle and up into the house into one of the bedrooms."

His blue eyes widened. "You sure?"

"I remember it, this is where he had me when he first brought me here, and I remember going out the tunnel to the cell you found me in. When he was ... touching me ... we came in through the tunnel and up to one of the bedrooms."

"That's perfect, sweetheart, you're amazing." Pride shone from his eyes and hers misted.

"I didn't cry," she told him. "When he was beating me I didn't scream."

"You cry if you need to, baby, I already know how strong you are, you don't have anything to prove."

"Come on, hurry up," Alex snapped.

"Just hold on a little longer," Ryder said, then touched his lips to her forehead.

With heavy steps Ryder crossed the cell. Alex had opened the door and held his arms out ready to take her while his men kept their weapons trained on them.

Abigail knew how hard it was for Ryder to hand her over to a monster, but he had no choice, and carefully placed her in Alex's outstretched arms. His fingers lingered on her arm as he let her go and took a step back.

The look Ryder gave Alex was beyond menacing. "I'm going to kill you, Alex. You have to know that."

Alex just laughed. "You're in no position to be threatening me. Open the cell opposite this one," he ordered one of his men. "And go bring me a mattress, I am a gentleman after all, I'm not going to do her on the floor."

He threw a mocking smile over his shoulder, and even though he had turned and she couldn't see their faces she knew Ryder, Grayson, and Charlie were shooting Alex death stares.

Her resolve was cracking, her heart breaking, of everything that Alex had done to her this was the worst. Raping her in front of Ryder would crush him, and even if they did make it out of this alive she wasn't sure how they would be able to recover from it.

It would change how he saw her.

Irreversibly.

Two men came down carrying a mattress between them, and they laid it down in the cell opposite the one he had just removed her from.

Alex carried her to it, and then an explosion shattered the world.

* * *

12:47 A.M.

Spider had told the others about the tunnels, and the explosion came at the perfect time. Right before Alex was able to do something to Abigail from which there might be no coming back.

He had been prepared for the explosion, he knew his men were upstairs because the two men who had been sent up to retrieve a mattress weren't the same men who brought it back down to the basement. Shark and Fox had brought the mattress down, and the second it was on the floor he saw Fox whisper something into his comms.

A second later the explosion boomed above them.

Unprepared, Alex's men startled, and that moment of

distraction was all it took for him and his team to take control.

Alex had made a mistake not asking them to remove their comms so he could relate what Abigail had told him to the others, and he had made a mistake in not collecting up their discarded weapons.

While Alex's men scrambled to figure out what was going on, King and Chaos lunged for their weapons as Shark and Fox began to fire, and Night came running down the stairs, also firing.

Spider threw himself at Abigail who was now on the mattress, covering her body with his own, protecting her from the bullets that were flying. She wasn't moving, but he didn't think she'd been hit.

Finally, silence filled the basement.

Cautiously he lifted his head, all of his men were standing, none of Alex's were.

"A head's up on the explosion would have been nice," said Abigail's weary voice from beneath him. "You're squishing me."

A relieved smile curled his lips up. "Better squished than dead, sweetheart."

"Can't argue with that," she said.

"I would have filled you in on the explosion if I'd had a chance," he told her as he maneuvered his body off hers. Running his hands over her body again to check for any new injuries, his team began checking the bodies, making sure that no one was left alive.

"I'm okay, Ryder," Abigail said.

"Untrue," he muttered. Her body was a mass of bruises, she had broken bones, was exhausted, and needed medical treatment, but at least she was alive. That was something to rejoice about.

"Uh, Spider, we got bad news," Fox said, positioning

himself between him and Abigail and the corridor. From Fox's stance, he knew that whatever the problem was it was a safety issue.

"What's wrong?" he asked, propping Abigail against his bent knee when she tried to struggle into a sitting position.

"Alex's body isn't here," Fox replied.

"What?" Abigail said, her voice wobbling. She'd held it together so well up until now, and he needed her to keep it together just a little longer.

"He won't get to you, Abby," he assured her, then to his team, "how did that happen?"

"He must have thrown Abby to the floor when the blast went off then hightailed it out of here leaving his team to distract us," Fox said.

"So it's not over." Abigail had tears shimmering in her eyes, and she looked like she had about reached the end of her rope.

"It will be, there's no way he's letting us leave without trying to take us out. So his plan to torture us by watching him rape and torture you is out the window. My guess is he's waiting out in the jungle for us, he'll try to pick us off one by one as we head for the evacuation point," he explained, already passing Abigail off to Fox so he could grab his weapons.

"Could also be waiting for us in the tunnel," Shark suggested.

"He'd do whatever he thinks we would least likely expect him to do," Chaos added.

"Options are he waits to pick us off in the tunnel which would leave us virtually trapped in here since we blew up the house. Or he waits to pick us off as we exit the tunnel, again leaving us virtually trapped in here. Or he waits until we're all in the jungle and goes after us there," Night said.

"We'd go with option A or B," Fox said.

"So Alex is going to go with option C then, wait until we're all in the jungle and then start shooting," Spider said as he reached out to take Abigail back from Fox.

"He knows the land better than we do," Shark said as they prepared their weapons and started down the corridor to where Abigail had said the entrance to the secret tunnels were.

"But we have him outnumbered," Chaos said, a grin on his face.

"But he wants you all dead," Abigail said, her cheek resting against his shoulder as though she were too tired to lift her head.

"Yeah, but we have an ace up our sleeve." He smiled down at her.

"An ace?" she asked, brow furrowed.

"We didn't come alone," he explained. "Wolf's team is here with us only Alex doesn't know that. They're going to be tracking us as we make our way through the tunnel and we'll let them know when we reach the end of it. They'll be watching as we come out, keeping an eye out for Alex, and following us to the helo. Alex will be focused on us, he won't even be thinking that we didn't come alone. He thinks that being a SEAL is all about having a massive ego because that's all it was to him. But that's not us, we came here to rescue you and to eliminate a threat. We came with backup because it was the smart thing to do. We're all going home, Abigail, all of us, alive and in one piece. Well, all of us but Alex," he finished darkly.

His answer seemed to be enough to satisfy her, and she sank down against him, allowing herself to rest, regain some strength because she trusted him to get her safely out of here.

Since his arms were full of Abby his team surrounded him, they made it into the tunnel without incident and through safely. The tunnels were long, close to two klicks by the time they finally reached the end, they were about five feet wide and lit sporadically with oil lamps. While they didn't know what was waiting for them on the other side, it was possible they were going to come up right in the middle of Perez's compound, right into another trap.

Wolf's team didn't alert them to any issues, so carefully King opened the door, and after clearing the immediate area, they all stepped out into the dark night.

Besides Abigail, they all put their NVG on then began the traipse through the jungle to where the helicopter would pick them up.

They couldn't leave without Alex though.

If they did this would never be over, Abigail would never be safe, and with a threat hanging over his team, he didn't know what that would mean for them.

"Want me to take her for a while?" Night asked, falling into step beside him.

It was selfish of him, but there was no way he was giving up his hold on Abby, not even for her brother. Her weight wasn't slowing him down, and they were just over halfway to the extraction point. "I got her."

All of a sudden, a black blur dropped down out of the trees above them, lunging at him and Abigail. Spider threw himself sideways and to the ground, rolling to take the brunt of the fall and then rolling again to cover her body with his own.

Alex was screaming something incomprehensible and Night tackled him. As much as Spider wanted to be there, bringing Alex down, making him pay for every bruise he'd put on Abigail's soft skin, every delicate bone he had broken, each piece of her psyche he had damaged by torturing her, this was more important. Holding the woman he loved safe beneath him, protecting her, not just her body but her mind as well. She needed him and he wouldn't abandon her for anything, not even to exact revenge.

"Got him," Fox's voice rang with a finality in his ear that had his entire body relaxing. They still had to get through cartel owned territory to the helicopter, they still had to get Abigail to a hospital to be examined, but it was finally over. Alex was dead, they were all safe. "You hear that, babe?" he asked.

"Hmm?" came her sleepy voice.

"We got him."

She blinked open her eyes and looked up at him in the dark. "He's dead?" Her voice shook on the last word.

"He's dead." Spider leaned down to touch his forehead to hers. "He's dead."

The tears he knew she had been holding back because she wasn't going to break down and show any weakness to Alex finally broke free and she began to sob. Dragging her up and onto his lap, he pressed her face to his chest in an attempt to muffle her weeping.

Rocking her, holding her tight but not too tight since he didn't want to cause her further pain, he finally felt like they were free to start their lives together. No secrets, no old hurt and doubts holding them back, free and clear to embrace their future.

* * *

3:50 P.M.

Most of the last twelve hours or so were a blur.

Abigail remembered bits and pieces, but everything was fuzzy like she had been experiencing it but also watching it happen to someone else at the same time.

She remembered being carried through the jungle, too tired to even offer to carry her own weight and walk on her own. She remembered the loud buzzing of the helicopter as she was loaded aboard and placed on a gurney where someone started an IV with fluids and blessed painkillers. She remembered being brought into the hospital where she had been treated.

And she remembered that through it all Ryder hadn't left her side.

She was sure he had other things he was supposed to be doing, like debriefing everything that had gone down in Mexico, but she also knew he couldn't leave her right now. He needed her just as much as she needed him.

Eventually the drugs and her own exhaustion had her drifting off to sleep, her hand tightly clutching one of Ryder's as he sat in a chair beside her bed. She'd woken up a couple of hours ago to find him asleep, his head resting on the mattress beside her hip, and since she hadn't wanted to disturb him she had been lying here thinking.

So many thoughts running through her mind.

Her problems with her parents, everything that Ryder had been through with his abusive father and what had happened to his mother, what Alex had told her while he was taunting her about what he had done to her, everything mixed together until it started to feel overwhelming. Abigail had been deluding herself into thinking that once Alex was captured or dead—preferably dead—it would all be over, but it was far from it.

In fact, she felt like she was just at the beginning of this journey.

Tears started to trickle down her cheeks. After so long trying to keep a tight lid on her emotions it seemed that lid had lost its seal and now her emotions kept bubbling up and out.

"Abby?" Ryder's worried voice said her name, and she felt him move so he was sitting on the edge of her bed, but didn't turn from staring out the window. "Baby, what's wrong?"

"Nothing, everything, I don't know," she said helplessly.

Strong arms wrapped around her and drew her up off the pillows and against his rock hard chest.

What would she have done if Alex had succeeded in killing him?

What would she do if she lost him on another mission?

Would she be able to get through this on her own?

Was she strong enough to survive losing him?

Things had been different when they had been together a couple of years ago, *they* had been different.

Now she both felt like she had gotten that missing piece of herself back when she got Ryder back, but also lost another piece of herself to Alex.

Alex had taken away something from her; she didn't know how to get back. He had touched her against her will, drugged her, and used her for his own pleasure, intended to sell her like she was just a piece of property. How did she get past that?

"Sweetheart, you're scaring me, would you please say something." Ryder's hand stroked the length of her spine in long, smooth movements.

"Just thinking," she whispered against his neck.

"About Alex? About what he did to you."

It wasn't a question, but she nodded anyway.

"I don't want you to keep anything from me, Abby." His hands closed around her shoulders and he pulled her back, holding her at arm's length, so he could see her face, pin her with those piercing blue eyes so she couldn't look away.

"I told you already," she reminded him.

"You're thinking about Alex drugging you and what he did to you while you were out." The tightness around his mouth and the darkness in her eyes had her dropping her gaze to the crisp white sheets. This was why she couldn't talk to him about it, it hurt him too much.

"He sexually assaulted me, I don't remember it, but yeah, it's hard to think about, hard to talk about, especially with you."

"Look at me, Abby." When she didn't the grip on her shoulders tightened. "Abby."

When she looked up at him the tightness was gone from his face, but the pain was still there. It seeped into her, merging with her own until she couldn't even tear them apart anymore. "I'm sorry," she whispered. This was so hard. How could she look at Ryder every day knowing that just the sight of her face caused him pain, made him feel guilty, made him blame himself just like he blamed himself for what had happened to his mother?

"Oh, honey, no, don't be sorry, what he did to you was not your fault."

"It hurts," she cried, not fighting him when he pulled her back into an embrace. "It hurts because it hurt me, but it hurts so much more because it hurts you as well. I want it to stop, I want it to go away, I want everything to be normal again, but I don't even know what normal looks like anymore. I don't want you to blame yourself, I don't want you to think that anything Alex did was your fault, I just want us to be a normal, happy couple, but I don't know if we can be."

His arms tightened reflexively around her. "What are you saying, Abby?"

"I don't know," she wept.

"Are you saying that this is over?"

Was she?

Was she at a point where she didn't know how to move forward?

Abigail felt stuck, trapped in quicksand, it was pulling her down fast and the more she struggled the faster she sank. How could she pull Ryder down with her?

And yet at the same time, how could she live without him?

Was it selfish to ask him to stand by her while she rebuilt her life?

One look up at his anguished face and she knew the answer. Knew it as surely as she knew that this would be the hardest thing she had ever done and the longest, roughest journey she had ever taken.

Dragging in a breath, Abigail prepared herself to say the one word that would change everything, that would dictate both of their futures. "No. I need you, Ryder, I just don't know that it's fair to ask you to wait while I sort out this mess Alex created."

"Fair? Abby, nothing that happened to you was fair, but I love you, and just like I would never have walked away from my mother, I would never walk away from you. We'll find a way to make it work, we'll get you back to Dr. Hancock as soon as you heal enough to go, we'll take our relationship slowly or fast or whatever you want. All I know is that I love you more than anything, and all I need is you."

Abigail melted against him. This man was her everything, he had saved her life twice, and yeah his decisions to keep his past from her had hurt her deeply, but in the end, he had proven how important she was to him, and she believed him.

"Ryder, in the jungle when you found me the first time, you said to trust you and we both knew I didn't, at least not with anything other than my life, but I trust you now, with all of me, with my heart," she told him, tilting her head so her lips could touch his jaw.

His big body shuddered against hers. "Abby, you don't know how much those words mean to me. I know I hurt you,

I know I lied to you and let you down, I know I broke your heart not once but twice, and for you to say that you trust me with your heart, sweetheart, that does crazy things to me. Abs, you think that I saved you, but the truth is your love saved me a long time ago. I feared for so long that with my father's DNA inside me I would turn out to be like him, but when a sweet, sassy, spunky, strong woman like you fell for me, I realized I was nothing like him and never would be. When you gave me a second chance and told me for the first time that you loved me the guilt I felt over my mother's death finally stopped choking me. And now, holding you in my arms and hearing you say that after everything we've been through that you trust me it heals the last of my broken pieces. *You* saved *me*, Abby, not the other way around."

Her lips were split, her eyes half swollen closed, she had a concussion, cracked ribs, a broken nose and cheekbone, and a broken arm all courtesy of Alex Irwin and his men, but none of that mattered as she wrapped her good arm around Ryder's waist and touched her mouth to his.

This man had owned her heart since she was a kid, she loved him with every fiber of her being, and finally the stars had all aligned and the universe had stopped frowning down at her, and now he was hers.

CHAPTER 17

June 30th

8:49 A.M.

Spider ran his hands through his hair as he closed Abigail's hospital room door behind him. Her doctor had gone in to examine her and hopefully give her the all clear to go home this afternoon.

Home.

With his girl.

They still had some things to work out, practicalities like where they were going to live and how soon they were going to get married, what Abigail's plans were for the future, and things like that, but the big stuff was out of the way. They were in love, and he had earned Abigail's trust back, that was all that mattered.

"How is she?" Night asked, storming through the hospital with a box in his hands.

"Yeah, she's doing okay," he said vaguely.

"That doesn't convince me," Night scowled. "Let me ask again, how is my sister doing?"

"She's struggling, okay, man? Not physically so much although she's in a lot of pain and she's going to be laid up for a while, but psychologically she's struggling. Finding out everything Alex did to her, it messed her up. She had nightmares last night, once the drugs wore off she struggled to sleep, tossing and turning, then she started screaming."

He dragged his hands down his face. He was exhausted, he hadn't left the hospital since Abigail was brought here. Someone had dropped off clean clothes so he'd changed, but he hadn't showered yet. His CO and his team had come here and they'd debriefed in Abigail's hospital room because he hadn't been able to leave her side. Now he just wanted to get her home and let her start healing.

"She going to see the doctor again when she gets home?" Night asked.

"Yes, she knows she needs help and she'd not resisting getting it."

"Good." Night nodded like that was a weight off his mind. "You're not going to bail on her again?"

"No. Never. It was a mistake to let my past keep me afraid of having a future with her, but if she can overcome what Alex did and still look to the future I can do the same. No more letting the past dictate the future, no more being afraid, she knows the truth, and she didn't run, I should have known that was how she would react from the beginning." There were enough mistakes made in his past to fill the ocean that he loved, but now he had everything to live for and everything to lose.

"Look, Spider, I know I apologized already, but again,

man, I'm really sorry for interfering. I should have made sure I knew why dad didn't want the two of you together before I got involved."

The pain in his friend's face wasn't what he wanted to see. Night had made a mistake in blindly going along with his father's wishes without having all the facts, but it was done and over with and Night had lost a lot too because of that decision, there was no need to keep beating a dead horse.

"It's okay, let's just move forward, you know I forgave you a long time ago."

Night gave a tight smile. "I won you over, but I think I have a way to go before I get my sister to forgive me."

"Actually, I think she just wants to move on too."

"Yeah, that's what she told me, but she's still hurt, and she's the only family I have left, and even though we weren't close as kids I would like us to be close now. Especially with the two of you together, you're my brother and she's my sister, we're family, and it's time to start acting like it. So I brought her a gift." Night held up the box.

"You two want some time alone together?" he asked, although he didn't want to leave Abigail for long, Night was right, the two of them did need time to reconnect.

"What did I just get done saying?" Night grinned. "We're family, I want you to know this too. Besides, you know she wants you back in there, and if I go in there alone all she's going to be doing is thinking about you and where you are, so we may as well bring you along and get her to focus."

Night smiled again, but he couldn't hide the worry in his eyes as they opened the door to Abigail's hospital room. Both she and the doctor turned as they entered and the doctor nodded at them.

"You can take your girl home this afternoon, Mr. Flynn," the woman said as she set Abigail's wrist down on the bed and patted her shoulder.

"Home," Abigail said with a content sigh as she rested back against the pillows piled behind her. "That sounds pretty good."

"I'll give you one last examination before I sign your release papers this afternoon, Ms. McNamara," the doctor said as she departed.

"I missed you," Abigail said, holding out her hand to him as he crossed over to her bed.

"I was out of the room for less than three minutes," he said as he clasped her hand and brought it to his lips and kissed it.

"You saying you didn't miss me?" she asked.

"That would be a nope." He stooped and kissed her quickly, then sat beside her and hooked an arm around her shoulders, carefully easing her against him without aggravating her cracked ribs. "Night came by for a visit, he wanted to check up on you."

Night was hovering by the door looking anxious, but when Abigail smiled at him he relaxed and came to join them, pulling up the chair and setting it beside the bed. "I brought you two things."

"Yeah?" Abigail eyed the box.

"That's the second," Night said.

"Then what's the first?" she asked, clearly curious.

"An apology."

"For what?"

"What I did to keep you and Spider apart," Night said.

"You already apologized for that."

"Yeah, well I wanted to do it again. I really am sorry. I guess since I always idolized Dad it was just automatic that I do what he asked without even bothering to find out why. That wasn't fair to you and it wasn't fair to Spider, and once I found out what my best friend had been through and how I added to that, I went to a bar to drink away my guilt, and let's just say I did something really stupid that I also haven't forgiven myself for."

Abigail reached out with her broken arm and touched her fingertips to her brother's hand. "Eric, it's okay, forgive yourself. I wish you hadn't done what you did, but Ryder and I are back together now and everything's okay. Please, for me, let go of the guilt. It's time."

"Yeah," Night said in a way that made it clear he hadn't decided to move on.

"So thing number two?" Abigail glanced from Night to the box he held and back again. "What is it?"

"Something to help you forgive Mom and Dad," he said, holding it out to her.

She took the box with curious fingers, set it on her lap, and pulled off the piece of tape holding the two sides closed. When she pulled out what was inside her brow furrowed at what she held. "I don't understand." She looked to her brother for clarification.

"Mom and Dad made mistakes with you, Abs, I'm not denying it, I did too, you were different and we didn't make enough of an attempt to understand the things that were important to you, but I don't ever want you to doubt again that they loved you. I'm not condoning what they did, messing with your life, but they did love you."

"These are all programs from the competitions that I did when I was a kid, there are dozens in here." She rifled through the box. "It looks like every competition I was ever in." She opened one, flicked through it. "It has my scores written in here. Were they there? They never came to any of my dance competitions."

"They did, they just didn't want you to know," Night corrected.

"Why?" Abigail asked as she started to cry. "Why would they keep that from me?"

"That I don't know," Night replied. "I wish I could tell you but I never even knew that they went. I found the box when I was cleaning out the house after Mom died. I wanted to give it to you, but I wasn't sure you would want to know. Now it just seemed like the time was right."

"Thank you, Eric, you're right, now the time is perfect. This makes me question everything about them and I hate I can't ever get answers, but it's nice to know that in their own way they cared." Abigail was crying openly now, and Spider curled an arm around her and held her close. "I want to start fresh, all three of us today, right now, as a family."

"I'm going to be a better big brother to you, Abs," Night promised.

"I love you, Eric, I always did even when we weren't close, and now, maybe just like Ryder and I are getting a second chance you and I can have a second chance too."

"I'd like that," Night said, taking her outstretched hand.

Spider had lost his biological family, been given a second one with the McNamara's that he had also lost, but in a different way by the betrayal of the only positive father figure he had ever had. Now he had a third family and this one he was never letting go of.

* * *

4:17 P.M.

"Lavender," Abigail grinned as Ryder carried her into her apartment and she saw her friend closing the oven door. "What are you doing here?"

"I just made you guys some dinner, I heard you were coming home today," the pretty redhead replied.

"How'd you hear?" Abigail asked, pushing at Ryder's

shoulders to get him to put her down so she could go hug her friend, but he ignored her and carried her over to the couch where he deposited her.

"Eric called, said you might like some of my awesome homemade vegetarian lasagna," Lavender answered, walking over to hug her.

Lavender worked as a waitress at her favorite restaurant, they'd met nearly four years ago when Lavender had first moved here after a particularly difficult time in her life. The redhead was a few years older than Abigail, but they had quickly formed a firm friendship. Lavender was outwardly confident, but she had the saddest gray eyes and an air of melancholy that she tried to hide. As hard as Abigail had tried, she hadn't been able to breach that barrier Lavender had erected around herself.

"Thank you so much," she said, squeezing her friend. "I do love your lasagna and it was so sweet of you to make it and bring it over."

"We'll have to catch up properly once you're feeling better," Lavender said, lightly brushing her fingertips across one of the colorful bruises on her face.

"I look forward to it."

"Good, because we have lots to talk about."

Abigail got the impression Lavender didn't just mean catching up on the whole Alex debacle but that she had her own news to share. "I'll text you tomorrow and we can make a time."

"Perfect. I'll let your guy have you all to himself now, he looks like he's about ready to devour you," Lavender said with a wink.

She laughed, wincing at the pain in her ribs, the pain that was quickly becoming annoying as it stabbed at her each time her lungs inflated. Still, it was a small price to pay to know that not only was she safe now but so were Ryder, Eric, and the team.

"So you want to devour me, huh?" she said as Ryder locked up the door and set the alarm.

"I do, but until you're fully healed there will be no devouring," he said as he came to sit on the floor beside the sofa.

"Spoilsport." She pouted.

"Uh, babe, don't stick your lip out like that, it makes me want to bite it," he groaned.

Heat pooled in her belly. "So bite it," she urged. She wasn't on board with Ryder's no making out policy. So it would hurt, probably every inch of her, but she didn't care, she could take the pain when the payout would be nothing but pleasure.

"Behave," Ryder warned.

"Make me," she shot back.

"Abby," he groaned again. "You are a very bad girl."

"Bad enough I need to be punished?" She laughed, she wasn't into that kind of thing but teasing Ryder like this was fun.

"Abigail Dana McNamara," Ryder said, standing and pacing around the room before coming back to her, lifting her legs, sliding in beneath them, then kissing her softly, doing absolutely nothing to douse the fire building inside her.

"We could just be careful," she suggested hopefully.

"You have broken ribs," he reminded her like she could forget.

"I'm not denying it will hurt, just saying it will be worth it," she shrugged.

"Abby."

"You keep saying that, but you know you want this as much as I do. Alex tried to make me afraid of sex, he tried to make it so every time I thought of it all I would see was his face, but I don't want that to be the case, Ryder. Please," she whispered, letting the vulnerability she felt seep through.

"Baby ..." His eyes met hers and she could see he was wavering.

"We can go slow, easy, I'll let you do all the work." She was almost begging and not too proud to get down on her knees if it would work. She knew that Ryder was just trying to do the right thing, protect her from more pain, but the truth was she just needed him right now. Needed to feel him inside her, needed to feel good, and needed to feel connected to the man she loved after so long deprived of everyone and everything.

"You just lie there," he said, standing with her in his arms and stalking toward the bedroom where he laid her down on the bed like she was made of spun glass.

That wasn't what she wanted.

"Don't, Ryder."

"Don't what?"

"Treat me like I'm a china doll. I'm not. I survived everything Alex did to me and I didn't break. I can take the pain. I don't care about it because you will be making my entire body come alive, you'll be making each nerve ending dance, you'll be flooding my system with the best antidote to pain available."

"Abby, you're so strong, I'm in awe of you." The expression on his face dulled her pain, that level of love was what she had always hoped to see shining from someone's eyes and directed all at her and seeing it had her tearing up.

Ryder slid her sweatpants down her legs just far enough that he could bare her, then reached into the nightstand for a condom.

"No," she stopped him. "I want to feel all of you, my blood tests are all clean, and I don't care if we make a baby."

Without taking his eyes off her, he freed himself and slid into her slowly. That feeling of being filled was heavenly and she curled her good hand around his shoulder, anchoring herself to him as he began to move.

"Baby, you're so beautiful." He kissed her. "So strong." Another kiss. "So kind." Kiss. "So big-hearted." Kiss. "You're my heart, my soul, my everything."

Balanced on one hand, he began to touch her with his fingers as he moved slowly, in and out. Each word he spoke, each touch of his lips, each thrust brought her higher and higher. Curling her insides until they were so tight that she felt like her entire being would explode if she didn't come soon.

"I love you, Abby."

Those words were all she needed, and she came like a rocket as pleasure sparked inside her, hot and powerful, and more than anything else she had ever experienced.

"Sex with you really does keep getting better and better," Ryder murmured as he found his own release and then pulled out of her.

"Yeah," she mumbled because it was all her wiped out body could manage.

"I'm going to clean you up and then you're going to sleep," he said, smoothing a lock of hair off her forehead as he stood.

Ryder walked into the bathroom then returned with a warm washcloth, he cleaned between her legs, then righted her sweatpants. After disposing of the cloth he came and eased the covers out from underneath her so they could both slide underneath them.

Abigail immediately snuggled up against his side. "Wouldn't it be awesome if we really did just make a baby?"

"You ready for kids?"

"I never really thought about it. I knew I wanted them,

and yeah when we were together last time I started wondering if we were ready, but now I don't know, if we did make a baby I would be thrilled. I know we just got back together, and I know that I have a long way to go to rebuild my life, but I know what I want. I want to start my own dance studio, I want to sell our apartments and buy a house together. I want to marry you and have babies with you. I don't care when it all happens but that's what I want," she said on a sigh as she tucked her head under his chin.

She felt his lips on the top of her head, and she loved the way his arm held her securely against him.

"I want all of that too, Abby. I want to plan the most amazing proposal and then I want to marry you and spend the rest of my life with you. I want a bunch of little girls who are just as strong and sassy as their mommy, and I want to grow old with you by my side."

"There's one little problem with that," she said sleepily.

"What?"

"I also want to have little baby SEALs."

"Ballerinas and SEALs, I can see there is never going to be a moment of peace in our house."

"You wouldn't want it any other way."

"I really wouldn't," Ryder agreed. "Sleep time now, sweetheart."

Rolling her carefully onto her side so he could spoon her against him, his body covered hers from her head to her feet, and with his arm curled under her neck and one around her waist his hand settled lightly against her breast, Abigail fell into a deep and dreamless sleep.

CHAPTER 18

July 1ˢᵗ

5:30 A.M.

This was perfection.

Spider could stay like this forever, just lying in bed holding his girl in his arms.

After amazing sex yesterday, Abby had slept for a couple of hours then they'd gotten up, eaten some of Lavender's lasagna, and taken a shower together before tumbling back into bed.

Abby had drifted in and out of bad dreams while she slept, but each time he had nuzzled his lips against her neck and whispered soothingly to her while making sure to keep her cocooned in his embrace, and her whimpers had quietened until she had drifted back off into a peaceful slumber.

What made last night even better was knowing that this was just the first of many wonderful nights they would spend together in the same bed.

Already he was trying to figure out the perfect way to propose to her. It had to be something special, something that made up for all the lost years, something that she would remember for the rest of her life. He had a few ideas and he would get to work planning something this morning. Maybe he would suggest Lavender come over so Abigail could catch up with her friend, and since the threat against her was over now he could leave the two women to talk while he started preparing what he hoped would be one of the best days of Abby's life.

Then his phone rang.

Spider groaned as he carefully eased out from the bed and picked up his phone, taking it into the living room before answering because he wanted just a moment or two more to live in this love-filled bliss before that little bubble was shattered.

"Yeah," he said when he knew he couldn't put it off any longer.

"We're heading out, Spider," Fox said.

Although that was what he had known he would hear, he couldn't help the lingering doubt about leaving Abigail alone so soon after her ordeal. She was far from being healed, physically she needed help, and psychologically she needed just as much support. She had an appointment with Dr. Hancock tomorrow, and she was still afraid of large groups of people, it was hardly the ideal time to be leaving her.

And he didn't want her to feel like he was abandoning her again.

"Spider?"

"Yeah, I'll grab my stuff and head straight out."

"See you soon."

"Yeah, soon," he muttered to the dial tone. This might not be what he wanted to do today, but Abigail had never given him a hard time about his job when they had been together before, and he had to believe her when she said she was strong enough to handle this if he wanted to keep the trust she had placed in him.

Since he didn't have time to dawdle, Ryder headed back to the bedroom to wake Abigail and tell her that he was being sent out.

Kneeling beside the bed, he gently stroked the unbruised skin of her temple and touched his lips lightly to hers. "Abby," he called out softly.

She moaned and her lashes fluttered on her cheeks before she opened her eyes to stare groggily at him. "Ryder?"

"Yeah, babe, I have bad news."

"You got called out?" she asked, awkwardly pushing herself into a sitting position with his help.

"Unfortunately."

"It's okay, Ryder, it's your job, I get it and you know I'll never complain about you getting called away. Miss you and worry about you, yes, but complain, no."

"I know, I just don't like leaving you like this. You're not up to staying on your own, and I don't know how long I'll be gone, could be a few days could be months." That was the worst part about being away when he was with Abby, the never knowing how long he would be gone made it hard for her. It was one thing to be able to count the days until he would be home but another to be stuck in limbo.

"I'll manage," she assured him. "And I don't just mean about missing you."

"I don't want you to just manage. You've been just managing for fourteen months all on your own, now you deserve to be taken care of. How about I call Caroline to see if you can go and stay in her basement while I'm gone. Wolf is home at the moment, and even if his team gets called out you and Caroline can keep each other company, and you can have someone around to help you out while you're healing."

Spider tried not to hold his breath as he waited to see what she'd say. He would feel much better about leaving her so soon if he knew she wouldn't be alone, but he wasn't going to force the issue. The harder he pushed the harder she would push back, and he did know that she would be able to manage on her own for however long he would be gone.

With a long sigh that he was pretty sure she was only putting on because she didn't want him to think she was conceding too easily, she nodded. "Yeah okay, my ribs do hurt, and I am covered virtually head to toe in bruises, it would be nice to have someone around. And ..." she ducked her head, "I am a little nervous to be alone so soon after what happened."

Leaning forward, he kissed her forehead. "You would have been fine on your own, but I will feel better knowing you won't be."

"And that will make me feel better, I don't want anything to distract you while you're gone. You better come home to me, Ryder." Her tone was light but he could see the concern hidden deep in her eyes.

"Sweetheart, I will *always* do whatever I have to in order to come home to you."

"And until you do you can believe that I will be here holding down the fort. We're a team, Ryder, you and me, together we can both have everything that we have ever dreamed of. I trust you again, Ryder, and I want you to trust me, I want you to believe in me, have faith that as long as I know you're coming back to me I will be okay. And ... I don't like to say it because I don't want to jinx it ... but even if you didn't come home to me I would find a way to be okay, I wouldn't give up, I would live and honor your memory. But I would only ever be yours." The last was a mere whisper, but he felt every drop of emotion in those seven words.

"I've only ever been yours too, Abby. You've always been mine."

"And you've always been mine."

"Always," he agreed. "Ever since you saved me."

Find out what has Eric "Night" McNamara consumed with guilt in the next book in this action packed and emotionally charged military romance series!

ALSO BY JANE BLYTHE

ABOUT THE AUTHOR

Jane Blythe is a *USA Today* bestselling author of romantic suspense full of sexy heroes, strong heroines, and serial killers! When she's not weaving hard to unravel mysteries she loves to read, bake, go to the beach, build snowmen, and watch Disney movies. She has two adorable Dalmatians, is obsessed with Christmas, owns 200+ teddy bears, and loves to travel!

To connect and keep up to date please visit any of the following

Email – mailto:janeblytheauthor@gmail.com
Facebook – http://www.facebook.com/janeblytheauthor
Instagram – http://www.instagram.com/jane_blythe_author
Reader Group – http://www.facebook.com/groups/janeskillersweethearts
Twitter – http://www.twitter.com/jblytheauthor
Website – http://www.janeblythe.com.au

There are many more books in this fan fiction world than listed here, for an up-to-date list go to www.AcesPress.com

You can also visit our Amazon page at:
http://www.amazon.com/author/operationalpha

PJ Fiala: Defending Sophie
Nicole Flockton: Protecting Maria
Alexa Gregory: Backdraft
Michele Gwynn: Rescuing Emma
Casey Hagen: Shielding Nebraska
Desiree Holt: Protecting Maddie
Kathy Ivan: Saving Sarah
Kris Jacen, Be With Me
Jesse Jacobson: Protecting Honor
Silver James: Rescue Moon
Becca Jameson: Saving Sofia
Kate Kinsley: Protecting Ava
Heather Long: Securing Arizona
Gennita Low: No Protection
Kirsten Lynn: Joining Forces for Jesse
Margaret Madigan: Bang for the Buck
Kimberly McGath: The Predecessor
Rachel McNeely: The SEAL's Surprise Baby
KD Michaels: Saving Laura
Lynn Michaels: Rescuing Kyle
Wren Michaels: The Fox & The Hound
Kat Mizera: Protecting Bobbi
Keira Montclair, Wolf and the Wild Scots
Mary B Moore: Force Protection
LeTeisha Newton: Protecting Butterfly
Angela Nicole: Protecting the Donna
MJ Nightingale: Protecting Beauty
Sarah O'Rourke: Saving Liberty
Victoria Paige: Reclaiming Izabel
Anne L. Parks: Mason
Debra Parmley: Protecting Pippa
Lainey Reese: Protecting New York
KeKe Renée: Protecting Bria
TL Reeve and Michele Ryan: Extracting Mateo

Elena M. Reyes: Keeping Ava
Angela Rush: Charlotte
Rose Smith: Saving Satin
Jenika Snow: Protecting Lily
Lynne St. James: SEAL's Spitfire
Dee Stewart: Conner
Harley Stone: Rescuing Mercy
Jen Talty: Burning Desire
Reina Torres, Rescuing Hi'ilani
Savvi V: Loving Lex
Megan Vernon: Protecting Us
Rachel Young: Because of Marissa

Delta Team Three Series
Lori Ryan: Nori's Delta
Becca Jameson: Destiny's Delta
Lynne St James, Gwen's Delta
Elle James: Ivy's Delta
Riley Edwards: Hope's Delta

Police and Fire: Operation Alpha World
Freya Barker: Burning for Autumn
B.P. Beth: Scott
Jane Blythe: Salvaging Marigold
Julia Bright, Justice for Amber
Anna Brooks, Guarding Georgia
KaLyn Cooper: Justice for Gwen
Aspen Drake: Sheltering Emma
Alexa Gregory: Backdraft
Deanndra Hall: Shelter for Sharla
Barb Han: Kace
EM Hayes: Gambling for Ashleigh
CM Steele: Guarding Hope
Reina Torres: Justice for Sloane

Aubree Valentine, Justice for Danielle
Maddie Wade: Finding English
Stacey Wilk: Stage Fright
Laine Vess: Justice for Lauren

Tarpley VFD Series
Silver James, Fighting for Elena
Deanndra Hall, Fighting for Carly
Haven Rose, Fighting for Calliope
MJ Nightingale, Fighting for Jemma
TL Reeve, Fighting for Brittney
Nicole Flockton, Fighting for Nadia

As you know, this book included at least one character from Susan Stoker's books. To check out more, see below.

SEAL of Protection: Legacy Series
Securing Caite
Securing Brenae (novella)
Securing Sidney
Securing Piper
Securing Zoey
Securing Avery
Securing Kalee
Securing Jane (Feb 2021)

SEAL Team Hawaii Series
Finding Elodie (Apr 2021)
Finding Lexie (Aug 2021)
Finding Kenna (Oct 2021)
Finding Monica (TBA)
Finding Carly (TBA)
Finding Ashlyn (TBA)

Delta Team Two Series
Shielding Gillian
Shielding Kinley
Shielding Aspen
Shielding Jayme
Shielding Riley
Shielding Devyn (May 2021)
Shielding Ember (Sept 2021)
Shielding Sierra (Jan 2022)

Delta Force Heroes Series
Rescuing Rayne (FREE!)

Rescuing Aimee (novella)
Rescuing Emily
Rescuing Harley
Marrying Emily (novella)
Rescuing Kassie
Rescuing Bryn
Rescuing Casey
Rescuing Sadie (novella)
Rescuing Wendy
Rescuing Mary
Rescuing Macie (Novella)

Badge of Honor: Texas Heroes Series

Justice for Mackenzie (FREE!)
Justice for Mickie
Justice for Corrie
Justice for Laine (novella)
Shelter for Elizabeth
Justice for Boone
Shelter for Adeline
Shelter for Sophie
Justice for Erin
Justice for Milena
Shelter for Blythe
Justice for Hope
Shelter for Quinn
Shelter for Koren
Shelter for Penelope

SEAL of Protection Series

Protecting Caroline (FREE!)
Protecting Alabama
Protecting Fiona
Marrying Caroline (novella)

Protecting Summer
Protecting Cheyenne
Protecting Jessyka
Protecting Julie (novella)
Protecting Melody
Protecting the Future
Protecting Kiera (novella)
Protecting Alabama's Kids (novella)
Protecting Dakota

New York Times, *USA Today* and *Wall Street Journal* Bestselling Author Susan Stoker has a heart as big as the state of Tennessee where she lives, but this all American girl has also spent the last fourteen years living in Missouri, California, Colorado, Indiana, and Texas. She's married to a retired Army man who now gets to follow *her* around the country.

www.stokeraces.com
www.AcesPress.com
susan@stokeraces.com

Made in the USA
Coppell, TX
03 December 2021